WALTZ WITH A LADY

"Molly tells me you know how to dance the waltz," Allyson said.

"The waltz? Oh. Yes, I do."

"Good. I should like you to teach me."

"Teach you? To waltz?"

"Yes. Teach me to waltz."

"The steps are really quite simple," he explained, and demonstrated with her standing beside him. She imitated his movements. "In a sense," he explained, "the lady is doing everything opposite of her partner—she sort of mirrors his actions. It is up to him to keep them from colliding with other dancers."

"I see. . . ." she said doubtfully.

"Here. Stand facing me. Put your right hand in my left hand, and your left hand on my shoulder. That's right. My right hand is at your waist to guide you in making the turns." He pressed her waist slightly to indicate directions.

She did as he told her. "Like this?" She looked into his eyes for confirmation. Their gazes locked, and he appeared as startled as she. His eyes momentarily shifted to her lips.

"Yes." There was something different—husky—in that one-word response. Then he began counting through the basic steps.

They were nearly an arm's length apart, yet she had never felt so intimate with another human being. . . .

Books by Wilma Counts

Willed to Wed

My Lady Governess

The Willful Miss Winthrop

The Wagered Wife

The Trouble with Harriet

Miss Richardson Comes of Age

Rules of Marriage

The Viscount's Bride

The Lady and the Footman

Published by Zebra Books

The Lady and the Footman

Wilma Counts

ZEBRA BOOKS
KENSINGTON PUBLISHING CORP.
www.kensingtonbooks.com

ZEBRA BOOKS are published by

Kensington Publishing Corp.
850 Third Avenue
New York, NY 10022

All Kensington titles, imprints and distributed lines are available at special quantity discounts for bulk purchases for sales
promotion, premiums, fund-raising, educational or institutional
use.

Special book excerpts or customized printings can also be
created to fit specific needs. For details, write or phone the
office of the Kensington Special Sales Manager: Kensington
Publishing Corp., 850 Third Avenue, New York, NY 10022.
Attn. Special Sales Department. Phone: 1-800-221-2647.

First Printing: December 2004
10   9   8   7   6   5   4   3   2   1

Printed in the United States of America

*This one is for the folks
at Carson Physical Therapy
who listened to me whine and plot
from day one,
especially Christine
and Marty
and Sheri
and Marge
and Karen.*

*Also
for Mona Prevel
who helps me keep my English English
and for Ramona Butler
who periodically rescues me
from my computer.*

Chapter 1

London, 1813

"Come along, Molly. Mama will fret if I am late for tea."
Lady Allyson Crossleigh gestured to her maid—that is, she
gestured as much as the packages she herself carried would
allow.

"Yes, my lady," the young maid mumbled, trying to balance a number of packages under her chin.

Allyson pursed her lips and looked about impatiently.
"*Where* is our coach?" she demanded. "I distinctly told John
Coachman to retrieve us at this corner!"

"I dunno, my lady. Traffic's heavy today, though."

Again Allyson looked about and recognized the truth of
Molly's observation. Even foot traffic was heavy here on one
of London's busiest shopping streets. She might not have noticed a man attired in the nondescript clothing of what appeared to be a dockworker, except for two things. He was
distinctly out of place in a street full of stylish shoppers and
fashionable fribbles out to parade themselves. And, unlike
others, he seemed in no hurry; he leaned nonchalantly
against a wall. A battered cap shaded the top half of his face;
the lower half revealed several days' growth of beard. She

frowned. Had not the same man been standing around in much the same manner when she and Molly arrived at this last millinery shop?

Suddenly, her attention was diverted, for a large woman wearing a shopkeeper's apron interjected herself between Allyson and the maid, knocking poor Molly to the pavement and sending her packages flying. At the same time, Allyson felt a hand jerk her elbow, causing her to drop what she was carrying. She also saw a closed carriage pull to a stop nearby.

"Now, *you* just come along, my lady," a harsh voice growled at her as its owner pushed her toward the open door of the carriage from which a hand extended to grab her.

Neither the man at her elbow nor the one in the carriage was apparently mindful of the sort of woman with which they dealt. Allyson Crossleigh was no milk and water miss who would submit meekly to rough treatment.

"Take your hands off me, you uncivilized brute!" She jerked away, but the man held firm, though she had thrown him off balance momentarily. She swung her reticule, which hung by a strap from her free hand, toward his head, and there was a dull clunk as it found its target. The man cursed angrily and pushed her another step closer to the carriage.

"Get 'er in here!" a voice called from the vehicle.

"I think not," yet another male voice said in a clipped tone.

Before Allyson could comprehend exactly what was happening, the grip on her arm was loosened and, off balance, she fell to the pavement.

The lounging worker had sprung to her rescue. She was vaguely aware of the sound of a fist colliding with flesh, and then running feet and a carriage team being whipped into action. She had a brief glimpse of her rescuer. His deep-blue gaze locked with hers for the merest moment. Then, she was surrounded by a crowd.

"Are you all right, miss?" a well-dressed gentleman asked as he helped her to her feet.

"Yes, I think so." Her voice shook.

"Can you believe this? In broad daylight, too," an indignant middle-aged woman demanded.

"We need a real police force in this city," a strident male voice offered.

Allyson had by now gathered her wits enough to look around for her rescuer and for Molly. She found only Molly. A very distraught Molly.

"Oh, my stars, my lady. Are you all right? I never seen anythin' happen so quick-like. Oh, my stars. What will His Lordship say?"

" 'I told you so,' " Allyson muttered to herself, but she offered soothing assurances to her maid and was grateful to see her own carriage draw near. Soon enough their packages had been restored to them and they were on their way to Rutherford House, but there was no sign of the man who had been the hero of the hour.

As she leaned back in the seat, the rush of excitement and emotion that had carried her through the incident began to ebb away. She felt herself trembling inwardly. She paid scant attention to Molly's babblings, which were punctuated by repeated exclamations of "Oh, my stars!"

What on earth happened? she wondered. Was she very nearly the victim of some random crime? Or was she a target? Why? Why had one stranger accosted her and another leapt to her rescue? It made little sense.

Or, perhaps it did. . . . Her father had hinted that the streets of London were becoming increasingly dangerous. Just this morning at breakfast he had urged his wife and daughters to be cautious in venturing out. However, his warning had been somewhat vague and Allyson had not thought him overly concerned, which therefore had caused her no undue alarm, though she had taken some extra precaution before going out.

"We must not alarm Mama and Clara overly much, Molly," she warned now.

She might as well have saved her breath. Disheveled and

distraught, Molly could not contain herself, and the house was thrown into an uproar the moment they returned.

In another section of London, a man dressed as a common laborer was admitted by a back entrance to the building housing offices of the foreign secretary and other important members of the government dealing with foreign matters, which, these days, were matters of war. The "laborer"—Captain Lord Nathan Christopher Thornton, late of His Majesty's Army in the Peninsula—was shown into a darkly paneled office that exuded authority and elegance.

"Well, Thornton?" asked the dignified white-haired man behind the desk.

"The information was right, my lord. There was an 'activity,' and it seems to have been aimed directly at you. There was an attempt to abduct your daughter."

Duncan Crossleigh, the Earl of Rutherford, sat up straighter and asked in an alarmed tone, "She is safe, though, is she not?"

"Yes, my lord. A bit rumpled, but safe. I saw her handed into her own carriage before I slipped away." He then gave Lord Rutherford a detailed account of the incident, ending with, "I'm sorry those villains got away in the melee that followed."

"I am, too." Rutherford gestured to a chair. "Have a seat, Thornton." When the younger man was seated across from him, Rutherford continued, "You think the culprits were the same ones we've been troubled with of late?"

"I certainly think our fellows were behind it, but these appeared to be hired ruffians, and I'm quite sure the woman who knocked Lady Allyson's maid aside was working with them."

"But you got a good look at them?"

"A brief look at the woman, and a fuller view of the man on the street, but not the one inside the coach—nor the driver." Thornton cursed himself inwardly. He had allowed himself to be distracted by a pretty face.

Today had given him his first glimpse of the daughter of the man who was currently his superior officer. Returned to England on convalescent leave, Captain Thornton had been seconded to the Foreign Office on his recovery. It was not an assignment he welcomed. However, he liked and respected Lord Rutherford, and when the man had asked him to take the place of an ill Bow Street Runner in keeping an eye on Lady Allyson, he had readily accepted the assignment for the day.

The surprise had come in seeing that she was not the schoolroom miss he had expected, but a woman of considerable physical charms. Very considerable. Brown hair, large brown eyes, a ready smile, and a delectable body had captured his attention. She had a determined, sprightly manner about her. However attractive she might be, though, Captain Thornton did not relish the job of playing ape-leader to some flighty female of the *ton*.

Rutherford broke into his musings. "Still, you can give us descriptions of those two, can you not?" He did not wait for Thornton's response. "We shall get the details out to our own agents and to Bow Street as soon as possible."

"Yes, my lord." Thornton started to rise. "Will that be all, sir?"

"No." Waving his visitor back into his seat, Rutherford steepled his hands over papers on the desk. "I doubt this failure will be much discouragement to Bonaparte and his friends across the channel. They will surely try again."

Thornton nodded. "Probably. The French are rather anxious for the kind of information you might supply them, my lord. You yourself are probably safe enough in your person, but those sorts work most effectively at extortion to get what they want. Were I you, sir, I would put extra guards around your house and set a particular watch on your daughter."

"My thoughts exactly," Lord Rutherford said with a note of satisfaction. "Someone who knows what's what and can pursue the real culprits behind these hirelings."

Nathan nodded, wishing the old man would get on with it so he, Nathan, could go home, have a bath, and get some sleep. He had been skulking around dingy taverns most of the last two days—and nights—and then trailing the comely Lady Allyson much of this day. Lord, that woman is a shopper!

"If you've nobody else in mind, my lord," Nathan offered, "I might recommend Harrison. He seems an able man."

"I do have someone else in mind."

"Oh?"

"You."

"Me? But, my lord . . ." He tried to wrap his tired brain around his protests in such a way that they might not offend the man before him.

Rutherford held up one hand. "I know. You are anxious to return to your regiment."

"Yes, I am. My wound has been fully healed for some time now. The Ninety-sixth will need every available man as they move into this summer's campaign."

"True. . . . But you are peculiarly fit for our purposes here in the Foreign Office, too."

"By which you mean, of course, that I make a good spy," Nathan said with a touch of bitterness. "Not exactly the kind of duty a soldier welcomes."

"I know, son, but necessary all the same."

The older man's tone was so gentle and matter-of-fact that Nathan was ashamed. Still, there was no way he could see himself nursemaiding a spoiled belle of the *ton* around London while his comrades fought and died on the sandy soil of Spain. He tried to keep his voice neutral.

"Surely, my lord, the Bow Street Runner is a capable man."

"He is, for what he does, but his job is not chasing down French spies. Yours is." This blunt assessment was accompanied by an equally blunt stare.

"Yes, my lord."

Rutherford smiled faintly. "If it is any consolation to you, those army sorts at Horse Guards were reluctant to send you over to us. But you are exactly what we need—new blood, an unknown face, and someone with a head on his shoulders."

"Thank you, I think."

"Whoever is behind this current business is someone who has particular knowledge of people connected to this office. It may, indeed, be someone in our midst. In any event, he— or possibly she—probably moves freely in the highest social circles."

"But, my lord, *I* have never moved in those circles! I took my commission right out of university. I returned to England briefly when my mother was ill, but for all intents and purposes, sir, I have been out of the country for seven years and more." Nathan's chuckle had an ironic note. "Actually, you should be recruiting my brother. He *does* move in those circles."

"I might have tried to do so, but the Marquis of Eastland is rarely in town. However, we *do* have other peers looking out for our interests."

Nathan placed his hands on the arms of his chair and again started to rise. "Good. Then you will not need my services."

"Hold on there. I have something particular in mind for you."

Nathan sank back, dreading what might be coming.

"I cannot order you to this mission, Captain, nor would I do so if I could, but I sincerely hope you will accept it."

Nathan did not hide his reluctance. "I assume duty requires that I consider what you have to say."

"You are to join my household in Grosvenor Square."

"In what capacity? I can hardly be a long-lost cousin or nephew."

"As a footman."

"As a *what?*"

Rutherford grinned. "A footman."

"Impossible. I don't know a thing about being a footman."

"You shall learn, I am sure. Melton, my butler, will teach

you how to get on. He is the only person on my household staff who will know you are not what you appear to be. In fact, aside from you, me, and the secretary himself, Melton will be the only one to know at all. Period."

"Not even your family?"

"Not even my wife."

Nathan shook his head. "Why? Why this charade?"

"As a servant you will have access to the servants of other houses from time to time—and everyone knows how difficult it is to keep anything secret from servants."

"True."

"Also, people tend not to notice a servant standing in the background."

"Hmm." Nathan sat silently mulling this over for a few moments. Well, at least he would not become some sort of male governess. "I'm not sure—what if I am recognized? I went to school with a good number of members of the *ton*— that is, with those of a certain age."

Rutherford shrugged. "Then it would be over, but it is worth a try. Bear in mind, though, that people usually see what they expect to see."

"That is true enough, I suppose."

"So . . . will you do it?"

"In the name of duty, honor, and country, do I have a choice?"

"Put that way, probably not."

"Very well, then." Nathan stood. "Is there anything else I need to know?"

Rutherford stood as well. "As a matter of fact, there is. One of your chief duties on my household staff will be to act as bodyguard to my daughter."

"Wha-at?" Nathan saw his worst nightmare coming true. He really was to play nanny to some frivolous female.

"Think about it. Allyson goes about in *ton* circles freely; it would be quite natural for her to be accompanied by a liveried footman, especially after her frightening experience this afternoon."

"With all due respect, my lord, the lady did not seem unduly *frightened* today. Surprised, yes. Angry, yes. But not frightened."

"That would be Allyson, right enough," Rutherford said with a note of pride.

The two men discussed the assignment in further detail, then shook hands. Lord Rutherford instructed his new footman to present himself the following morning.

Allyson was not nearly as composed as her recent rescuer had thought her to be, but she was determined not to make a Cheltenham tragedy of the matter. Prompted by Molly's tale to another maid who relayed the information to Lady Rutherford, Allyson found herself relating the story to her mother, her sister Clara, and Clara's husband, Lord Edmund Lawton.

This would *have to happen when Clara and Edmund are visiting,* Allyson fumed to herself.

Clara had taken to the sofa and resorted to her vinaigrette several times, clinging pathetically to her husband as she listened with evident horror to Allyson's matter-of-fact telling. Lady Rutherford, too, was clearly alarmed, though less theatrical.

"Really, Clara! Mama! I am perfectly well." She forced a little laugh. " 'All's well that ends well.' You two must not carry on so."

Edmund patted his wife's shoulder. "Allyson is right, my love. In your condition, you must remain calm."

Clara sniffed and gazed at her husband with adoring, big blue eyes. "Oh, Edmund, the city is too dangerous. We never should have come. We must return home immediately. We should take Allyson with us, too."

"Of course, my love, if that is your wish. . . ."

"A splendid idea," Lady Rutherford agreed.

"Oh, nonsense," Allyson said. "I am not removing to Lawton Manor in the middle of the Season. Nor can I believe you seriously entertain the idea, Clara. There's the Worthingtons' ball next week, and Lady Satterly's soiree in two days. Everyone who is anyone will be there. And you *know* you have dress fittings all this week." She tried to draw on all the things that would most appeal to her sister, and added silently to herself, *Besides, I would suffocate in the reflection of all this marital bliss.*

"Well, yes. . . ." Clara raised her blond head from her husband's shoulder. "I would hate to miss the ball. I have the new blue gown, and soon enough I shall have to go into seclusion." She glanced at her husband and blushed prettily at this admission.

Allyson thought Clara was overdoing it a bit. After all, the Lawtons' blessed event was a good seven months away. She watched with a mixture of amusement and impatience as Lady Lawton basked in the concerned attentions of her husband and her mother.

There followed a good deal of genuine concern from Lady Rutherford and more than a good deal of dramatic posturing from Lady Lawton, punctuated by Lord Lawton's occasional "There, there, dear" or "Whatever you wish, my love. . . ."

Allyson finally escaped to her own room. She was mildly annoyed. Was *she* not the one who had narrowly escaped being abducted for who knew what nefarious purposes? Now, suddenly the whole affair was about *Clara*. She quickly dismissed this thought as petty.

She removed her outer garments and lay on the bed, staring unseeing at the canopy overhead. Reviewing the events of the day, she shuddered at what *might* have happened. Thank goodness for that dockworker—or whatever he was.

She frowned in concentration, trying to conjure up his image again. He was tall. Even slumped against the wall, he appeared to be tall. His cap had obscured his hair. He had a strong profile—at least that was the impression she had had from what she could see of it—what with the cap and his being unshaven. But there had been that one intense instant when their eyes had met. What was he doing on that street at that time? Why was he not on the river tossing cargo around, or doing whatever those types did? Still, she was grateful that he had been there, out of place or not. Strange that he had disappeared like that. Those of the lower orders usually expected to be compensated for such services.

She must have fallen asleep, for the next thing she knew, Molly had come to help her dress for dinner. In the drawing room before dinner, and in the dining room later, her mother and sister repeated their concerns for the benefit of Lord Rutherford, who had returned as Allyson slept, and for Miss Pringle, Allyson's one-time governess who now served as her mother's companion-secretary.

Allyson greeted her father with a kiss on the cheek and smiled cheerfully at Miss Pringle. "I suppose Mama and Clara have told you of my adventure."

He nodded and put his arm around her waist. "They have. I am sorry you went through that, but it bears out what I told you all earlier."

Allyson laughed lightly. "I knew it! I knew your reaction would be 'I told you so'!"

"Well," he said gruffly as he released her, "I did, did I not?"

"Yes, Papa, you did." She tried for a mollifying tone. "But it truly was a minor incident, and, thankfully, it is behind us." She sat in a comfortable round chair.

"That may or may not be." He seated himself next to his wife on a sofa. "Until this business with Bonaparte is settled, we in government need to be cautious. And that caution extends to our families as well."

Lord Lawton, who had been leaning casually against the mantel, straightened. "Just as I have been telling Clara, my lord. We have thought of returning to the country. Lady Rutherford and Allyson would be most welcome to accompany us, as would Miss Pringle."

Lady Rutherford placed her hand over her husband's. "Allyson may certainly do so, but I could not leave Duncan here in London alone." She gave her husband a teasing look. "Who knows what mischief he might get into?"

"I do not want to miss the Worthington ball," Clara pouted. Had she been standing, Allyson thought, Clara would have stamped her dainty foot.

"No, no. Of course not, my love."

"It has not come to our having to take refuge in the country—not yet at least," Lord Rutherford said dryly. "And, while I urge caution, I think the Lawtons are less vulnerable than a Crossleigh."

"Well, then we *can* stay." Clara gazed happily at her husband.

"Yes, dear."

"What about Oliver?" the countess asked.

"Not to worry, my dear. I have taken care to see that the remarkable Viscount Sothern is adequately protected." The earl gave his son and heir—away at school—his proper title.

"Wonderful," the countess responded.

Lord Rutherford turned toward his elder daughter. "As for you, my independent miss, there *will* be some changes, but as I see Melton is about to announce dinner, we shall discuss them later."

This had a faintly ominous ring to it, but Allyson shrugged it off. She had always been able to get around her father.

Chapter 2

Somehow the family never quite got around that evening to discussing Lord Rutherford's edicts regarding "changes." The next morning, as was her wont, Allyson rose early to ride in the park before it filled with less-capable riders and drivers whose primary interest was not riding, but in seeing and being seen. She had not slept well and a vigorous ride would be just the thing to clear the cobwebs. However, when she arrived at the stables, the head groom refused to saddle her favorite mare.

"I'm sorry, my lady. Lord Rutherford sent down orders about an hour ago I wasn't to do that."

"Why? Is Princess lame?"

"No, ma'am."

"Well, then, Alfred, put a saddle on her for me," she said firmly.

Alfred looked downcast. "I'm so sorry, Lady Allyson, but if I went against His Lordship's set order, it'd be my job, don't you see?"

"Well," she said in disgust, "I can certainly saddle a horse for myself."

"I'm real sorry, Lady Allyson." Alfred looked as if he

might cry. "Lord Rutherford thought you might feel that way, and he said not to allow it."

Allyson was furious, but she knew it was not poor Alfred's fault. She stormed back into the house, muttering to herself. In the hallway, she encountered Melton.

"I should like to see my father immediately," she demanded.

"He's in the library, my lady. But he has someone with him."

"Who is with him?"

Melton looked uncomfortable and coughed. "I believe he is interviewing a new footman."

"Interviewing a footman? Whatever for? I thought *you* hired male members of the staff just as Mrs. Simpson hires the females."

"Yes, my lady. Ordinarily I do."

Allyson frowned, but she proceeded to her room. She might as well change. By the time this contretemps could be sorted out, it would be too late for the kind of ride she wanted.

She had no sooner donned a soft green print muslin than there was a knock on her door.

Molly opened the door. "Yes?"

A footman responded. "His Lordship wishes to see Lady Allyson as soon as she may be available."

"Tell him I shall be there directly," Allyson said. She straightened the scooped neck and puffed sleeves of the morning dress.

"But your hair, my lady," Molly protested.

"Oh, just tie it back with a ribbon. I don't want to keep Papa waiting." She did not add that she wanted to see him before her own sense of abuse dissipated.

She knocked on the library door and entered even as her father's voice bade her to do so. She was surprised and annoyed to find him not alone.

A man dressed in the black pantaloons, the silver-gray waistcoat, and the dark blue jacket of Rutherford livery rose from a chair in front of her father's desk.

"Allyson, this is Nathan, our newest staff member. My daughter, Lady Allyson."

The stranger bowed low and murmured, "My lady."

She inclined her head slightly, but said nothing, though her mind was working furiously. First of all, what was a footman doing sitting in the presence of the master of the house? Then there was his name: Nathan? Not James or Robert or Tom as most footmen were designated, but *Nathan*. Then, too, there was the mere fact that her *father* was questioning him. She looked more closely at the man.

He was tall—well, that would qualify him as a typical footman—and he had light brown hair with lighter streaks. His clean-shaven face was well tanned. *This man must spend a great deal of time in the sun. In England?* He had deep-blue eyes framed by dark brows and lashes. He looked quite dashing in the Rutherford livery. She caught a gleam of amusement in his eyes as he observed her observing him. She deliberately returned her attention to her father.

"I was not aware that we were taking on extra staff, Father."

"After yesterday's incident, I thought it a prudent measure, my dear. Nathan here was a soldier in the Peninsula."

That explains the hair and the tan, she thought. "Oh, indeed?" she asked in a disinterested tone. She waited for her father to explain the unusual circumstance of hiring household staff instead of leaving such a task up to Melton, and the even more unusual event of his requiring *her* presence at such an interview.

"Nathan will be accompanying you on any future outings, my dear, including your morning rides."

So that is it. She lifted her chin and tried to ignore the third person in the room. "I am perfectly satisfied with Alfred, Father. He knows horses and is an excellent rider, a range of expertise that neither a *foot*man nor a *foot* soldier might be expected to have mastered."

She heard a muffled sound from Nathan, but he, of course, said not a word. She went on.

"Alfred accompanies me when I have need of him, and Molly attends me on other occasions."

"And may continue to do so," her father said affably, and then added in a sterner tone, "but Nathan will be there as well."

Allyson recognized that tone, but she was not going down without a fight, or, at the very least, a strong protest.

"Papa," she wheedled, in a manner that usually swayed him, "you know I don't need some male nanny. I can take care of myself."

"Yesterday—" her father started.

"Yesterday was something quite out of the ordinary and cannot be expected to happen again, not at least to me. Those men were surely just out to grab the next well-dressed woman they saw. I doubt not that their only motive was robbery."

"Nevertheless—"

She rushed on. "And besides, I could have handled the situation. I had my pistol in my reticule, and you know I am a good marksman—well, markswoman."

From the corner of her eye, she saw the new footman lift a brow at this.

"Yes, I know," her father agreed. "I was your tutor, remember? But I believe your confidence is perhaps overdone." His voice became more stern. "Now you can either accept Nathan's services, return to Rutherford Hall, or pay an extended visit to the Lawtons'."

"Papa!" she wailed. "You would banish me to the country?"

Lord Rutherford looked distracted. Allyson knew very well how much he hated refusing her anything. "Daughter, please. I cannot spend my time worrying every time you step out of the house."

The anxiety in his voice made her ashamed. She knew her father had too many worries without her adding to them. Were not the newspapers full of such concerns every day? Still, she offered one last protest.

"I am sorry, Papa. But, really, I have no need of a nurse-maid."

Her father seemed to recognize and accept her capitulation. "I rather think Nathan shares your sentiments," he said ruefully, "but it will please me immensely if you both abide by my wishes."

She glanced at the footman, who gazed at her directly. His eyes still held that amusement, but there was challenge in them as well. She averted her gaze.

Only later did it occur to her to wonder about her father's paying the slightest bit of attention to a mere servant's "sentiments."

When his interviews with Lord Rutherford and then with the inimitable butler, Melton, were over, Nathan spent the rest of the morning polishing silver. Melton had outlined the duties of footmen in detail.

"Footmen see to cleaning the silver on a daily basis, though before a party, the others will help, of course. They serve at family and company meals. They keep the lamps in the public rooms properly trimmed and cleaned and ensure that they are kept adequately filled with oil. Also, they keep these same rooms supplied with sufficient coal for the fire-places and see that the ashes are disposed of properly each morning."

"Oh, is that all?" Nathan did not curb the irony in his tone.

Melton gave him a stern look. "No. They may also answer the door and announce visitors when Robert or I are unavailable to do so. However, no one person does all these chores; they are assigned separately."

"That's a relief!"

"When visitors are being entertained, footmen are expected to present a positive impression of the household."

"What does *that* mean?"

The austere Melton seemed to have a hint of a twinkle in

his eyes. "You stand around looking imposing and pretend to be unconcerned about the affairs of your betters."

Nathan had been cleaning silver for some time when Melton looked in on him.

"Why are you not using paste to clean those things?" the old man asked in surprise. He pointed to the smears on Nathan's waistcoat. "And why did you not use the apron hanging there on the door? And those work gloves? Good heavens, man, you'll never get that black tarnish from under your nails!"

"Paste? What paste?" Nathan asked in frustration. He had been rubbing pieces of silver with a cloth for what seemed hours but saw little result from his labor.

"There—on the sideboard—are chalk and ammonia. You make a paste of them and rub it on, then rub it off. Like this, see?"

Nathan watched in some chagrin as the butler made short work of a fancy candlestick. "You might have told me," he muttered under his breath. He was glad none of his regiment were here to observe his ineptness.

"I apologize, Captain. I just assumed—"

"That a footman would know his business, eh?"

"I, uh, suppose so," Melton said.

"I usually learn quite quickly, Mr. Melton. I will try not to embarrass you." Nathan cleared his throat. "But we had best drop that 'Captain' business. Don't want to be caught out needlessly, you know."

Melton nodded his agreement and shared a few more tricks for producing gleaming silver. He then moved on to details of serving drinks and a meal.

"When it is just the family, as it will be tonight, the supper will be rather a simple one of only three removes," Melton explained. "A new footman is always assigned this duty immediately with just the family—they like to observe his performance, you see. Of course, I shall be there to oversee the meal, but I am sure you will agree that it would not do to raise questions among the staff by changing the routine."

"Quite. I just hope I manage to survive without spilling soup down Lady Rutherford's neck."

Melton gave a restrained chuckle and proceeded to give the new employee tips on the fine art of serving. He finished by saying, "You can practice on the staff at our midday meal."

Nathan had always vaguely realized that, in any London house of the peerage or gentry—and, indeed, in many country houses as well—the basement and attic were the servants' domain. Melton gave Robert, the head footman, the task of showing the new man around. Robert, a redheaded young man whom Nathan judged to be about his own age, served as underbutler and was clearly aware of the prestige that accompanied his position. He reminded Nathan of a certain corporal still in Spain. Nevertheless, Robert greeted Nathan with a degree of warmth.

"Glad to have another set of hands, don't you know? With only four of us aside from Mr. Melton, it gets hectic at times. We've even had one of the grooms double as a footman on occasion."

The basement of the Earl of Rutherford's house was larger than one would have expected from viewing the house from its street front. Larger than many of its neighbors, Rutherford House had five bays of windows across the front, instead of the more usual three. Nathan had, of course, entered through a side alley that led to a servants and tradesmen's entrance, but he had noticed the main entrance, an elaborate wrought-iron bridge over a declivity between the street and the house. This deep moat-like space allowed light and air to permeate the basement from the outside. To the rear of the house, the basement extended partway under the back garden. Here, skylights allowed for light and ventilation.

Besides the kitchen and various storerooms, the base-

ment contained the servants' hall and separate quarters for
the housekeeper and the butler, and a smaller room for the
cook. The kitchen maids and scullery maid, he was told in
passing, had pull-down beds in the basement hallway.
Nathan had simply assumed he was passing storage cabi-
nets.

In the attic were rooms for female servants at one end of
the house and for male servants at the other end. Some were
small and rather cramped for one person, and others were
larger to accommodate two or three beds and a large chest to
be shared by the occupants. A common room separated the
two areas of bedchambers. Here, the maids spent afternoons
mending linens and gossiping.

Nathan was grateful for one of the cramped single-
occupancy rooms. It was sparsely furnished with an iron cot,
a chest, a small table, and a single chair.

He had met some of his fellow servants during his orien-
tation tour, but it was at the midday meal that he found them
all congregated in the servants' hall. There were some twenty-
five or thirty people in all. *A whole company or more,* he
thought, still seeing life in military terms.

The new man occasioned questions, curious looks, and
some good-natured joking. One of the maids, a girl named
Beth, openly flirted with him. She was a black-haired, dark-
eyed lass who had a knowing look about her.

"Careful, Beth," one of the other girls cautioned. "Harry
aint goin' ta like your smilin' so at a new fellow."

Beth tossed her head. " 'Arry knows I don't mean nothin'
by it."

Harry was one of the grooms and, noting the man's
scowl, Nathan vowed to steer clear of the flirtatious Beth. He
certainly did not need an added complication to this mission.

Their initial curiosity satisfied, the others engaged in separate conversations. Nathan listened closely and found the
chief topic to be Lady Allyson's adventure of the day before.
Molly, personal maid to Lady Allyson, preened as the focus
of others' questions. Nathan thought Molly extraordinarily

young for such a position: she could have no more than fifteen or sixteen years.

"Must a been terrible," one of the grooms commented.

"Oh, my stars, yes!" Molly said. "I was never so scared in my whole life!"

"From what I hear, we're lucky to have Lady Allyson still with us," one of the other maids offered hesitantly.

"Right. An' we wouldn't have," Molly replied, "had it not been for some stranger who just showed up out of the blue an' chased them ne'er-do-wells off! He was a real hero, he was."

"Who was he?" the saucy Beth asked. "I'll wager His Lordship will reward him handsomely if he saved his precious daughter."

"You know? That is so very strange," Molly said. "He just disappeared like. It all happened so quick and we were so scared—"

"Lady Allyson was scared?" the youngest footman asked in a disbelieving tone. Jamie was a lad of about fourteen, Nathan surmised, wishing the topic would shift away from the "hero."

"Well, she *should* have been," the housekeeper, Mrs. Simpson, said. "But I rather expect Lady Allyson was more angry than scared."

Others nodded sagely.

"His Lordship had me in this morning and asked me all kinds of questions." Molly was clearly reluctant to give up the center of attention. "But I couldn't remember much, except that big cow of a woman what pushed me. She had a big black mole close to one of her eyes—the right eye, I think it was."

Nathan stored this bit of information away, but gleaned nothing more from Molly's account.

He made it through serving the staff's meal with only a few mistakes. Melton took him aside later and gave him extra pointers. Even later in the afternoon, Nathan had a few minutes to himself before it would be time to serve at the family's evening meal. He lay on his cot, his hands behind his head, and stared at the ceiling.

If nothing else, he told himself, *I am gaining a whole new appreciation for the Thornton family's servants!*

His mind drifted to his earlier encounter with the intrepid Lady Allyson. He made several mental notes. The lady obviously did not find him a welcome addition to her life. She had agreed to his presence only in deference to her father's wishes. So, she was headstrong, but the old man seemed able to control her. She was proud—even arrogant, perhaps—but the servants seemed genuinely fond of her.

There might be *some* bright spots in this assignment. The woman was quick-witted, and that cascade of reddish brown hair tied back in schoolgirl fashion had made his fingers fairly itch to test its softness.

Oh, good grief, Thornton! Remember your place.

The family customarily gathered in the drawing room prior to the announcement of dinner. Allyson was late arriving. She had thought herself over her pique at her father's high-handed orders of the morning, but when the new footman entered the drawing room bearing a tray of drinks, it all came back to her. She tried to paste a serene look on her face, but a questioning look from her mother told her she had failed.

The footman approached Lady Rutherford first. "Ratafia, my lady?"

"Thank you." Lady Rutherford took the glass absently and returned to her conversation with Miss Pringle and with Clara, to whom he offered lemonade.

He learns quickly, Allyson thought sourly. Then he turned to her.

"My lady, lemonade. Or ratafia?"

"I shall have sherry," she said, her voice rather haughty.

He inclined his head and she had the impression that he would have accorded her a mocking bow had he not been encumbered with the heavy tray. She took the glass and turned away, vexed with both him and herself. She deliberately entered the conversation of her mother and sister as the footman served her father and Lord Lawton and then quietly left the room.

She knew she was being childish. It had nothing to do with the footman—Nathan, was it?—but she could not seem to stop resenting the power her father had given a servant over his daughter's comings and goings.

"Is that a new man?" Lady Rutherford directed the question to her husband.

"Yes, my dear."

"I was not aware we were taking on new staff." She sounded somewhat surprised. Allyson knew her mother prided herself on taking a direct hand in managing her household.

"Only this one, my dear," her husband responded, in a we-will-discuss-this-later tone that his wife undoubtedly recognized.

Lady Rutherford shrugged her shoulders and returned to her discussion with Miss Pringle. The two men escorted their wives down to dinner; Allyson and Miss Pringle brought up the rear. Melton and the new footman would be serving. As the two husbands seated their ladies and Melton helped Miss Pringle, the footman held Allyson's chair.

"My lady?" he intoned politely.

"Thank you." She was intensely aware of those strong gloved hands on her chair, and of something else she could not quite identify. This unnerved her, for Lady Allyson was used to being in full command—at least of herself.

Initially, the meal proceeded uneventfully. Allyson noted that Melton occasionally gave the man—Nathan—directions with a gesture, or in a low voice. The family were all seated at one end of the huge dining table to facilitate conversation, which touched on a wide range of topics, including political issues and news of the war in the Peninsula. At one point, the footman was replenishing wineglasses. He had a carafe of red wine in one hand and a pitcher of water in the other, for the Rutherford ladies drank their wine with liberal doses of water. Just as Allyson reached for her glass, intent on making a conversational point with her father, the new servant reached toward the same glass. She bumped his arm, and water splashed onto the table and into her lap.

"Oh!" she gasped, but managed to set the glass down.

"I am so sorry, my lady," he said. Setting his two vessels on the sideboard, he grabbed up an extra napkin and offered it to her, repeating his apology.

Conversation at the table came to an abrupt stop.

She dabbed at the wet spots on her dress. "Never mind," she muttered. "It was surely my fault as much as yours."

Clara's officious voice dropped into the silence. "So few servants are trained properly these days."

"It was an accident, Clara," Allyson said rather testily.

"Still," Clara went on, "are you sure you do not wish to change your gown?"

"For a few drops of *water?* I think not." For some reason, Allyson wanted to smooth over the incident for the hapless footman whom Melton had now dismissed to the kitchen. She saw Lady Rutherford send a questioning glance toward her husband. Allyson took this as a hopeful sign, for if her mother objected to the man, he would surely be gone in a twinkling.

Melton served dessert, and afterward the ladies withdrew. Clara was still talking on about the spilled water, but in truth the gown was hardly spotted as the three women took up positions in the drawing room. The two men joined them there in short order. Lord Rutherford usually found his son-in-law an absolute bore. Allyson noted that tonight was no exception.

Chapter 3

As soon as she could politely do so, Allyson excused herself to retire early, glad to escape the sort of chitchat that passed for conversation whenever her sister was involved. Not that she *disliked* Clara. It was just that the two of them had so little in common. Allyson had been a self-contained child, clinging to adults far less than her younger sister, whose very "neediness" struck a chord in Lady Rutherford's heart. Often, as they were growing up, Allyson had felt like an outsider with her mother and sister, though she had to admit that her mother had always tried to include her. Moreover, Allyson and her mother had grown closer since Clara's marriage. Nevertheless, both parents and their daughters had long since acknowledged—albeit tacitly—that Clara was Her Ladyship's daughter and Allyson was her father's.

Allyson reveled in the relationship she had with her father. She shared his love of books and politics, as well as his love of horses. In the country, the two spent hours riding. Unfortunately, the earl had little time for such a pastime in the city. Rutherford had also taught Allyson how to fish and fence and shoot. He might have taught her how to box as well, had Lady Rutherford not put her foot down at such beyond-the-pale unladylike behavior.

Yet, much as she enjoyed these traditionally male activities with her father, Allyson often envied the ease with which her mother and sister settled into more feminine interests and social situations. For the last year or so, she had felt a sense of emptiness—an undefined longing—in her life. She had even begun to consider seriously the possibility of marrying. True, at twenty-four she was probably "on the shelf," but she still had her share of suitors each Season.

She did not want what she saw as the simpering superficiality of her sister's marriage, though there was no doubt that Lawton doted on his wife. No, she wanted a relationship more like that of her parents: they understood and respected each other as equals, although they had their own interests. She thought each genuinely *liked* and enjoyed the other *person,* whereas Clara and Edmund seemed to care more about image than reality. Perhaps she was being unfair to the Lawtons.

"Will that be all, my lady?"

Allyson was pulled out of her somewhat melancholy musing by Molly, who had all this time been helping her mistress prepare for bed. The maid had just finished plaiting Allyson's hair into a single thick braid.

"Oh, yes," Allyson responded. "I seem to have drifted away there for a moment."

"Yes, my lady. I hope you wasn't dwellin' on what happened yesterday."

"No, I wasn't. I trust you have recovered sufficiently?"

"Once I got over bein' so scared, I was fit as a fiddle, though my stockings was ruined."

"I shall see that you have some new ones."

"Thank you, my lady." Molly seemed to perceive a change in the demeanor of her mistress, for she launched into chattering of below-stairs gossip as she gathered up discarded clothing. Allyson only half listened until Molly mentioned the new footman.

"Ain't he a handsome piece, though?" Molly did not wait for a response. "Beth's already makin' eyes at 'im an' I daresay all the women—even Cook and Mrs. Simpson—are taken with him."

"Already?"

"Oh, my stars, yes! Even me."

"Well, you had best see you all behave yourselves," Allyson said in mild reproval. "You *know* how Mama would feel about a scandal in her house."

"Yes, my lady."

When Molly left, Allyson sat reading in a comfortable chair before the fireplace, a lamp on the table at her elbow. Rather, she was *attempting* to read Mr. Scott's newest work. When she had read the same paragraph for the third time, she closed the book, her finger marking the place, and stared into the fire.

Her mind kept drifting, and the recurring image was of that infernal footman. The sooner he was gone, the better—obviously he had set hearts aflutter among the female staff. She sighed. *Unfortunate that he is a mere servant.* She immediately chastised herself for *that* unworthy thought.

"Perhaps not so very unworthy," a soft young voice said.

"Wha-at?" Startled, Allyson looked in the direction from which the voice had come.

She was astonished to see a young girl, of perhaps ten years, sitting cross-legged in the middle of the bed. Or seeming to sit. Allyson saw no indentation in the coverlet and, indeed, she was able to see right through the child's figure, yet she clearly discerned pink cheeks, dark hair, and a sprinkling of freckles. The girl clutched a rag doll with tight yellow yarn braids springing from the head.

Amazed, but somehow not afraid, Allyson said inanely, "That was my doll. My favorite, actually. Her name is *Leah.*" She remembered finding the doll in the attic and preferring it to the china-faced doll that Clara loved so.

The girl jumped down from the bed and stood next to the bedpost, which Allyson could discern clearly through the old-fashioned blue dress the child wore.

"It was mine long before it was yours," the girl said, hugging the doll closer. "And her name is *Caroline*—after the queen, of course."

"The queen's name is *Charlotte*," Allyson corrected. "You mean the Princess of Wales." She could not believe she was having a conversation with some figment of her imagination.

The figment stamped her foot and said sharply, "No! I mean *my* queen—Queen Caroline."

Allyson dug around in the recesses of her brain and then said in some wonderment, "Queen to King George II?"

"Precisely!"

"Good heavens!" Allyson muttered to herself, "I cannot be having this discussion." Aloud, she said to her uninvited guest, "But they died in . . . in the last century."

"Of course they did. So did I," the child said cheerfully.

Allyson was beginning to believe this was *not* a figment of her imagination, but, oddly enough, she felt no fear or apprehension, just curiosity. She recalled that the servants had several times complained of misplaced items; of unexpected, but not always unpleasant, smells; and of seeing strange, but fleeting, images. She and her parents had dismissed these notions as flights of fancy.

"Who *are* you?" she asked. "More to the point, *what* are you?"

The girl drew herself up proudly. "I am Lady Maryvictoria Elizabeth Watkinson." She put the doll on the bed and curtsied prettily.

"Watkinson. Watkinson. I know I should know that name."

"My papa was the Earl of Valmere, but the title died when Papa died."

"Valmere. Valmere. Ah! I believe he built this house . . . in . . . in 1730 if I recall correctly. You—you must be a—"

Maryvictoria giggled. "A ghost."

Allyson jerked to full attention at this revelation. "A ghost? Oh, come now. No thinking person believes in ghosts." She was not sure whether she directed this pronouncement at the child or at herself.

"Well, thinking people should. And *you* should, too."

Maryvictoria put her small hands on her hips and skipped to the center of the room. Allyson wondered if the child realized she had just insulted her hostess.

"What are you doing here?" Allyson asked.

"I come here quite often, actually," the child said matter-of-factly. "This was my home, you know. In fact, I died in this very room."

Allyson shuddered and looked at her bed.

"No, not this bed." She examined the big four-poster carefully. "Mine was much smaller, but far prettier."

"Oh?"

"I'm not allowed to come as often as I would like," Maryvictoria said with a note of regret. "But I like to see the pretty clothes and jewelry of the ladies, and smell the perfume." She moved about the room, gesturing here and there.

"You can smell?" Allyson asked.

"Well, of course. And I must say that bit in the blue bottle is too heavy and too sweet. You are much wiser to stick to that light flowery one as you do."

Allyson raised her brows. "Why, thank you." Then another thought occurred to her. "You have been going through my armoire and my jewelry box? And moving things around on my dressing table? And here I thought Molly—"

"I tried to leave things just as I found them. That's one of the rules."

"Rules?"

"For my coming here from time to time."

"What was your name again? I was caught by the name *Watkinson*."

"*Maryvictoria Elizabeth Watkinson*," she repeated with a profound degree of patience.

"That is a great deal of name for a little girl," Allyson observed. "Are you—were you—called *Mary?* Or perhaps *Vicky?* Or *Eliza?*"

"No!" She stamped her foot again, but Allyson noted no

sound from the action. "I am Maryvictoria. I *like* my name. The *Victoria* part comes from Latin, you know. Papa said it was quite noble. But you need not call me *Lady* Maryvictoria."

Allyson inclined her head in acknowledgment. "Very well, *Maryvictoria* it is." She was beginning to find this whole dream—if that was what it was—vastly amusing. "So, tell me, Maryvictoria, why are you here? *Now,* that is?"

Maryvictoria looked at her in surprise. "Why—I am here to help you, of course."

"Help *me?* Help me what?"

"Sort out your life. You are making rather a muddle of it, you know."

"I beg your pardon!"

"Well, you can't seem to make up your mind what you want, and I will help you decide."

"If you think for one moment that I will tolerate some ten-year-old . . . ap-apparition—"

"Actually, I have eleven years."

"—run my life, you had better think again."

"Oh, I'm not allowed to do *that*—I just help."

Allyson raised her voice. "I do not need your help!"

Before Maryvictoria could respond, there was a knock on the door.

"Allyson, dear," her mother called.

"Come in, Mama."

"I heard your voice." Lady Rutherford looked around blankly. "To whom were you speaking?"

Maryvictoria stood by the bed in what should have been plain view, but her mother apparently had no inkling of the child's presence.

"Oh . . . uh . . . I suppose I was thinking aloud, arguing a point with Mr. Scott," she said, holding up the book. Heavens, her mother would never countenance what Allyson had just experienced, if, indeed, she had "experienced" anything at all.

"You must not allow your father's orders to overset you, my dear. He means only your best, you know."

"Yes, Mama."

Her mother closed the door softly behind her.

Maryvictoria said, "I'll be going along now. But I shall be here when you need me." Her image began to grow fainter; then it suddenly took form again. "I almost forgot Caroline!" She picked up the doll and, this time, simply faded away.

"Wait! Come back! I have some questions—" But the visitor had gone.

Allyson sat for a long while, thoroughly nonplussed.

When she awoke the next morning, after a night of—at best—fitful sleep, Allyson wondered if it had all been a dream. But then, before she rang for Molly, she noticed that her perfume bottles had been rearranged—again. *That little imp,* she thought.

She had slept later than she intended, but it was early enough that if she hurried, she would have time for her ride. She finished her morning ablutions and sent word to the stable for Alfred to saddle her horse and one for himself. When she arrived at the stable, though, it was not Alfred who was waiting to accompany her, but the new footman.

"I had thought you would be gone from Rutherford House by now," she said by way of greeting.

"Why would you think that?" he asked, not impolitely.

He flashed her a grin that showed even white teeth and deep dimples in his cheeks. *I see what Molly and Beth like,* she thought, then was instantly annoyed with herself. She was also annoyed that he seemed so expressly unintimidated by her brusque manner.

"My mother rarely tolerates ineptness in a staff member," she said.

"Perhaps *she* recognizes an apt pupil when she encounters one," he replied. "And as you well know, my lady, I am beholden to His Lordship for my job."

"Do not be impudent. You would do very well to remember your place, Nathan." Her tone was haughtier than she intended, haughtier than she ever used with servants.

"Yes, my lady."

The words were correct and the tone subdued, so why did she have the distinct feeling he was amused?

Alfred interrupted the exchange by bringing two saddled horses from the stable. One was her own Princess; the other, a black gelding she did not recognize. She *did* recognize the animal's very fine lines, however.

"Alfred, where did *that* mount come from?" she demanded.

"I dunno, my lady. Lord Rutherford brought him in yesterday and said Nathan here was to have the use of him."

She openly gaped at this information. Her father had purchased a new horse—a very superior one at that—and was allowing a new untried servant to ride him? And why had he not discussed the new acquisition with *her* as he usually did regarding new cattle? She was rather miffed that he had failed to do so.

"Are you quite sure of that, Alfred? Papa said exactly that?"

"Yes, my lady. His Lordship was very definite." Alfred's tone and a curious glance at the footman suggested that the groom found this behavior as extraordinary as she did.

"Well, all right. . . ." she said reluctantly. She turned to the footman. "Then let us be off. I do hope you are up to handling that horse. It would be a shame if he were mistreated through ignorance or ineptness."

"I shall do my best, my lady." He cupped his hands to give her a boost into her saddle, then quickly mounted his own horse.

They made their way in relative silence to Rotten Row, where at this early hour Allyson could have the vigorous ride she had missed the day before. Until they reached the park, the only sounds were the steady clopping of the horses' hooves on the street, and the squeaks and groans of such vehicles, and the calls of tradesmen who were out at this hour. She sneaked a covert glance at her companion from time to time. Well, he *seemed* to know what he was about.

"You needn't try to keep up with me, Nathan. I like a hard ride, you see."

"Yes, my lady. I do remember my place, you see."

She gave him a caustic look, wondering if he was mocking her. She dug her heels into Princess's flank, fully intending to leave the brazen footman far behind. Ten minutes later, she pulled up to give both Princess and herself a breather. The footman was right there, a discreet distance behind her. Moreover, neither rider nor horse seemed especially winded. In fact, she had the impression that the footman, instead of being hard-pressed to keep up, had been deliberately holding his mount back.

The crisp coolness of the early morning and the exhilaration of the ride had improved her mood remarkably. She swung the mare to be beside the black.

"You do seem to know your way around riding," she conceded.

"Thank you, my lady." He flashed her that grin again.

"I should like to see how well Papa's new hack performs." She gave the black's rider an arch look. "Are you up to a bit of a race?"

"Here? Now?"

"Yes, here and now. As far as that large elm that seems to be leaning over the Row." She pointed with her riding crop.

His gaze followed where she pointed, and he did not answer for a moment. He appeared to be weighing whether he should engage in such unseemly conduct. Finally, he shrugged. "From here to the elm?"

"Yes. By the way, do you know if the black has a name?"

"I . . . I believe it is Bucephalus."

"Bucephalus?" She laughed. "Whoever named him must have had delusions of grandeur!"

"I beg your pardon?"

"Imagine giving a modern horse the name of Alexander the Great's warhorse. That is quite a name to live up to."

He patted the black's neck. "I think this fellow will probably hold his own."

"We shall see."

"Bucephalus is bigger and stronger than your mare. It seems only fair to give you a head start."

She looked his mount over again carefully, then nodded. "As you please." She dug her heels into Princess's flank again and leaned forward to urge the horse on. She glanced behind her once to see that the black was yet standing still. But soon enough she felt the breeze of the other horse and rider beside her, and then ahead of her and Princess. She noted that the horse and rider were very well matched. They drew up at the designated elm tree.

"Well—" She drew in a deep breath. "I am happy to see that Papa has not lost his touch in choosing horse flesh."

"No, my lady."

Just then, another early rider approached. "Lady Allyson!" he called, and came up beside her. "I thought you might be out this morning. I missed you yesterday."

"Lord Braxton, how nice to see you." She noticed fleetingly that Nathan dropped back out of earshot, but not out of sight.

Lord Braxton was a handsome man, almost pretty, she thought. He was dressed moderately, but in the latest fashion, with buff-colored pantaloons and a maroon jacket. His neckcloth was tied in a rather intricate knot. He tipped his hat to her and smiled.

"I see you've not curbed your hoydenish ways, my dear," he teased. "You should have let me know. I would have spared your having to race with one of your family retainers."

She laughed. "You know very well that that slug on which you insist on being seen in public cannot hold a candle to Princess."

"Oh, do be careful of injuring Sheik's tender sensibilities." He patted the horse's neck. "Pay her no mind, my boy. I'm sure she doesn't mean it."

They rode along at a rather slow pace, chatting of inconsequential matters. Having had her energetic run, Allyson did not mind the slower pace now. She was aware of the footman, who maintained a proper presence—and distance. Only later did it occur to her that on similar occasions Alfred had been just as correctly circumspect, but she had always been more or less impervious to the groom's presence.

Richard Ritter, Viscount Braxton, was a friend of some years' standing. He had been an ardent suitor during her first

Season, but she had discouraged him. Since then, theirs had developed into an easy relationship, though Allyson suspected his ardor would return in full force if she but encouraged him. As it was, they both enjoyed a bantering flirtation.

"You *will* save me a dance—maybe two?—at the Worthington ball, will you not?" he asked as he took his leave of her.

"Of course."

She watched him ride away and smiled at his slight clumsiness in the saddle. Thank goodness Lord Braxton was far more capable on the dance floor than on the back of a horse. He was a comfortable companion. Perhaps she *should* encourage him. . . .

She glanced behind her and gestured for Nathan to close the distance between them. "The traffic has increased considerably. We shall return now."

"Yes, my lady."

There was nothing even slightly clumsy about the footman's expertise as a rider.

Although he had not intruded so far as to eavesdrop on the conversation between Lady Allyson and her friend, Nathan had observed with interest the comfortable camaraderie the two seemed to enjoy. He tucked the name *Braxton* away in his mind. *Probably a long shot,* he thought. He seemed to Nathan's practiced soldier's eyes to be a follower of the Beau Brummell crowd, to whom fashionable dress and being up to the mark on the latest *on-dit* was the very center of life.

He turned his attention to the female he had come to view as his "charge." She rode slightly ahead of him, and he noted that she had a good seat, in every sense of the word. She wore a tan riding habit trimmed with dark brown braid. The garment was perfectly designed to show off her best features. *The woman has style,* he mused. He found himself envying a fop like Braxton, for he had heard her promise the fellow a dance.

He thought her personal antipathy to him had lessened somewhat during the course of their ride. Which was just as well, for

Lord Rutherford had made it clear to Captain Thornton that he would *not* be relieved of this duty, regardless of any fault the countess might find with the new footman's serving skills.

Nathan leaned over to pat his horse's neck and said softly, "I think Lady Allyson admires you, old fellow." Bucephalus, who had been with him throughout his sojourn in the Peninsula, and before, pricked his ears at the sound of his master's voice.

Perhaps it had not been wise to have Rutherford stable Nathan's own horse, but there had seemed little choice. He certainly would not ask to stable the animal at Halstead House. He had not seen or spoken to his father or brother in some years now, and cared but little if he ever did. And who knew when he might need his own trusty mount?

Arriving at the stable, he quickly dismounted and offered his assistance in helping Lady Allyson dismount. For a moment she hesitated, but then, she accepted his offer. He reached to settle his hands on her waist, and she put her hands on his shoulders as he lifted her down. For the briefest, most impersonal moment, he held her close. The top of her head brushed his chin, and he smelled a flowery, woodsy scent from her hair. He quickly released her.

"Thank you." Her tone was dismissive and she turned to Alfred, who had emerged from the stable. "Alfred, please inform John Coachman that I will need the carriage shortly after noon." She turned back to the footman and said in an overly casual tone, "You need not bother to accompany me, Nathan. I shall take Molly with me as I make a few morning calls."

"I beg your pardon, my lady. His Lordship's orders were quite clear."

"But I do not *need* you hanging about," she insisted.

"Nevertheless—"

"Oh, very well." She sounded annoyed. "But it is quite unnecessary—a waste of time—in my opinion."

"Be that as it may—"

But she had already turned away from him. He watched as she walked toward the house, her anger apparent in her determined stride. Yes, indeed. The woman had style.

Chapter 4

Allyson changed from her riding habit into a pale yellow day dress before she went down to breakfast. Her mother and the Lawtons were already seated and tucking into their repast.

"Good morning, all. Papa has left already?" she asked.

"Yes," her mother replied. "He mentioned an early meeting this morning."

"I had hoped to catch him."

"Something I can help with?" Lady Rutherford asked, accepting a stack of letters Melton handed to her.

"The post, madam."

"Oh, no," Allyson responded to her mother. "It is just that I cannot have a footman following me about all the time, but the man seems to think the earth will stop moving in its orbit if he is not dogging my every step!"

"The earth might not change its customary cycle," the countess said calmly, "but your father might join it in orbit if you protest too strongly. Rutherford apparently thinks the fellow has qualities that surpass those of an ordinary footman."

"But, Mama—"

Clara set her fork down. "I do not understand why you

are making such a fuss, Allyson. You are always wanting your own way—"

"And I usually get it," Allyson said with a childish smirk at her sister.

"Yes, but sometimes a lady must bow to the wishes of the men in her life," Clara said sweetly. "Isn't that right, dear?" she addressed her husband.

"Absolutely, love."

Allyson rolled her eyes and gritted her teeth. Ever since Clara had beaten Allyson to the altar, she adopted an insufferable air of condescension toward her elder sister. Poor Edmund had probably not had an idea or wish in the last three years that his ever-so-dutiful wife had not put into his head.

Melton placed a plate of eggs and muffins in front of Allyson. Lady Rutherford sorted through the mail, Edmund devoted himself to his plate, and Clara apparently equated Allyson's silence as agreement. The countess handed Clara and Edmund several missives.

"Oh, finally," Edmund said of one.

"You will not mind if we read these?" Clara asked, already breaking the seal on another. "It has been so long since we had any word of home."

Allyson and Lady Rutherford murmured their assent, and the Lawtons were quickly absorbed in their mail. Allyson was thus the only one who noticed the slight intake of breath and the sudden pallor in her mother's complexion as the countess turned over a certain letter. Lady Rutherford quickly put it on the bottom of her stack. Her hand shook as she did so.

"Is something amiss, Mama?" Allyson asked.

"Nothing important, dear." However, her mother sounded distracted, and there was a stricken look in her eyes. "If you will all excuse me," she said, rising, "I will finish dealing with the post in my sitting room." This was a room off the master bedchamber in which the countess had a writing desk and from which she conducted household business.

"Of course." Clara looked up vaguely and returned immediately to her letter.

Edmund jumped to his feet and then promptly resumed his seat as the door closed behind his mother-in-law. "She did not finish her breakfast," he observed.

Allyson was concerned, but obviously her mother did not want to share whatever had overset her. At least, not yet. She finished her breakfast slowly, making small talk with Clara and Edmund, neither of whom seemed aware of Lady Rutherford's agitation.

Breakfast over, Clara and Edmund invited Allyson to join them on a shopping trip. She politely refused, and when they had gone, she sought her mother, whom she found in the sitting room. The older woman was seated at her desk, staring blankly at a piece of paper with some heavy writing on it.

"Mama? What is it? Can I help?"

The countess laid the paper on her desk blotter and folded her hands over it. "It is nothing to worry you, my dear. I daresay it will work itself out in a day or two." She paused. "You are going out, my dear?" Allyson thought the cheerful tone had a false note to it.

"I had planned to do so. *We* had planned to—"

"Oh, goodness. It quite slipped my mind, and now I find I have a small matter that I must see to. Can . . . can we make our calls tomorrow? Or . . . ?"

"I do not mind going alone," Allyson falsely assured her. "That is, unless you would like me to accompany you."

Lady Rutherford sighed. "No, dear. This is something I must see to myself. The new curtains in the west drawing room . . ." Her voice trailed off, and then she said brightly, "Please give Lady Beauchamp my regrets. Oh, and do remember the Satterly do this evening."

"Yes, Mama." But Allyson thought her mother had something very different than the west drawing room curtains on her mind.

Allyson left the house later in the day in a state of apprehension. She knew from Molly's chatter that her adventure and rescue two days ago was still the subject of drawing room gossip all over town. Now she would have to face the harpies without her mother's support. But face them she would. She was also still vaguely worried about her mother's behavior. Something was definitely amiss, but if Mama did not want to discuss it, well, so be it.

Nathan was standing at the carriage door ready to hand her and Molly to their seats.

"Oh!" Allyson said. "I had quite forgotten about *you*." This was a lie, but the fellow annoyed her—that is, that she *had* thought of him annoyed her.

He put his fist on his heart. "My lady, you have quite wounded my self-esteem."

"I doubt that," she said sourly. When she was settled in her seat, she muttered, "Insolent fellow."

"But ever so handsome," Molly said dreamily. "An' so polite, too. And he can read! Not very many footmen do that."

"He reads? Are you sure?" Allyson's interest was piqued in spite of her determination to remain indifferent to the man.

"Yes, my lady. I heard him ask Mr. Melton to please not burn the old newspapers."

"Hmm." It was unusual, but not unknown, for a servant of Nathan's station to be literate. After all, the Methodists and other dissenters had been teaching the lower orders to read the Bible for over two decades now.

"I think he's real innerested in the war news," Molly went on.

Allyson nodded. "He was a soldier."

"Wonder why ain't one now? I thought once you signed on for the king's shilling you were there a good long while."

"Almost for life," Allyson said absently.

Then it struck her: that was true. So why was an able-bodied soldier employed as a footman? Had the man deserted? Desertion was a hanging offense. It would be a shame to have such a handsome face and form consigned to a gibbet. She shrugged off this ghoulish thought by reminding herself that her father had hired the man and seemed to have confidence in him. She deliberately turned her attention to the order—that is, the ordeal—of the day.

She made several calls. At each of them, just as she had feared, she found her foiled kidnapping to be the latest *on-dit*. However, she had reasoned that she might as well face the gossips sooner as later, so she answered all questions as matter-of-factly as possible.

"You are so very brave, Lady Allyson," gushed Miss Loretta Longworth, a blond beauty who was this Season's "diamond of the first water." She glanced around to be sure she had the attention of most of the gentlemen in the Longworth drawing room. "I know I should have taken to my bed for a week if something so terrible had happened to me! I suppose I just have a more delicate nature."

"Is it true that three gentlemen were riding by and rescued you? I heard that one of them swept you up onto his horse as the other two chased the culprits away. 'Tis all so very romantic," Emily Prentiss said, clasping her hands over her heart.

Allyson laughed. "I suppose it might be considered romantic, though a bit awkward to be swept up onto a moving horse, if it were at all true. There was only one man, a common laborer on the pavement. The would-be criminals took flight immediately. Do you not think that rather cowardly behavior?" she asked lightly.

Miss Longworth gave a dramatic shudder and fluttered her eyelashes. "I say, it makes one reluctant to go *shopping*." This announcement had the desired effect, for two gentlemen instantly volunteered to escort her any time they could be of service to such a lovely damsel. She murmured sweetly and batted her lashes some more.

The dark-haired, slightly plump, but pretty Emily Prentiss thrust herself back into the conversation. "I heard your father had hired two *huge* men to protect you."

Allyson drew back, pretending to be more appalled than

she really felt. "Wherever did you hear such nonsense as that?"

"It is not true, then?" Miss Prentiss asked.

"My father insists that I be accompanied on most excursions by one quite ordinary footman," Allyson admitted, and added caustically, "That is far fewer servants than many gentlemen and ladies of the *ton* must have whenever they venture a step away from their own houses."

Miss Caroline Dawson was a squint-eyed little thing with mousy brown hair and a rather splotchy complexion. She had been a devious sneak in the exclusive girls' school many of the young women in the room had attended. She was now tolerated in *ton* circles because to exclude her would subject one to the most malicious of rumors—and because she was heiress to a fabulous fortune. She now entered the conversation with an arch look and a high-pitched voice. "If by an 'ordinary footman' you mean the Adonis in Rutherford livery in the park this morning, dear Lady Allyson, well, I would have to say 'the lady doth protest too much.' "

Miss Prentiss said, "You saw him?"

"Oh, yes," Miss Dawson said airily. "Very handsome as servants go. Puts one in mind of that groom Lady Ferrington used to go about with in the park."

Miss Prentiss and Miss Longworth gasped. One of the gentlemen said, "Here, now."

Miss Dawson was all innocence. "Oh, I meant nothing untoward. Lady Allyson has chosen a *very* fine-looking man—just as Lady Ferrington did."

Allyson was embarrassed and furious. The Ferrington scandal was a fairly recent one. Lady Ferrington, it was rumored, chose her male retainers for qualities other than their efficiency as servants. She had, only a few weeks ago, gone off to Italy with one of her grooms.

"One does not have a great deal of control over how one looks, does one, Miss Dawson?" Allyson asked.

There was a moment of tight silence, and Allyson inwardly cringed at her own spiteful behavior. When *would* she learn to keep her tongue between her teeth? Miss Dawson did not reply, but she sent a searing look in Allyson's direction.

Lord Merrivale, a pudgy young baron, relieved the tension by observing, "Very wise of your father to take such precautions, Lady Allyson."

"Hear! Hear!" another of the gentlemen said and tactfully changed the subject.

Lord Braxton sidled over to Allyson and said softly, " 'Tis a good idea, you know. You are far too independent."

"Oh, Richard. Not you, too," she said just as softly.

Allyson was glad to move on to another drawing room, but with each call, she found herself subjected to essentially the same conversations. It was clear that in certain quarters the feeling was that the toplofty Lady Allyson Crossleigh was getting a bit of a set-down. Keeping a polite smile pasted on her face was taking more and more effort. After each visit, she came face-to-face with Nathan standing at her carriage, waiting to hand her in before taking his position on the rear of the vehicle. Finally, she determined that she had endured enough of society's inquisition and returned home.

At each stop of the Rutherford carriage, Nathan noted that the earl's equipage was not the only vehicle out and about, nor were he and Molly the only servants attending those engaged in "morning" calls. Among the servants, as among their employers, the principal topic was the attempted abduction of Lord Rutherford's elder daughter. Nathan thought Lady Allyson must have warned her maid about undue gossip, for the usually ebullient Molly was far more subdued than she was in the Rutherford servants' hall.

She answered questions as they were addressed to her, but offered little else, though much speculation was offered here and there. At one point, when she evaded a pointed question, Nathan winked at her and nodded approvingly.

Molly blushed and lowered her gaze, but during a moment alone as they waited for Lady Allyson to say her good-byes, the loyal maid let loose her emotions.

"Cuckoo old cows, what do *they* know?"

Nathan laughed. "You have your metaphors mixed, Molly, but your sentiments are right enough."

"Meta—what? Oh, never mind. You would not believe the nonsense I've been hearin'."

"I probably would."

She ignored his response and went right on. "Some would have it that it was a disappointed lover as tried to grab 'er. An' that silly Longworth abigail—you won't believe what *she* said!"

Nathan suspected he would not have to wait long for Molly to divulge this bit of information.

"She said—she had the *nerve* to say—Lady Allyson probably brought it on herself, that she's always flirting with this man or that one. Well, I put her in her place, I did."

"I hope you did not create yet another line of talk," Nathan warned.

"I didn't, I'm sure. I just told her she should not judge all ladies by her own mistress. Flirting, indeed! As though my lady had to put herself forward so. Why, she's turned down more proposals than . . . than . . . well Princess Charlotte, probably."

Nathan grinned at this extreme indication of Molly's loyalty.

"You don't believe me, but it's true. At least two each Season since she's been out. And it ain't just her fortune as brings 'em around, either!"

"Is that so?" Nathan asked, not really liking this line of discussion, but a rejected suitor just might factor into the picture. Perhaps he and Rutherford were chasing the wrong fox in tying the abduction attempt to French intrigue.

"Yes, it's so." Molly began to tick names off on her fingers. "First there was Mr. Cummings, but he were only a second son—to a baron, I think. And after all, Lady Allyson is the daughter of an earl! Then Lord Braxton—I know as she turned 'im down, but he still calls regular-like. And Lord Swinburne. And the Comte de Pommeraie. And Mr. Hamilton . . . And there was another Frenchman, but I forget his name—Arnaud, perhaps—and . . . and countless others."

"I shall take your word for it," Nathan assured her, and dropped the subject as Lady Allyson appeared. However, he filed away each of the names Molly had mentioned.

As he handed his mistress into her carriage after each visit, he thought he saw increasing signs of strain about her eyes. He wanted to tell her to take no notice, that this, too, would pass, but he carefully kept his place.

In the carriage on the way home, Molly was relatively quiet, a fact for which Allyson was grateful. She could have sworn Nathan gave her a look of understanding and sympathy as he handed her down at Rutherford House.

Before repairing to her own room, Allyson knocked at the door of her parents' private sitting room. Her mother bade her enter, and Allyson assumed the strain of the afternoon showed in her face when her mother greeted her.

"Was it so very bad, my dear?"

"It was simply awful, but at least I have put to rest some of the more wild speculations."

"I am proud of you, Allyson. Few young women would have faced the dragons as you did today."

Allyson shrugged. She looked keenly at her mother. Had she been crying? "And you, Mama? Are you all right? You seemed overset earlier."

"I am quite fine. 'Twas a trifling matter only. Goodness, look at the time, and we have the Satterly soiree this evening. Just time for a short lie-down."

Allyson went on to her own chamber, aware that her mother had more or less dismissed her. But she thought she herself would welcome a short rest. Molly helped her remove the outer garments and left. When the door closed behind the maid, Allyson lay on the bed but soon became aware of another presence in the room.

"I thought your visits went quite well."

Allyson lifted herself on one elbow. Maryvictoria perched on the stool in front of the dressing table. There was, however, no reflection of the child in the mirror.

"You thought . . . You mean you were there? At every house? I did not see you."

Maryvictoria giggled. "Of course not. You see me only when I want you to. No, not at *every* house. I find Mrs. Dalrymple a dead bore, don't you? Always prattling on about those silly dogs."

Allyson grinned in spite of herself, then sat up straighter to gaze at her visitor more directly. "If you did not want to be seen, why were you there then?"

"I'm to keep an eye on you."

Allyson wiped her hand across her brow. "Heavens! It is not enough I must put up with that infernal footman? Now I must contend with *you* as well?"

Maryvictoria hopped down from the stool. She had a very determined look on her face. "I told you, I am here to help you. You *did* see the Dawson chit spill her tea in her lap?"

"You did that?"

Maryvictoria grinned slyly. "Well, I helped her. She deserved it, you know."

"That is entirely beside the point," Allyson said firmly. "I have told you that I do not want, I do not need, and I do not welcome your 'help.' "

"But you will."

"I will? I suppose you can see into the future?" Allyson asked scornfully.

"Hmm . . . Mostly."

"Oh, good!" Allyson's voice dripped with sarcasm. "Then you can tell me all, and I can shout it to the world and thus become a modern Cassandra, though without her tragic end, I would hope."

"It does not work that way."

But Allyson, caught up in her own rhetoric, ignored this and went on. "Why, we can change history, I and this figment of my imagination. We shall single-handedly—well, *together,* at any rate—change history. We shall curb Napoleon's ambition; we shall see the Prince Regent become a man of moderation and common sense; and we shall turn his wife into a paragon of female virtue."

Maryvictoria soundlessly stamped her foot. "I am not a f-f-ficament—"

"Figment."

"And I *told* you, it does not work that way. Nothing can be changed. What will be will be."

"Then how on earth—or elsewhere, if you please—can you possibly 'help'?"

"You'll see."

With that, she was gone again.

Allyson lay back, thoroughly confused. She was not at all sure she was not hallucinating these visits from her ethereal friend. Still, she found the conversations diverting, and there *was* the matter of moved objects among her possessions. She grinned as she recalled the shocked expression on Miss Dawson's face and her accusing a servant of jostling her elbow, though the servant had been quite out of reach.

Chapter 5

Dressed in a vivid blue silk gown, Allyson met her parents and the Lawtons in the drawing room before leaving for the Satterly soiree. Lady Rutherford and Lady Lawton were also attired in silk—in lavender and light green, respectively. With a quick kiss on his wife's cheek, Lord Rutherford went off to his club.

"Your very correct black shows us off to good advantage, Lawton," Clara said to her husband when the earl had left.

"I shall be the envy of all the gentlemen there," he replied. "I thought Miss Pringle was to come with us."

"She is not feeling well," the countess explained. The others murmured sympathetically.

Allyson thought both her mother and her sister were looking especially fine. "I vow, Mama, you will outshine both Clara and me this evening."

Her mother smiled and patted Allyson's cheek. "Thank you, my dear. 'Tis pure flummery, but I do thank you for lifting my spirits so."

"It is not flummery," Allyson protested, and both Lawtons murmured their assent.

Nor was it flummery. In her early forties, the Countess of Rutherford was still a very beautiful woman with auburn hair and the same brown eyes she had passed on to her elder daughter.

Allyson thought the problem that had troubled her mother must have been resolved, for Lady Rutherford chatted cheerfully as they prepared to depart.

Jamie, the youngest footman, held the carriage door as Lord Lawton assisted the ladies to their seats, Allyson being the last of the three. She gave the young man an inquiring look and could not resist asking, "Are we to be spared the presence of the ubiquitous Nathan, then?" She immediately wished she had said nothing at all.

Jamie had a puzzled expression. Finally, he said, "This here's Nathan's half-day off, my lady."

"Oh, of course," she murmured as she stepped into the carriage, glad the faint light hid the color she felt in her face. She scarcely heard the conversation of the others. She found herself wondering what the handsome footman would be doing with his free time. Did he perhaps have a sweetheart in some other house? This thought was briefly dismaying, then annoying. He was probably in some alehouse, she decided. And, anyway, why on earth should a servant's activities on his time off concern *her?*

The gathering sponsored by the Satterlys was rather informal by *ton* standards, but Allyson preferred such affairs over the interminable receiving lines favored by many hostesses. The focus of attention was on the Satterly daughters, a set of golden-haired twins who had recently made their curtsies to the queen. The two young women performed admirably as a team, one playing the pianoforte as the other sang a plaintive ballad. Soon the guests were free to mingle as they wished. Card tables had been set up in an adjoining room, and servants were available with food and drink.

Clara was deep in conversation with three young matrons who, Allyson knew, had attended school with her sister. Lawton was undoubtedly in the card room. She looked around for her mother but did not see her.

"Have I somehow offended you that you look right through me?" a masculine voice asked.

She smiled at the familiar teasing tone. "Lord Braxton! No, of course you have not offended. I was merely searching for my mother."

He gestured. "She was over there by the terrace doors, talking with Cranston. Would you like me to escort you over there? Or get her for you?"

"No, no. It was idle curiosity more than need." She glanced in the direction he had indicated and spied her mother's lavender-clad shoulders. A good-looking man of middle years smiled down at the countess. "Cranston? I do not know that name," Allyson said to Braxton.

"Mr. Cecil Cranston. Nephew to Viscount Templeton. Cecil thought he would inherit until the old fellow had the lack of grace to marry a much younger woman and immediately get himself a direct heir."

"Lord Braxton!" She gave him a mocking frown and tapped his arm with her fan.

He grinned and shrugged. "Well, 'tis true, you know."

"But Mr. Cranston has not been in society much. I do not recall meeting him."

"I understand he has been on the Continent for, maybe, twenty years. He used to be a crony of Fox and our Prince Regent, though he is a year or so younger than the prince, I think."

Allyson glanced across the room. Her mother backed away from the man Cranston, who put out a hand to detain her. The countess ignored the gesture and moved away in a determined manner. Intrigued, Allyson looked more closely at the man. Mr. Cecil Cranston was a handsome man, even with the fifty-some years he would have to have. He was tall with still-dark hair and appeared to dress in a manner fashionable, but not ostentatious.

Even as she continued to converse with Lord Braxton, Allyson noticed her mother leaving the room through a door that led to a hall at the end of which was the ladies' withdrawing room. Something in her mother's bearing alarmed Allyson. Then she saw Mr. Cranston follow the countess. He did so discreetly, pausing to speak to other guests as he went. He smiled and laughed and left the impression of an amiable, personable gentleman.

Was he, indeed, following her mother? Allyson could not be sure.

"Excuse me," she said to Braxton. "I think I should check on my mother."

He bowed politely. "My lady."

She proceeded to the ladies' withdrawing room, fully expecting to find her parent there. There was no sign of the countess. Allyson turned and started back down the hallway. As she passed a door that was slightly open, she heard a familiar feminine voice full of distress.

"No, I cannot do that."

"Oh, I rather think you can, my dear Katherine," a honeyed male voice said, and added in a firmer tone, "And you *will*."

Allyson turned to stone. Despite every admonition against eavesdropping that she had had drilled into her as a child, she could not bring herself to move. Something was terribly wrong here.

"How can you—? I—you were once a gentleman." Shock and disappointment filled her mother's voice.

"Poverty has a way of hardening one." The tone was flat, indifferent.

"Please, Cecil. . . ."

Allyson noted both the begging tone in her mother's voice and the use of Mr. Cranston's given name.

"Please, I implore you—" the usually proper and proud Lady Rutherford said again.

"I am sorry, Katherine." Actually, there *was* a note of regret in his tone. "But I *do* have the letters. They ought to be worth, say, a hundred guineas each?"

"A hundred—oh, good Lord! I could never—"

Allyson heard a rustle of silk as her mother apparently sank into a chair.

"Then perhaps your noble husband would be interested in purchasing them. . . ."

"No! No! Duncan does not deserve—"

"Then I suggest you find some way of compensating me for . . . uh . . . my discretion, let us say." He no longer seemed either amiable or personable.

"I—need time. . . ."

"A fortnight, then," he said.

"That is not enough time for me to gather such an enormous amount of money." Her voice was strained, but even.

"I am not an unreasonable man," he said smoothly; then his voice turned harsher. "A month then. But not a moment more. If I have not your cooperation by then, the letters will be delivered to your loving husband and to Rutherford's daughters."

"Cecil, what happened to you? You were never such a hard-hearted creature before." She sounded genuinely concerned and mystified.

"Times change, my dear, and so do we. Not always for the better, but we do what we must in order to survive. Now, if you will excuse me—"

Panicked at the thought that Cranston would catch her eavesdropping, Allyson quickly turned and went back in the direction of the ladies' withdrawing room. She heard the door open behind her, but, her heart in her throat, she did not look back. Shaken, shocked, and overwhelmed, she sat stunned for she knew not how long.

Extortion. Her mother was being subjected to extortion. But, over what? Letters? The man had letters. Her mother and Mr. Cranston had a first-name acquaintance with each other. Had they been lovers? No. Impossible. Everyone knew Lord and Lady Rutherford were disgracefully devoted to each other. Besides, had not Braxton told her Cranston had been on the Continent for many years?

Perhaps it had something to do with Aunt Winston, her mother's sister. Yes. Surely, that was it. Aunt Winston was very straitlaced now, but family legend had it that she had been a terrible flirt in her youth. And the ever-so-pompous Lord Winston would take a very dim view of such a matter as this apparently was. As soon as this thought popped into her mind, she knew instinctively it was not Aunt Winston at all. But, what, then?

"Oh! There you are!" Clara said brightly. "I have looked all over for you. We are ready to return now."

"Mama, too?"

"Yes, of course Mama, too. She has the headache."

Allyson did not wonder at that news. In the carriage, Lady Rutherford said, "It just came upon me in such a flash." She sat with her head against the back of the seat, her eyes closed. Clara and Edmund said proper words of sympathy; then all four were quiet. Allyson was grateful not to have to make small talk. She doubted she could have done so.

Allyson's conjecture that Nathan was "probably in some alehouse" was not far from the truth. He had readily—even eagerly—accepted Robert's invitation to join him and some friends at a public house frequented by those in service to the *ton*. Although certainly not located in the same neighborhood as the elegant houses in which its clients served, The Pear Tree was only a short walk away. That is, it was a short walk as Robert led the way, through a series of back alleyways and mews.

Robert was hailed the moment the two of them stepped through the door. "Over here, Rob."

Three men sat at the table, all dressed as Robert and Nathan were, in a mishmash of commoners' clothing. Robert introduced his friends as Howard, a footman for Lady Eggoner; George, a groom for Lord Kitchener; and Jock, also a groom, but employed at a mews shared by several houses.

"Nathan Christopher." Nathan offered his hand to each in turn and repeated the names as he did so.

"Nathan's new to service," Robert explained to the others, and to Nathan, he said, "We use our own names 'mongst friends. I was just lucky; my name really is *Robert*."

"Ye are that," Lord Kitchener's groom said. "My ma an'

da named me *George* for the king himself, but in the Kitchener stables I am Toby. Their first groom was a Toby, so—" He shrugged. George seemed an amiable young man of perhaps twenty. He had red hair, freckles, and clear blue eyes.

Jock, on the other hand, was ten or fifteen years older. He was a stocky man with thinning black hair and a face that showed remnants of many a fight. "Damned nobs can't even learn a man's name," he groused.

Lady Eggoner's footman, Howard, who was of an age with Robert and Nathan, had light brown hair and gray eyes. He laughed now and said, "Now you wouldn't be expecting the grand lords and ladies to keep track of everyone on their staff, would you?" He effected the voice of a woman and wiped his brow dramatically. "Why, I declare, I just cannot keep the members of my household straight—they change so often."

They all laughed at his imitation. Then the young one named George asked Nathan with just a touch of awe, "You the one Rob says was a soldier?"

"I *was*." He deliberately kept the tone neutral.

"How come you ain't now, then?" Jock's question held a hint of suspicion and even challenge.

Nathan was ready for just such a reaction. He patted his left thigh. "Got a game leg."

Jock's expression remained suspicious. "Game leg, eh? I never noticed when you come in."

"It only really shows up when I've been marching two or three hours or standing in ditches of cold water for any length of time. Then, it just gives out on me."

"Hmm." Finally, Jock nodded his acceptance.

Meanwhile, at a signal from Robert, the barmaid had brought them additional mugs and another pitcher of ale. They all drank deeply, and then the others began to share what Nathan recognized as the types of complaints and observations common to any occupational group. For a moment, he felt a keen sense of nostalgia for the campfire camaraderie of the campaign trail. He only half listened to the others until Howard spoke most emphatically.

"I swear, that . . . that *female* is driving me to drink!" He punctuated this statement with a deep swig of his ale.

"Lady Eggoner?" Robert asked in mocking surprise.

"No, it ain't Lady Eggoner, an' well you know it! It's that infernal Frenchie. Teasing tart, she is. First she will, an' then she won't. Don't make sense."

"Jus' like a mort," Jock said. "Women never make any sense."

"Frenchie?" Nathan asked in what he hoped sounded like idle curiosity.

Robert leaned closer to Nathan to effect privacy, but he spoke loud enough for all to hear. "Howard here is in lo-o-o-ove with Lady Eggoner's French maid."

"I see." Nathan grinned and the others chuckled, except for Howard, who looked doleful.

At last the conversation was veering in a direction that might prove useful to Nathan. "I suppose there are quite a few French people serving in the big houses," he observed casually.

"Some," Robert said. "Now, the Irish will take any job they can get, but most of the French immigrants want a higher-toned position."

"Shopkeepers or dressmakers, at least," George said.

" 'Course some of 'em come out o' frog land with a good deal o' the ready. Them that got out early enough," Jock said.

"Like that one calls hisself *Comte Pommroy*," George said.

"*Pommeraie*," Robert corrected.

"That's what I said," George retorted slightly testily.

The name rang a bell with Nathan, for it was one of the names Molly had mentioned in her litany of Lady Allyson's suitors. Now, Robert confirmed the Frenchman's identity.

"Well, that *is* his name, and he held the title in France. Don't think Lord Rutherford would have him coming around if he weren't respectable, do you?"

"Didn't say he weren't respectable," George said, sulky now. "Just that he musta been one of them got out with money in his coat linings."

" 'Twas his father's doing, that was." Robert seemed to be enjoying being the informed one on this subject. "The old man made a fortune in shipping in France and moved it over here before the frogs started chopping off the heads of all the aristos. Comte Pommeraie, of course, don't dirty his hands with trade, but he lives off it well enough."

"Many of 'em weren't so lucky, though. They was lucky to get out with the clothes on their backs," Howard put in.

"Must a been a real comedown for some o' them aristos to have to make their way in the world like real people," Jock sneered. "An' they're everywhere now. Can't even walk down the street—in London, by God!—without hearing that crazy lingo they got."

"There are a good many about," Robert agreed in a conciliatory tone. "The Seymours even have a French butler. And there are dancing masters and language teachers that come around to teach the schoolroom set."

"Kitcheners have both come in real reg'lar like for their boy and the girls," George said.

"An' don't forget about all those French chefs in English houses and clubs," Robert put in.

"Bleedin' frogs takin' good jobs away from English men and women," Jock muttered.

So far Nathan had heard little that was news to him, but the conversation did serve to remind him of just how pervasive the French presence was among the higher echelons of English society and politics. Lord Kitchener was an important member of the government, a close friend of the prime minister, in fact. Even Lord Rutherford apparently had no qualms about his daughter's French suitor. Finding a spy among this lot would, indeed, be most difficult—or, as Cervantes had put it, "As well look for a needle in a bottle of hay." Was Captain Lord Nathan Christopher Thornton little more than a modern-day Don Quixote, chasing windmills?

But where to start on his windmills? *Think, Thornton. Think.* He would begin by sorting through those of French nationality or sympathies who had even the remotest of ties to Rutherford, from the French chef at His Lordship's club, to the comte paying court to the Rutherford daughter. He wondered briefly why he would welcome finding something scurrilous about the comte. The Foreign Office itself, of course, used French nationals to further its own ends. Most of these were Royalists intensely opposed to the upstart Napoleon, but might one of them, in fact, be a double agent?

In his own room later that night, Nathan made a list of all those with connections to France who might have access to Lord Rutherford's affairs, and those of his family. He would check with the earl tomorrow for additional names. *Someone* had known that Lady Allyson would be out shopping that day—and where.

Was it really less than a week since that woman had become the focus of his life?

Allyson was not surprised when her mother sought her own rooms immediately on their return from the Satterlys'. Indeed Allyson was so overset herself that she dismissed Molly as soon as possible and sat in her night rail staring blankly into the dressing table mirror, the hairbrush forgotten in her hand.

"Don't worry so! Everything will work out all right."

Allyson dropped her brush and swung around to see Maryvictoria peeping around the edge of the winged back chair near the fireplace. "Why am I not surprised to see *you?*" What did surprise her was the degree to which just seeing the child lifted her spirits.

Maryvictoria turned around on her knees, folded her arms along the back of the chair, and rested her chin on them. "Maybe you no longer think of me as a filament of your imagination?" There was a hopeful note in her voice.

"Figment. A *figment* of the imagination."

"Very well. *F*igment. Rhymes with *pigment*. That will help me remember!" she said triumphantly.

Allyson waved this aside. "Never mind. What did you mean 'everything will work out'? How? When? Who?"

"I can't say."

"You *cannot* say? Or *will* not? I thought you knew what was going to happen, and when."

"I wish I could tell you more, but they don't trust me with details, you see. Michael says I chatter too much. He's always telling me to be 'less enthusiastic.' Michael is a bit of a bother sometimes," Maryvictoria said as though she were sharing a confidence.

" 'They'? 'Michael'? What *are* you talking about?" Allyson asked the question with dawning suspicion.

"Well, you know, they're in charge; they manage things." Maryvictoria's voice turned ultraserious. "They won't let me come here to play anymore if I don't obey all the rules—and I really, really like coming here—and so they say if I don't know everything, I am less likely to break the rules. You see?"

"Then *how* can you be so sure everything will work out all right?"

"Well . . . I don't have any bad feelings. I get these . . . these immer— . . . inter— . . . no, *intuitions,* Michael calls them, and mine are only good now."

"Were you there at the Satterlys' tonight? Did you see and hear everything?" Allyson wailed.

"No. I only came to play with Caroline for a while tonight."

"Then you cannot possibly know—"

Maryvictoria jumped down from her chair and shook an accusing finger at Allyson. "I *told* you, I just know things."

"Well, nothing just *happens,* now, does it? Someone—someone *real,* if you please—actually has to *do* something."

Maryvictoria plopped herself on the carpet before the fireplace and sat cross-legged with her dress spread over her knees. "Nanny didn't like it when I sat like this, she said it wasn't ladylike," she confided.

"It isn't," Allyson said, "but it is comfortable sometimes." She crossed her legs and gracefully lowered herself into the same position facing the child. "But to get back to the point—"

"Yes. You will have to get those letters back."

"What?" Allyson squeaked. "You just said you were not there!"

"I wasn't. I heard you thinking about them just now."

"You heard—oh, good Lord! Now you are reading my mind?"

"Only sometimes. It wouldn't be polite to listen to the personal stuff."

"And you are always polite?" Allyson was half disbelieving and half curious.

Maryvictoria bit her lip. "Hmm. Sometimes it is *very* hard, but I do *try* to be."

Allyson put her hands on either side of her face and pressed hard. "I *cannot* believe I am having these . . . these discussions—or sessions—with you!"

"You still think I'm a pigment?" The little girl laughed. "Your face looks funny that way!"

"Figment," Allyson corrected absently and put her hands in her lap. "I just do not know *what* to do. Should I confront Mama with what I know? She would be *so* embarrassed. Perhaps I should tell Papa and let him handle it. But he has so much worry now. I wish . . . I wish *I* could do something to help!"

Having forgotten her uninvited visitor, she mused aloud— or had it been aloud?—for the sprite responded.

"Perhaps you can retrieve the letters yourself."

Allyson scoffed, "What? Just say to some strange man, 'If you please, sir, do give me my mama's letters'?"

Maryvictoria giggled. "No, widgeon. Find out where he lives, and when he is out, just get them."

"By myself? Just like that?" Allyson snapped her fingers. "The man surely has servants."

"If he is out, they are likely to be, too. 'Tis often the way of gentlemen's establishments."

"How does a child of ten—pardon me, eleven—know that?"

"You forget. I have been around a *long* while." Maryvictoria chewed on her thumb absently for a moment or two, then added, "But you really should not go alone."

"Right. Molly? No, she is a dear, but she is far too excitable. She would wake the household and its neighbors exclaiming, 'Oh, my stars!' Perhaps Alfred. No. He would feel impelled to tell Papa immediately. And Lawton would be less than useful. Who then? Braxton? Hmm. He might do."

"What about Nathan?"

"Nathan? Why, I hardly know him," Allyson protested. Yet the man did inspire confidence, she supposed.

Maryvictoria echoed her thought. "He is very well thought of."

"He is? How do you know?"

"Well, your papa hired him. And trusted him to guard you, did he not?"

"True. . . ."

Maryvictoria rose and straightened her dress. "I must go." She paused at the winged back chair and picked up Caroline, and then simply faded away.

Allyson shook her head as though to clear it. Was Maryvictoria real? Or was Lady Allyson Crossleigh more depressed and under more strain than she had thought? There was this about the situation: Maryvictoria seemed to think along the same lines as Lady Allyson.

But *Nathan?*

That idea would bear some consideration.

A month. Cranston had given her mother a month.

Chapter 6

For the next few days Nathan went about the routine duties of a footman, but always with part of him alert to his particular assignment. Since much of that assignment involved Lady Allyson, he was especially attuned to her moods and actions. She seemed to present the same cheerful, confident personage to those around her, but he thought there was something troubling her. In unguarded moments she seemed strangely introspective, even worried. He found himself wanting to lighten her load. After all, it *was* his job to protect her, was it not?

His view of the spoiled, arrogant social flutterby received a jolt one afternoon. It began with Melton's informing him that Lady Allyson had ordered a carriage to be ready immediately after nuncheon.

"Thank you, Mr. Melton," Nathan said. "You *do* manage to keep me more or less efficient. Left up to Lady Allyson, she would contrive to leave me behind."

"I am just doing as Lord Rutherford bade me," the butler replied somewhat stiffly. He then added, "You'd best not wear your livery for this outing, Nathan. Lady Allyson does not like to attract attention when she visits the sisters, and Lord Rutherford would prefer that you go armed when she does so."

"The sisters?" Nathan asked, but Melton had already turned away. Nathan shrugged and changed into the plain but clean clothing he had worn to The Pear Tree. He added his pistol to an inner coat pocket. He was surprised to see a very plain landau out front rather than the fancier berline Lady Allyson seemed to favor. This vehicle was obviously well kept, but it was over ten years old, he thought, and there was no crest on the door.

Nathan attempted to satisfy his curiosity by engaging John Coachman in idle conversation.

"Lady Allyson asked for *this* carriage?"

"Aye."

Not much conversation in that monosyllabic response, idle or otherwise. He tried again. "It is not the one she has taken before. Does she often use this one?"

"Nay."

"Is there a particular reason for the change?"

"I just drive 'em," the coachman said.

Nathan noted several bundles and covered baskets already in and on the carriage. "Do you know where we are going?"

"Aye."

"Well, man—?"

"Lady Allyson will tell you—maybe."

Just then the lady herself emerged wearing a plain gray walking dress, a darker gray cloak, and a straw bonnet with yellow ribbons that were her only adornment. Molly, wearing equally subdued attire, was close behind her, carrying yet another small bundle.

It had begun to rain, one of those cold, drizzly rains that London endured in early spring. This was one aspect of home he had not missed in Portugal and Spain. Hanging on to the back of this vehicle, or even riding next to John Coachman, was going to be no fun today.

As he handed her into the carriage, Lady Allyson gave him a look that was at once rather resigned, yet penetrating. He felt a strange tightening of his body at the depth of her gaze. She looked away.

"I see you've dismissed Alfred again," she said, but her testiness seemed to come from habit more than disgust or impatience.

"No, my lady. I would not be so presumptuous." He handed Molly in and reached to close the door.

"Nathan," Lady Allyson said, "in view of this rain, you may as well ride inside. There is little sense in two of you becoming soaked. Molly, move that large basket over onto this seat with the others to make room for him."

"Thank you, my lady," he said.

"You are welcome, but it was not benevolence alone that prompted me to take pity on your body—that is, your comfort. I had thought to discuss something with you, but it will wait."

Her voice was serious, almost solemn. "No, my lady. I did not take it for benevolence." She gave him a sharp look, and he grinned fleetingly. " 'Tis most generous of you, all the same."

She merely nodded, and all three settled back into their seats as the landau entered heavier traffic. Horses' hooves on cobbled streets, along with the squeaks of dozens of wheels and the occasional curse or shout of various drivers, formed the musical background of the journey. The rain had dampened down some of the offensive smells to which the city was subject.

Nathan asked, "Would it be considered impertinent of me to ask where we are going, my lady?"

"Impertinent? Probably," she replied. "However, we are going to Spitalfields."

Nathan felt himself openly gaping at this announcement. "Spitalfields? A demons' lair in the best of times, and with so many of the silk weavers out of work now, it is ripe for riot. It is certainly no place for a gently bred young lady!"

"Now you truly are being impertinent," she said, lifting her chin.

"I apologize, my lady. But I must caution you against this journey. Even during daylight hours, Spitalfields is a very dangerous place. I wonder that your father approves."

"In truth, he does not approve, but—"

"But he denies you few of your wishes," Nathan said, shaking his head.

Molly gasped. Lady Allyson took a deep breath, and he could see the muscles of her jaw working. Finally, she said in a tight voice, "Unfortunately, he *did* ignore my wishes recently." Her glare left no doubt about *what* wish her father had denied. "Besides, Molly and I have made this journey before without mishap, have we not, Molly?"

"Yes, milady. Several times."

"Are you telling me you do this on a regular basis?" He knew he was going too far, but he was genuinely alarmed. Spitalfields was not only home to a vast number of impoverished silk weavers, it was also a haunt for thieves, prostitutes, and other elements of society's refuse. Truly nasty ruffians roamed the streets at all hours. Few gentlemen ventured into the area at any time, and these two were blithely going where angels might well fear to tread.

"Not *regularly*." She sounded defensive. "About once a month, I believe. It takes that long to gather things." She gestured toward the baskets and bundles.

"What are these things? And where *are* we taking them?" He hoped he sounded merely curious.

"Clothing. Bed linens. Some food. We are taking them to the Fairfax sisters who take care of . . . of unfortunate women and girls and children."

He looked at Molly, who seemed to stiffen more and more as they neared their destination. She merely nodded to confirm what her mistress had said. There was some sort of mystery here, he thought, but perhaps it would be best not to pursue it just yet. Good Lord. Spitalfields. And delicate women. He was glad he had his pistol, and a knife in his boot. He noted a peculiar bulge in Lady Allyson's reticule. She, too, was armed. Perhaps not so "delicate" after all.

They stopped in front of what must have once been a modest London residence. This house, of gray stone with a newly painted bright blue door, seemed cared for, while its neighbors were victims of neglect. It was like a single flower in a plot of weeds. Unlike the rest of the street, there was no trash around this abode or in front of it.

Jumping out first, Nathan said, "Wait a moment."

He scanned the street. There was a beggar huddled in one doorway, and a half-clad woman who looked at him hopefully in another. *She must be freezing,* he thought. The noise coming from a building two doors down, along with a metal sign proclaiming it The Bears' Den, told him it probably housed one of the gin mills of the poorer sections of the city. There was another some distance down and across the street. Seeing no other street activity, he conjectured that the rain was on his side. He turned back to hand Lady Allyson down. Her eyes sparkled with amusement.

"You see? I told you there was little to worry about."

"Perhaps," he said.

Molly handed out a bundle, which Nathan hurried to take. At Lady Allyson's gesture and the single word, "Here," he handed it over to her. Molly handed out two more packets, which he took even as he awkwardly helped her from the carriage.

"You and Molly can come back for the others," Lady Allyson said. She turned to look up at the coachman. "We shall be the usual length of time, John."

"Aye, milady."

The door opened before she could lift the knocker. A rather burly man, obviously a servant, greeted her warmly. "Lady Allyson, the sisters will be pleased to see you. Lady Paxton has already arrived."

"Wonderful," she responded.

As the servant took her bundle and laid it on a hall table, Nathan saw that his left sleeve was pinned up over a stump below the elbow. *An ex-soldier?* He followed Molly's lead in putting his own bundle on the floor near the table; then the two of them went back to the carriage for the rest.

When they returned, a tiny sprite of a woman was greeting Lady Allyson warmly and helping her remove her cloak.

Nathan judged the woman to be fiftyish. Her black hair, pulled back in a tight bun, was profusely streaked with gray. She wore a plain dark brown dress. She would have seemed austere, were it not for her fluttery motions, cheerful chatter, and twinkling brown eyes.

"Thank you, Miss Priscilla," Lady Allyson said.

"Now you just come along in," Miss Priscilla urged her guest. "Samuel probably told you Lady Paxton is here, too. We are so honored to have both of you on the same day! And just look at what you are doing for our girls!" She handed the one-armed servant the cloak and clasped her hands in front of her. "Samuel, you will see to Lady Allyson's people, will you not?"

"I will, Miss Priscilla."

As Lady Allyson disappeared into what must have been a drawing room, Nathan and Molly followed Samuel down a flight of stairs to the basement kitchen. Like the rest of the house he had seen, it was warm, dry, and impeccably clean. Samuel introduced the rather plump woman who was clearly in charge of the kitchen as his wife, Mrs. Boskins.

Mrs. Boskins gestured to another, younger woman. "And this is our Betty Lou. Thank goodness, she's permanent. Don't know what we'd do without her."

Betty Lou, a young blond woman—only a girl, really—smiled shyly and gave a slight curtsy to acknowledge the introduction. Molly introduced Nathan, who greeted them all rather formally. Molly, whose demeanor had changed once they arrived and were inside the house, hugged Betty Lou and said, "I've *so* much to tell you!"

Mrs. Boskins rolled her eyes and smiled indulgently. "I imagine we have lost those two for a bit. Now you just sit here, Mr. Christopher. I'll make us a pot of tea. Help yourself to those biscuits. I made 'em fresh this morning."

Nathan took the seat she indicated at a large, well-scrubbed worktable, and Samuel sat across from him. Nathan nodded at Samuel's arm.

"Army? Or navy?"

"Army. I was with Moore at Corunna."

"*We* were with Moore at Corunna," his wife corrected.

"You?" Samuel asked Nathan. "You have a look of the military about you."

"I was on the Peninsula, too. Got mine in the leg at Burgos."

"You musta been at Badajoz earlier, then."

"I was."

"That were a nasty one, too, I hear," Samuel said.

"It was, especially in the aftermath. I missed most of that, thank heavens." He did not add that he had been out on patrol much of the time as one of Wellington's "correspondents."

Mrs. Boskins served tea and then busied herself at some other task, leaving the two men to trade war stories for a while. They were interrupted by a bell.

"The ladies will be wanting more tea, I'm sure," Mrs. Boskins said as her husband answered the summons.

Molly and Betty Lou, who had been off in a corner sharing secrets, joined Nathan at the table, and the three of them chatted as Mrs. Boskins prepared another tray. Samuel returned, balancing a large tray awkwardly on his stump.

"Allow me." Nathan took the tray from him.

"Thank you. I manage most things pretty well, but this is not one of them."

"I'll take the other one in, if you would like me to," Nathan offered.

"That would be fine," Samuel said, and Mrs. Boskins shot Nathan a look of gratitude.

As he entered the drawing room, four women looked up from their positions bent over a table covered with papers and drawings.

"Over there, young man." A tall, angular version of Miss Priscilla pointed to a smaller table.

"Thank you, Nathan," Lady Allyson said.

Nathan took in the scene around him. The drawing room was modestly furnished with a tasteful selection of outdated, but well-cared-for, furniture. A woman who was dressed in stylish mourning and looked to be in her midtwenties was the fourth occupant of the room. This was no ordinary visit. The table strewn with drawings and what looked to be reports of some sort resembled a field table over which army officers planned strategies.

When the angular Miss Fairfax told him, "That will be all. I shall pour," he set the tray down and returned to his seat in the kitchen.

He accepted a second, weaker, dish of tea just as a young girl burst into the room carrying a pail. "Mrs. Carter says we got to have more hot water," she said excitedly.

"Calm down now, Sally," the stolid Mrs. Boskins said. "It will be a while yet."

"Yes, ma'am."

Sally fidgeted as Mrs. Boskins filled the pail from a huge cistern next to the hearth. The girl left as hastily as the full pail allowed.

Mrs. Boskins chuckled. "I expect Mrs. Carter sent her down here just to get her out of the way for a bit."

Nathan's curiosity finally won out. "May I ask what is going on here?"

"One of our girls is lying-in above stairs," Mrs. Boskins answered. "Mrs. Carter is the midwife."

"I surmised something of that sort," Nathan said, and gestured widely. "But I mean all of it—the Fairfax sisters, Lady Allyson, Lady Paxton—this house."

Mrs. Boskins shot Molly a surprised and reproving look. "Neither Lady Allyson nor Molly enlightened you?"

Molly blushed and mumbled something about its not being her place.

Mrs. Boskins sighed, refilled her dish of tea, and sat down next to her husband. " 'Tis a long story, but we'll try to give you a shortened version." She paused and seemed to be thinking. "The Fairfax sisters come from a trade family—lived in London all their lives. Their father owned one of the smaller silk mills here in Spitalfields. He left them a modest fortune."

"Even if they had wanted to make a showing in London society, that smell of trade would have kept them out," Samuel put in.

His wife continued. "Acceptance by society means little to those two. They grew up together and they are growing old together—that is enough."

"Neither of them ever married?" Nathan asked.

"I think they both had their chances," Mrs. Boskins said. "Don't know what happened with Miss Fairfax, but she broke off an engagement. Miss Priscilla's young man was killed in one of those battles with natives in India."

"Sometime in the nineties," Samuel said.

"Anyway, they did not want to spend their lives embroidering fire screens and chair covers and the like, so, since they had control of their own funds, they decided to put their money to good use," his wife went on.

"At . . . ?" Nathan prompted.

"Establishing this house for women and girls who have nowhere else to go when things get bad," she replied.

"What kinds of females—in this part of the city?" Nathan asked, though he thought he knew.

"What you would expect," she said, with both challenge and defense in her tone. "Women beaten down by poverty, or by the men in their lives. Many have been forced by circumstances or have otherwise been tricked into prostitution. Like that poor girl trying to give birth up there." She jerked a thumb upward. "She has only fourteen years! But at least she and her babe will have a chance now."

As Nathan mulled this over, Samuel added, "The Fairfax sisters are truly fine people. They gave me—us—a chance when no one else would."

His wife nodded and patted him on the shoulder. Nathan admired the closeness of this couple who must have been through some very hard times together.

He looked at Molly, who was looking at her friend in serious, silent communication. Molly then shifted her direct gaze to Nathan and said with a touch of defiance, "And they helped get me and Betty Lou away from that beldam Francis Fish and her horrible husband."

"If he even *is* her husband," Betty Lou said.

Nathan must have looked confused.

"A . . . a procuress. She runs a brothel two streets over," Mrs. Boskins explained. "The sisters rescued these two saucy misses." She again smiled indulgently at the girls, of whom she was obviously very fond.

Her husband chuckled. "Don't forget—the sisters had help. That Fish woman hardly knew *what* to do when she was face-to-face with not only the Fairfaxes—formidable enough in themselves—but also with Lady Allyson and Lady Paxton!"

"Samuel!" his wife admonished. "I don't think any of the ladies wants that bruited about. The Lords Rutherford and Paxton would probably suffer apoplexy at the very idea."

"With cause, I should think," Nathan said.

"You won't be tellin' the others at Rutherford House about me, will you?" Molly worried. "Only Lady Allyson and Alfred and John Coachman know where I come from."

"Is *that* why you were so quiet on the way here?" Nathan asked.

"I . . . I suppose so."

"Don't worry—your secret is safe with me, too."

"Thank you." She gave him a brilliant smile. Betty Lou poked her in the ribs and giggled.

For the next several minutes, the Boskinses and the two girls sang the praises of the four ladies in the drawing room above. When the Fairfax sisters found themselves overwhelmed both physically and financially with the need around them, they had enlisted the aid of others. First, Miss Pringle, whose resources were severely limited, and then Lady Paxton and Lady Allyson, had answered the call.

Nathan made appropriate comments occasionally, but his mind focused on what he had learned. From his previous prowling among London's low life, he knew the names of Francis Fish and her male companion known only as "Bart."

Both were nasty pieces of work. If Lady Allyson had gained their enmity, perhaps it was they, not the French, who had perpetrated the near-abduction.

Lady Allyson Crossleigh *did* keep complicating matters.

As she settled into the carriage for the return trip, Allyson was feeling quite pleased with what had been accomplished. The new rescue center would become a reality in a few months, if they could find the right people to staff it. Surely that could be done.

Molly sat beside her mistress now that bundles no longer filled the seat and the empty baskets were tied to the back of the vehicle. Nathan sat across from them with a contemplative expression as the carriage got under way. She wondered what he was thinking. Then she was abruptly startled out of that reverie.

There, on the seat next to Nathan, sat Lady Maryvictoria Elizabeth Watkinson.

"What—what are *you* doing here?" Allyson asked, staring at the ghostly child.

"Sitting," Nathan answered in a confused, but ironic, tone. "You saw me get in. And you may have noticed, my lady, that it *is* still raining. However, if you wish me to ride outside, I will signal John Coachman."

Her gaze shifted to his. "No, of course not. That will not be necessary." She knew she should explain herself, but how? She could hardly announce to her family and friends, let alone servants, that she was seeing and communicating with ghosts! Why, they would be for sending her off to Bedlam for sure.

"Are you not freezing with so little clothing on?" she asked Maryvictoria, who was again attired in the gauzy blue concoction. "I am sure there is a lap robe, perhaps under the seat."

Nathan looked confused. "My coat is quite adequate, as it was earlier."

"I did not mean you," Allyson said.

"Molly?" he asked. "Do you need the robe?"

"No, not at all," Molly answered.

Maryvictoria's eyes danced with mischievous glee. "They cannot see me, or hear me."

"Then how can I do so?"

"Do *what,* my lady?" Nathan asked, regarding her intently. "Surely you can have the robe if you wish it."

"My cloak is sufficient," she said impatiently, and continued to stare at Maryvictoria.

That little imp responded with, "In your mind. You may talk to me in your mind. Otherwise, yes. They *will* be considering you for Bedlam."

"Just think—" Allyson started aloud, then tried only thinking her response. *You mean I just think* my conversation with you?

"Just think *what,* my lady?" Molly asked.

"Precisely. That is, when others are present," Maryvictoria said.

"I am not sure—" Allyson said to Maryvictoria, then realized she had said it aloud. She wiped her hand across her brow and looked at Molly and Nathan in turn. "I am sorry. I quite forgot what I was going to say. I . . . uh . . . I did not sleep well last night."

She thought Nathan looked skeptical, but why should she care what a footman thought? Still, she had hoped to broach the question of retrieving her mother's letters with him. Well, not now. She leaned her head against the seat, looked at Maryvictoria from nearly closed eyes, and willed herself to think, *You and I will discuss this later. Now please go before I make an utter fool of myself.*

"As you wish." Maryvictoria sounded slightly hurt, but she was gone in an instant.

Allyson breathed a sigh of relief and pretended to nap.

Chapter 7

The next day, Nathan was still mulling over that extraordinary visit to the Fairfax house. Lady Allyson had seemed distracted on the return journey; her conversation was downright strange, almost as though there were a fourth person in the carriage. He supposed that people burdened with worry might take to talking to themselves. What worries would she have, though? She had taken the attempted abduction in stride—outwardly, at least. It probably was not a broken heart, for she did not seem overly enamored of any of the ninny-hammers who called frequently and sent tokens of their admiration. He wished he might lighten her load. Meanwhile, there were other matters to see to.

Nathan had arranged with Melton to be assigned to wait upon guests during the Countess of Rutherford's monthly "at home." The countess filled her drawing room with artists, writers, politicians, and anyone capable of discussing topics other than the weather and which *ton* dandy was making a cake of himself or managing to lose the family fortune at the gaming tables, though there was a fair share of these types, too. Nathan's job of seeing that there were sufficient cakes, tea, and lemonade allowed him to scrutinize the guests. He concentrated his attention on Lady Allyson's suitors, especially the two Frenchmen, each of whom had a smooth, sophisticated air about him.

The Comte de Pommeraie was tall, dark-haired, and dressed in the latest fashion of high shirt points and an elaborate neckcloth. He looked every bit the aristocrat he was. His demeanor suggested a natural hauteur, though he unbent enough to make himself agreeable to the ladies. He seemed well aware of the devastating effect of his smile on them, for he flashed it often enough, Nathan thought sourly. However, given that few exiled French aristocrats favored the republican cause, in general, or Napoleon, in particular, the comte seemed an unlikely candidate for kidnapper of the week.

Monsieur Arnaud, on the other hand, was a far more mysterious figure. He seemed to move in the best of circles, but others in those circles knew little of him—at least little was known among the *ton*'s network of servants. He was of average height with brown hair and even, but not especially handsome, or memorable, features. The kind of person, Nathan thought, who could blend into nearly any group with ease.

As he passed among the guests, bearing a tray, Nathan listened closely to snippets of conversations.

Lord Livermore, with a hearty chuckle: "Smuggled brandy just seems to taste better. . . ."

A white-haired man who bore the look of a military man despite the walking stick on which he leaned: " 'Twas sheer madness to engage the Americans in war before we had done with Bonaparte."

"Oh, my dear, you should have *seen* the look on the prince's face!" This from a dowager who apparently wanted others to know that *she* had been in a position to see that look.

From another member of the House of Lords: "The ideas Robert Owen puts out about a 'new society' are nothing short of seditious! This is England, not France, by heaven."

A scholarly looking fellow: "As you well know, I generally find little of value in novels, but this woman who wrote *Pride and Prejudice* is very amusing."

A mother in a constrained whisper to her daughter: "Do

control yourself, you silly chit. You know very well Bentley has pockets to let."

"But, Mama—"

As Nathan offered his tray to tempt Lady Eggoner, she—unlike others who saw him merely as part of the furniture—gave him a bold look. "Ah ha! You must be the new addition to this house about whom one hears so much!"

"I am new here, my lady." He kept his voice modulated and neutral.

As she reached for a glass of lemonade, her expression changed to one less bold and saucy. She studied his features thoughtfully. "You look rather familiar to me. You must resemble someone I know."

Nathan chuckled in what he hoped was a deprecating manner. "Unlikely, my lady." He moved on and swore under his breath. The late Lord Eggoner had been a friend of the father from whom Nathan had inherited a slightly aquiline nose and distinctive blue eyes. He would have to try to steer clear of Lady Eggoner.

He worked his way around the room dispensing drinks and unobtrusively picking up empty vessels. He paused near a settee on which Lady Allyson sat conversing with the Comte de Pommeraie.

"You are breaking my heart, Lady Allyson, in refusing my invitation for a drive." His tone and the hand over his heart were ridiculously dramatic, Nathan thought.

Her voice was equally insincere. "*I,* sir? You exaggerate. Did you not tell me that your heart had been previously broken by a pretty milkmaid? Or was it that beautiful Spanish princess? Or perhaps—"

He laughed. "Enough, my lady! Each of those times it mended, but I fear you have shattered it beyond repair."

"I am sure it will mend this time, too."

"Only if you promise to allow me two dances at the Worthington ball."

She made a show of pretending shock. "Two? Two would be positively scandalous."

"Now who exaggerates?" he asked. "But I must bend to your understanding of English customs. We French are more liberal. One, then?"

"One," she agreed, with what seemed to Nathan a distinctly flirtatious laugh.

Another young woman strolled over on the arm of an equally young dandy. Nathan knew them to be Miss Loretta Longworth and a certain Viscount Sawyer. Nathan had noticed Miss Longworth casting not-so-subtle glances at the comte. He wondered how Lady Allyson felt about the Longworth chit's attempt to attract one of her own suitors.

"Did I hear you mention the Worthington ball?" Miss Longworth chirped as the comte rose and bowed over her hand, kissing the air above her wrist.

"Ah, Miss Longworth," he said, with one of those syrupy smiles, "looking lovely as always."

Miss Longworth fairly preened. "Why, thank you, Monsieur le Comte. How is it that French gentlemen always know what will please a female?"

"Practice, perhaps?" Lady Allyson said dryly. She happened to catch Nathan's gaze. He clamped his lips tight over what threatened to be a teasing grin, and deliberately looked away. In that instant, though, he was sure she was as amused as he at these mating games.

"In my country," the comte explained, "a gentleman strives to make himself agreeable to the ladies. I think Englishmen have less . . . warmth?"

Nathan thought he heard Lady Allyson mutter, "Rubbish," but the word was covered by Miss Longworth's speaking again.

"I understand Lady Worthington is offering *two* waltzes in her program. I am *so* excited about this prospect." She added in a little-girl voice, "My mama has engaged a special lesson with a dancing master so I will not make a fool of myself on the dance floor."

As she undoubtedly expected, both the comte and Lord Sawyer protested the idea of something so preposterous as Miss Longworth's ever making a fool of herself.

Miss Longworth spoke again, her tone rather condescending. "Have you learned the waltz yet, Lady Allyson?"

Lady Allyson's response was an airy, "Has not *everyone* done so?"

Nathan moved on to another area of the room as the other Frenchman approached Lady Allyson. Later, he observed Lord Braxton making his way toward her. Well, at least Braxton was not *quite* such a popinjay as the comte.

Aware that Nathan had overheard some of her conversation with the comte, Allyson was mildly discomfited. Viewed from the footman's position, what passed for discourse among the *ton* was often shallow and silly. Never before, though, had she been concerned about how things might sound to a servant. Of course, one did not discuss things of a private nature in front of staff members, and most servants just melded into the background. Not this one, though.

She had been so disconcerted by this truth that she had foolishly allowed Miss Longworth to goad her into an extremely unwise statement, for Lady Allyson Crossleigh had *not* yet learned to waltz. This new, shocking dance had only recently been introduced in England. Dancing masters themselves were scrambling to learn it so they could teach their clients.

The Worthington ball was only a few days away. How on earth could she find someone to teach her the steps? Clara and Edmund? Hardly. Clara had seen the dance performed but once and pronounced it "scandalous."

To dance or not to dance the waltz was not a major issue, however. Embarrassing, yes, but hardly of profound proportions. Allyson still had not hit upon a way to help her mother without humiliating the countess or involving the earl. Despite Maryvictoria's suggestion of Nathan as an accomplice, Allyson had only briefly considered such a possibility. One did not involve servants in one's personal affairs. His apparent disapproval of her association with the Fairfax sisters had also turned her away from such an idea. So now, here were *two* problems—one rather trivial but potentially discomfiting, and one of much deeper import, and potentially dangerous.

A young voice sang in her ear, "You are making a mista-a-ake."

"I am?" she asked in surprise before catching sight of Mary-victoria standing at her elbow. Too late, she realized that Monsieur Arnaud had directed an inane bit of flattery in her direction.

"Oh, dear me, I had not expected to see *you* here," Allyson said to Maryvictoria.

Monsieur Arnaud said in a rather hurt tone, "But my dearest Lady Allyson, I attend Lady Rutherford's 'at homes' regularly."

"Oh. Uh . . . I meant . . . I had not expected to see you looking so well. You see, I had heard your carriage had overturned." Allyson stumbled through this made-up excuse and turned to glare at Maryvictoria.

That imp had the temerity to say, "You may remember, Lady Allyson, that—in a manner of speaking—I live here. Besides, I like parties."

"Overturned a carriage?" Monsieur Arnaud was surprised and outraged. "*Who* can have told such a scurrilous tale? I admit to one wheel's being in the ditch, but it was nothing. Nothing, I assure you."

Maryvictoria giggled and pointed at a dowager dressed in purple and sporting a purple turban with long yellow plumes. "Did you ever *see* such a silly headdress?"

"It is most impolite—" Allyson said to Maryvictoria, forgetting that she need not speak aloud. She continued silently, *to point and make negative comments.*

"Impolite, my lady?" Monsieur Arnaud was clearly puzzled.

Allyson recovered with, "It is most impolite of me to monopolize your time so when I know so many other ladies are eager to speak with you after your recent trip to Paris."

He swelled with self-importance. "Ah, yes. I do suppose you are right, dear lady. So kind. One of your most charming traits." He rose and moved around the room like a bee sipping at flowers.

Allyson sighed. *You are going to have me in Bedlam, yet,* she told Maryvictoria, *and what is more, you virtually forced me to drive Monsieur Arnaud away.* She must have managed this communication properly, for no one sitting or standing nearby stared at her as though she had two heads.

Maryvictoria shrugged. "It does not matter. That man will not suit."

Allyson glared at the child. *If you do not mind, I shall make such decisions myself!*

Maryvictoria shrugged again. "Oh, *I* do not mind in the least. But at your advanced age, do you think you should waste time on a pointless dalliance?"

Allyson fairly spluttered, although she did so silently. *Maryvictoria Elizabeth! That comment was even more impolite than the one about Lady Morton's headdress.*

Maryvictoria managed—with some effort, it seemed—to look contrite. She innocently questioned, "Do you not find it strange that truth is so often considered impolite, but lies are perfectly acceptable?"

That is simply not so.

"Yes, it is. For instance, what would you say if purple turban asked you what you thought of her headdress?"

Why, I should probably tell her it is an interesting style or that feathers are very popular now.

"See?" Maryvictoria said triumphantly. "But you think it is as ghastly as I do!"

Trying to avoid offending another is hardly dishonest, Allyson argued.

"And what about your allowing Miss Longworth to think you waltz?"

I admit that was a foolish mistake, but I did not precisely *say I could perform the waltz.*

"Well—" Maryvictoria started, but she was interrupted by a strong male voice.

"Lady Allyson." Lord Braxton stood before her and gave a slight bow. "You are looking especially fine this day, my dear, but you seem truly lost in thought. Is something troubling you? Is there a dragon you would like me to slay?"

Allyson laughed and patted the cushion beside her. "Do sit, Lord Braxton. I . . . I suppose I was a bit distracted." She glanced at Maryvictoria, but the sprite was already disappearing in the familiar aura.

"Troubles?" Braxton asked.

The question reminded her that, yes, indeed, she was troubled. She wondered briefly if she should ask him about that man Cranston. Then she thought better of it. "Nothing of import." She paused, then asked, "Do you waltz, Lord Braxton?" She asked the question softly so others in the immediate vicinity might not hear.

"Do I what?"

"Waltz."

"Oh, the new dance. Not yet. But my sisters have engaged a dancing master and have coerced me into joining them. If you can put up with a neophyte, I shall hope to show to good advantage at the Worthington ball."

"We shall be a pair of neophytes. Let us hope we do not step on each other's toes."

They chatted amiably a while longer, then strolled about the room, stopping now and then to talk with others. Allyson covertly glanced at her mother occasionally and marveled at the smooth grace with which the countess conducted herself. Only someone *very* well acquainted with her would have sensed the strain beneath her easy manners, and then only if that someone were aware that a problem existed. Allyson noted a certain tightness about her mother's eyes and that the usually ready smiles appeared less frequently this day.

Allyson happened to be standing near, but not within her mother's conversational group, when Lady Morton—she of the purple turban—approached her hostess. Lady Rutherford was standing with her longtime friend, Lady Eggoner, and Lord and Lady Houghton. They were discussing a new play they had all seen, and welcomed Lady Morton, who added her comments, which mostly consisted of which actress or dancer certain male members of the *ton* currently favored. Lady Morton was an inveterate purveyor of gossip.

During a pause in this discussion, Lady Morton gave her hostess a sidelong glance and said, "Is it not marvelous that Mr. Cranston has returned at last to our shores?"

"Come home to repair his finances, I would venture," the outspoken Lord Houghton said with a snort.

"Cranston's estate is near ours," his wife added.

"The land takes care of those who give back to it," Houghton went on. "Unfortunately, ever since reaching his majority, Cranston has consistently taken, giving very little back."

"He has always enjoyed the finer things of life," Lady Rutherford said lightly. Allyson admired the control with which her mother spoke.

Lady Eggoner sniffed. "You mean he was a rakehell."

Lady Morton gave a laugh that sounded false to Allyson. "Do not be so hard on the man, Lady Eggoner. In our younger days, many ladies who are now 'of a certain age' were quite thrilled with his attentions." She turned directly to her hostess and asked slyly, "Was he not a *particular* friend of yours, Lady Rutherford?"

"He was a friend, yes."

"Oh, but of course. I had quite forgot," Lady Morton said, but Allyson suspected the woman's memory was needle-sharp. "You and Rutherford were already married when Cranston broke so many hearts."

Lady Rutherford merely nodded her assent to this comment.

Lady Morton went on in the same sly tone. "I observed you talking with him at the Satterly do. It must be *so* wonderful to renew an old . . . friendship . . . after such a length of time."

"Only if you still have something in common," Lady Eggoner said. "I recall meeting an old acquaintance after a lapse of some years, and we scarcely had anything to say to each other."

"Perhaps you were not so close as were Cranston and Lady Rutherford," Lady Morton replied.

Allyson decided it was definitely time to rescue her mother from the talons of this harpy. She moved into her mother's circle.

"Pardon me for interrupting," she said sweetly, "but I must drag my mama away for a few minutes to deal with a trifling domestic crisis."

Lady Rutherford shot her daughter a look of gratitude and excused herself. "What is it?" she asked Allyson.

"Actually, nothing. I happened to overhear some of what Lady Morton said, and I did not like her tone."

"You dear girl!"

Lady Rutherford left the room briefly and joined another group when she returned. Allyson noted the Houghtons and Lady Eggoner, too, quickly separated themselves from the loquacious Lady Morton. However, the woman's poisonous comments had stirred Allyson's curiosity even further.

After supper that evening, when the ladies retreated to the drawing room, Allyson mentioned that the waltz would be offered at the Worthington ball.

"I am not surprised," Lady Rutherford said. "Even when we were still in school, Lady Worthington was always alert to the latest trends."

"It is nothing short of scandalous!" Clara said. "That dance is immoral."

"It cannot be so very bad, Lady Lawton," Miss Pringle observed. "I hear the patronesses at Almack's are approving it for their assemblies."

"Are they? Still. . . ." Clara was obviously surprised at this news. Allyson knew her sister set great store by the opinions of Almack's self-appointed arbiters of society.

"It is becoming quite popular," Miss Pringle said. "Why, I believe there was a chart showing the steps in the last issue of *London Ladies* magazine."

"Was there? I should like to see it," Allyson told her.

"I will get it for you." Miss Pringle rose and left the room. When she returned with the journal, the gentlemen had rejoined the ladies.

"Here you are." Miss Pringle sat herself next to Allyson on a sofa and opened the magazine. Lady Rutherford leaned over her daughter's shoulder from behind the sofa.

"Hmm," Allyson murmured as she examined the chart. "It *looks* simple enough."

"What is that?" Lord Rutherford asked from his favorite chair.

"The waltz," Allyson and her mother spoke jointly.

"Oh."

"It is improper," Clara said piously. "Papa, you must tell Allyson not to make a spectacle of herself—and us."

Her father grunted. "Improper, eh?"

"Really, Clara!" Allyson did not bother to curb her impatience. "You are becoming quite straitlaced. Have you taken up one of those strange dissenting religions?"

"Of course not," Clara said primly. "But marriage and motherhood make one more cautious in life. You shall see one day, I hope."

Allyson willed herself not to roll her eyes at this too-familiar refrain.

"I have seen the waltz performed." Lord Lawton's tone was as pompous as his wife's. "It requires a shocking degree of closeness between males and females, even those who are not married to each other."

"I, too, have seen it." Lady Rutherford lifted her head to look at her husband. "You remember, Duncan. It was at Grantham House three or four weeks ago. The Granthams had just returned from the congress in Vienna."

"Ah, yes," her husband said. "Hmm. I seriously doubt a dance in a crowded ballroom is likely to degenerate into an orgy of lust and lasciviousness. Do you not agree, my dear?"

"I am ever the dutiful wife; of *course* I agree with you," his wife teased.

"Hah!" He gave her an intimate grin.

Allyson saw Clara and Edmund exchange a look of disapproval.

When she retired to her own bedchamber, Allyson took the magazine with her, where she studied the chart as Molly brushed her hair.

"What is that strange drawing, my lady?"

"It is a chart of the steps to the waltz. I must learn these by Thursday."

"You can learn a dance from just looking at a drawing?" Molly asked in surprised admiration.

"Perhaps not. But I must try, or that infernal Loretta Longworth will crow like a rooster."

Molly giggled. "Roosters are males."

Allyson grinned. "All right, then—preen like a peacock. No, that is male, too. You know what I mean. I just can*not* have that woman condescending to me in her supercilious way!"

"Supercilious?"

"Haughty. Superior."

"Oh." Molly was quiet for several strokes of the brush. "Still, it must be hard to learn a dance from a book."

"I know, but it is too late to find a dancing master. They are all engaged. I must simply make do. Miss Pringle will help me by playing the pianoforte tomorrow so I may become acquainted with such music."

Again Molly was silent for several strokes. Then she said, "I know someone as could teach you."

Allyson jerked around so quickly, the brush caught in her hair, pulling it. "You *do?*"

"Hmm-mm. Nathan."

"Nathan? The footman?"

"I don't know no other named *Nathan*," Molly said.

"Of course not. But how does *he* know this dance? And how did you find out he knows it?"

"He said the king's German legions taught it to the soldiers in Portugal and Spain. Mrs. Simpson was carrying on in the servants' hall about how indecent she heard it was to waltz, an' Nathan said that was nonsense an' he could show her. So we pushed the tables out of the way, an' he did. You should've seen Mrs. Simpson dancing with him!"

Allyson smiled at a vision of the short, plump housekeeper and the tall footman doing this elegant dance.

So—Nathan could teach her to waltz.

Did she dare ask him?

Chapter 8

By the next morning, Allyson had made her decision. She would *not* ask Nathan to teach her the waltz, nor would she involve him in her mother's personal business. One simply did not breach that invisible wall that existed between master and servant, employer and employee. True, a family might feel closer to some members of the staff than to others. A secretary, say, or a governess—Miss Pringle was a good example of such—but a footman? Hardly.

She was no longer surprised or annoyed to find Nathan waiting for her at the stable each morning, nor that he continued to ride the new horse. Allyson had asked her father about that magnificent animal and his allowing a servant such free use of a special mount. The earl had said something to the effect that he had not the time it took to exercise the horse properly and, besides, he wanted the footman well mounted "just in case."

She had to admit, though never to the footman himself, that there was a certain degree of comfort in his presence. Alfred was a capable stable hand, but she doubted he would be able to handle an untoward incident as well as, say, that laborer had some days before. Nathan Christopher might be the most impertinent servant of her acquaintance, but one could feel *safe* with him around.

Once they reached the park each day, he kept a discreet distance between them and accorded her privacy in her conversations with other riders. On the way to and from the park, however, he rode inordinately close, and she was aware that part of him was ever vigilant to the traffic around them.

Her resentment at having his presence foisted upon her had dissipated to the point that they had taken to having real conversations. Having learned of his interest in the newspapers, she found herself looking forward to sharing ideas on this or that issue of the day. She was surprised at how often their views coincided. Even when they did not, he listened and considered what she had to say. Most men of her own class were apt to take a condescending attitude of "do not worry your pretty little head about such matters." In other situations and in company, he kept to the role of servant, but there was definitely a sense of equality when they rode together.

Still, she could not bring herself to confide the most pressing matter of her mother's problem. After all, it was not hers to share, was it? Nor had her pride allowed her to bring up the waltz during this morning's ride. She knew very well that Nathan had heard her ill-advised comment to Loretta Longworth. She would just have to muddle through on her own.

Later that morning, however, muddling through on one front proved frustratingly impossible. She and Miss Pringle had retired to the music room after breakfast. As the former governess played an unfamiliar waltz tune, Allyson attempted to walk herself through the steps.

"This is ridiculous!" she wailed. "I am not sure that I am following this chart properly, and I simply do not know *what* to do with my hands!"

"I would help you, dear, if I could," Miss Pringle said, "but even if I *could* dance, I could not play and do so at the same time." Miss Pringle had been born with a clubfoot.

"I know."

"Perhaps Lady Lawton or her husband—?"

"No. You heard them last night. They would not help if they could. Besides, Edmund has two left feet."

"Well, dear—" Miss Pringle folded her hands in her lap.

With a sigh of resignation, Allyson went to the bellpull and gave it a sharp tug. After a few minutes, a maid answered the summons.

"Please find Nathan and have him report here immediately," she ordered.

"Yes, milady."

A childish voice from the window seat chirped, "I wondered how long it would take you to recognize the obvious."

"Oh, no, not—" Allyson, startled, said aloud, then shifted to thinking, *you, Maryvictoria. I hope you are not here merely to plague me. Hmm . . . I do not suppose you waltz?*

"What is it, Lady Allyson?" Miss Pringle asked.

"Oh . . . uh . . . nothing. I just remembered something I should have done, but I shall take care of it later."

Maryvictoria grinned. "No, I do not waltz. The minuet was our raciest dance. But I should like to see it. I promise not to say a word if you allow me to stay."

Which no one but I would hear anyway.

"True."

And do I really have a choice about your going or staying?

"But of course. I never stay where I am not wanted—or needed."

You have rather peculiar ideas of "need," Allyson replied.

"Well, may I stay or not?"

Miss Pringle broke in with, "Are you feeling unwell, Lady Allyson?"

"Yes," Allyson said to Maryvictoria. "I mean, no. I am quite well," she said to Miss Pringle, who gave her a questioning look but said nothing as the footman rapped on the door at just that moment.

"You sent for me, my lady?"

"Yes." She hesitated only briefly. "Molly tells me you know how to dance the waltz."

"The waltz? Oh. Yes, I do."

"Good. I should like you to teach me."

"Teach you? To waltz?"

"Yes, teach me to waltz." Her embarrassment at making this unorthodox request caused her to sound more impatient than she intended.

He looked puzzled, then amused. "But I thought . . . Did I not hear you say just yesterday 'everyone' knew this dance?"

Maryvictoria giggled. Allyson glared at her before replying to Nathan, "Never mind what I said. Can you or can you not teach me this dance?"

"I suppose so," he said. "It depends on how apt a pupil you might be."

"How apt—? You are being impertinent—again."

"Yes, ma'am." The twinkle in his eyes belied his contrite tone.

She smiled, unable to suppress her own amusement at the situation, embarrassing or not. "Well, then, let us not waste anymore time. Miss Pringle will provide the music. I have this chart—" She lifted the magazine from the pianoforte to show him. "But I cannot seem to master the steps."

He studied the chart for a moment, then laid it aside. "The steps are really quite simple," he explained, and demonstrated with her standing beside him. She imitated his movements. "In a sense," he explained, "the lady is doing everything opposite of her partner—she sort of mirrors his actions. It is up to him to keep them from colliding with other dancers."

"I see. . . ." she said doubtfully.

"Here. Stand facing me. Put your right hand in my left hand, and your left hand on my shoulder. That's right. My right hand is at your waist to guide you in making the turns." He pressed her waist slightly to indicate directions.

She did as he told her. "Like this?" She looked into his eyes for confirmation. Their gazes locked, and he appeared to be as startled as she. His eyes momentarily shifted to her lips.

"Yes." There was something different—husky—in that one-word response. Then he began counting as he moved her through the basic steps. "One, two, three, and one, two, three . . ."

They were nearly an arm's length apart, yet she had never

felt so intimate with another human being, not even when she had occasionally been kissed. There was a clean, spicy smell about him, and the touch of his hand holding hers was sending incredible sensations through her entire body. Every nerve seemed alive to *him*. She tried to concentrate on the simple mechanics of the dance.

"Now, we shall try it with the music," he said, "if Miss Pringle would be so kind."

Miss Pringle played a few bars of music until they each had command of the rhythm. They started off awkwardly. Allyson stepped on his toes twice.

"Ouch," he said softly, teasing. "I just polished these boots."

"Sorry." She felt herself blushing in embarrassment, though he obviously was trying to keep the mood light.

He stopped and signaled Miss Pringle to stop playing. "You must not try to lead, my lady. You simply follow where your partner directs you. Listen to the music and obey my commands." He gave her a devastating grin that nearly undid her.

She could not help smiling in kind. "I suspect you take great pleasure in ordering me about."

"It *is* a change in roles for me," he said. "Shall we try again?"

She nodded, and Miss Pringle began to play again. Lost in the music and the swirling movements of dance, Allyson simply gave herself up to following his lead. She was hardly aware of when the last note sounded.

He, too, seemed a bit startled at the end. He released her and bowed from the waist. "You possess a natural grace, Lady Allyson. I predict you will be the belle of the ball."

She laughed. "Thank you. You are an able teacher. But Lady Worthington would likely take it amiss if any but her daughter were the belle of this ball."

When Nathan returned to his duties, Allyson caught a considering, concerned look on Miss Pringle's face and a knowing grin on Maryvictoria's.

* * *

Since Lords Rutherford and Lawton were both attending the Worthington ball with their ladies, Nathan had thought he would be free of duties that night; not so. In need of extra servants for the huge number of guests she expected, Lady Worthington had "borrowed" from her friend, Lady Rutherford.

"At least it ain't rainin'," Robert said cheerfully as he and Nathan took their positions on the rear of the coach.

The two days since the waltz lesson had passed quickly and fairly normally—if anything about this assignment might be called "normal." The morning rides had continued as before, with only a slight awkwardness at first. So, she, too, felt that waltz was something significant. Perhaps it had been a mistake. He had never before been distracted from official duties by recurring thoughts of a light, flowery scent, an enticing smile, and a pair of dazzling brown eyes. If that waltz *was* a mistake, though, he would happily do it again, even as he recognized an inherent danger. He had never wanted to kiss a woman so much in his life.

Nathan was standing against the wall of the wide entrance hall when the ladies of Rutherford House came down the stairs to the waiting men. All three women were, he supposed, attired in elegant ball gowns, but Nathan's attention focused on Lady Allyson. She wore a green dress of some clingy material, with a lighter green, fuller overskirt of gauze. Gold embroidery scattered across the overskirt was repeated at the scooped neckline, which allowed a generous hint of cleavage. Emeralds—a pendant and earrings—completed the ensemble. Green and gold—nature's perfect spring colors—adorning what had to be one of nature's perfect creations.

He wished he had the right to tell her how incredibly beautiful she looked. As it was, when her gaze shifted to him, he merely raised an eyebrow and nodded his approval. She gave him the briefest of smiles in acknowledgment. He was sure none of the others had noticed the byplay, until he heard a soft clearing of a throat and saw Lord Rutherford glance from his daughter to the footman. The older man's eyes held a definite twinkle of amusement.

Forget it, Thornton. She's not for you. Just picture such elegance on a military campaign trail. A twinge of regret accompanied this thought.

Lord Worthington was a powerful member of the government and worked closely with Rutherford. Worthington House was a huge dwelling for the city, more a palace than a mere house, Nathan had thought when he visited the day before to be apprised of his duties. The house boasted a proper ballroom on the first floor with a shell-shaped alcove for the orchestra and a wide balcony overlooking a garden below. A library and several smaller rooms claimed the rest of that floor. On this night, two of those rooms had been set aside as withdrawing rooms, one for ladies, one for gentlemen.

Nathan's "duties" were light. He was, in Melton's words, largely assigned to roam around looking imposing but somehow manage to blend in with the woodwork. He was also to direct guests to the supper room, the card room, and the withdrawing rooms. He suspected Rutherford had somehow managed this eagle's view of the crowd for him, or was it a worm's view? In any event, it also allowed for some unobtrusive eavesdropping.

As Lady Allyson had predicted, the Worthington daughter was the belle of her own come-out ball, but Rutherford's elder daughter came in for a great deal of male attention. Nathan watched with pride—and no small degree of envy—as she waltzed first with the French comte and then with Braxton. Of course, she danced other sets as well with a variety of partners, including that other Frenchman, Arnaud. Nathan made a point of identifying every man who spoke to her. After all, it was his job, was it not?

Nathan had never been one to dress flamboyantly or behave outrageously to attract attention. While it was his *job* this night to blend into the woodwork, he found it slightly annoying that he could so easily be ignored. At one point, just before the supper dance, he found himself blending very well, indeed—not into the woodwork, but into the shrubbery.

Lady Worthington had had numerous large potted plants

hauled into her ballroom and arranged in groups. Nathan was standing in the midst of a cluster of this foliage when he noticed Lady Rutherford standing nearby. He was about to make his presence known and ask her if she would like him to fetch her a drink, when she was approached by a darkly handsome gentleman who had been previously identified to Nathan as one Cecil Cranston.

Nathan stayed where he was. To move now would be most awkward. There was a certain tenseness about the countess that caught his attention. This woman was no more of a shrinking violet than her elder daughter, so what was it that made her apprehensive?

Cranston bowed elegantly. "Ah, my dear Katherine, you are looking as lovely as in our youth. Actually, lovelier. Maturity suits you, love."

"Mr. Cranston." Her tone was civil. "I would prefer, sir, if you would forgo the endearments. I have been 'Lady Rutherford' to most acquaintances for years."

"Oh, Katherine, love, how can you be so cold to me after we were once so *very* close?" His voice was silky smooth, but Nathan sensed an undertone of sarcasm and sadistic enjoyment. "I seem to recall that you were in fact 'Lady Rutherford' when we became 'Katherine' and 'Cecil' to each other."

"That was a long time ago," she said coldly.

"But *I* remember it as though it were yesterday." This sounded to Nathan like a line from a bad play. Cranston's voice turned harsher. "Have you obtained what I want from you? You've only a fortnight or so left."

"I am *trying*. Truly, it is not easy. Can you not give me additional time?"

"Oh, my love, I should like to, but time is simply not on our side." He reached into an inner pocket of his coat and thrust a folded paper at her. "Here, I counted on your being here tonight and thought you might need some stronger incentive."

She put up her hands in a gesture of rejection. "No. What is it?"

"Take it." His voice was low, the tone menacing. "I

copied out some of your more . . . uh . . . colorful lines, just in case your memory had dimmed."

She took the paper as though it were something loathsome and stuffed it into her reticule. "You are despicable," she said.

"No, just somewhat desperate." Nathan felt chilled by his next words. "Bear in mind, my love, the risks to the lovely Allyson." He emitted a nasty chuckle. "It must have been a relief when your firstborn was a female."

Lady Rutherford clutched her reticule so tightly her knuckles must have been white beneath her gloves. "I take it back—you are *worse* than despicable."

"I'll be whatever you want, so long as I get what *I* want. Ah, I see the inimitable Lord Rutherford returns to claim his bride. Talking with you, my love, has been most . . . pleasant." He gave her a perfunctory nod and strode quickly away.

"What did *he* want?" Lord Rutherford asked his wife.

"I . . . uh . . . I am not really sure," she said. "Nothing of importance—just chitchat."

"You . . . You are not thinking to renew your—our—acquaintance with him, are you?" It was a casual question, but Nathan sensed something deeper behind it.

"Good heavens! No!" she said and took his arm. "Some acquaintances are best left in the distant past, and Cecil Cranston is one of them. Come, let us mix with the company and see if those lobster patties are as delicious as Martha claims."

"As you wish." He patted her hand on his arm.

Nathan was dumbfounded. Here was yet another source of danger to Lady Allyson. French agents, that Fish woman, and now this man Cranston. Could they somehow be connected? How much of this Cranston business should be shared with Lord Rutherford? Nothing yet if both Rutherfords were to be protected. Whatever Cranston held over the countess was clearly of a personal nature. But did what Cranston "wanted" pose a serious threat to the countess, to Lady Allyson, or to her father? More important to Captain Lord Nathan Thornton, did it pose a threat to England's national interests?

These musings occupied him as he circulated about the room. As he neared the door of the card room, he stepped aside to allow one of the guests to enter, and looked into his brother's eyes. The two men gasped simultaneously.

"Eastland! What are *you* doing here?" Nathan asked.

The elegant Eastland raised his quizzing-glass and gave Nathan a long condescending stare. "I was invited. A far better question, oh, brother mine, is what are *you* doing here, and in that getup? Father and I have long thought you on the Peninsula. He checks the casualty lists religiously."

The usually subservient footman instantly transformed into a military commander. "Come with me," he demanded, ready to grab Eastland should he resist the order.

Perhaps it was Nathan's tone, or Eastland's reluctance to create a scene, or even simple curiosity, but Nathan was gratified when Eastland readily accompanied him to the library across the hall.

As he opened the door, Nathan heard a swish of silk. He hoped he was not interrupting a romantic tryst. Lady Eggoner, seated on a sofa, was alone in the room. The only light shone from a lamp on a huge mahogany desk. Thank heavens it was a rather dim light, for if Lady Eggoner had thought a *footman* looked familiar to her, she would surely recognize the Marquis of Eastland. Nathan deliberately steered his brother to shelves away from the lady.

"I think Lord Worthington said the piece was in that glass case over there," he said for the woman's benefit. He had suddenly remembered that both Worthington and Eastland collected small jade figurines.

"Thank you." Eastland apparently had no wish to be seen having a tête-à-tête with a footman. He barely nodded at the other guest.

Luckily, Lady Eggoner, occupied in gathering her shawl and fan, scarcely glanced at the newcomer. "I came in here only to rest for a moment," she said. "My moment is over."

Then she was gone, and Nathan breathed a sigh of relief. Eastland turned. "All right, out with it. Are you so determined to smear the family name that you would do . . . do *this?*" He gestured at Nathan's livery, but did not allow a response. "God knows our grandmother left you a small fortune."

"Which you have always felt should be *yours.*" Nathan struggled to control himself.

Eastland—blond, equally as tall as his brother, and seven years older—drew himself up proudly. "Part of the Halstead properties, yes. It should have been in Father's marriage settlements."

"Well, it was not," Nathan said flatly, "and Halstead is as rich as Croesus anyway. Besides, this is an old issue."

"Yes," Eastland agreed. "The issue now is your continual need to embarrass the family. First, there was that sordid mess with the squire's daughter, then a duel—a *duel,* for God's sake—and finally your running off to the army."

"I was *sixteen* when the squire's lovely Sylvia—twenty, if she was a day—decided she wanted a more noble name for the brat she carried than some farmer's. Jarvis accused me of cheating at cards. We were both drunk and the next day we both deloped."

"And the Oxford dons decided the university would be a better place without Halstead's second son."

"Actually, they sent both of us down," Nathan corrected. "And, as I recall, both you and the duke were happy enough to have me out of England." Nathan rarely referred to his father as anything but *the duke* or *Halstead.*

"Which brings us to the current indiscretion," Eastland said. The two had been standing in the middle of the room like two roosters squaring off against each other. "Let us sit while you attempt to explain this away." He gestured again at the livery Nathan wore.

They sat in opposite chairs. Eastland sat back, one leg crossed casually over the other, his hands folded in his lap. Nathan sat forward on his chair, his elbows on his thighs, his hands dangling loosely.

"Well?" the Marquis of Eastland demanded.

Nathan wondered how much he should reveal. Eastland,

following their father's example, had always taken a superior, condescending attitude toward his siblings, and, like their father, the heir to the dukedom expected nothing less than absolute obedience. Nathan's independent nature had never set well with either his father or his brother. However, both the duke and his heir were loyal subjects of England, so Nathan told his brother everything.

He explained that he had been approached while he was in the hospital immediately after his return to England, and that he was encouraged not to contact his family—not that he had much inclination to do so. He also explained briefly about the problem of certain information ending up in French hands and how the government was trying to find the source.

"Why *you?*"

Nathan shrugged. "Story of my life—I was in the wrong place at the wrong time."

"I cannot argue with that," his brother said, but Nathan sensed less arrogance in his tone than earlier. "You are bound to be found out, you know."

"Perhaps. But meanwhile I shall do my duty." This sounded pompous and self-righteous, but sometimes the sincerest beliefs did sound so. Besides, it was an argument any Thornton could understand; it was part of the family motto on the duke's crest.

Eastland gave him an oblique look and nodded. "Nor can I argue with that."

"Does that mean you will not expose me?"

"Yes, that is exactly what it means. You are probably a fool to think you can keep up this charade, but so be it."

"Thank you." Nathan rose and gave his brother an ironic little bow. "I must be about my duties, trivial and otherwise."

Chapter 9

Allyson had looked forward to waltzing at the Worthington ball. She loved the sweep and grace and freedom of this dance. In the event, she *had* enjoyed it, but she sensed something missing—a certain excitement that had been there when she swept around the Rutherford music room in the arms of the footman. No green girl, Lady Allyson Crossleigh recognized that indefinable physical attraction to the man for what it was. However, Nathan Christopher was a *footman* and *Lady* Allyson was no Lady Ferrington, willing to bring shame and scandal on her family. In time, he would move on to another position; footmen often did.

Meanwhile, she would try to limit her association with him, though that would be difficult with her father insisting the man accompany her everywhere she went. She was honest enough with herself to note that while she recognized the wisdom of limiting contact with him, she welcomed the fact that it would be difficult, if not impossible, to do so. She was aware of his presence in the Worthington ballroom. She had even seen him leave at one point with none other than the Marquis of Eastland, undoubtedly performing some small service for Eastland.

She had also seen her mother talking briefly with Mr.

Cranston, which reminded her forcibly of her nebulous plan to try to retrieve those letters. Tomorrow. She would definitely come up with a plan tomorrow.

"You seem somewhat distracted, my lady," Lord Braxton said as he escorted her in to supper.

"No. How could I be distracted when I have such charming company?"

"Doing it too brown, dear girl," he chided.

They joined two other couples, and Allyson deliberately set about enjoying herself and amusing her companions, which she did with remarkable success. This, despite the fact that one of the couples they joined was Loretta Longworth on the arm of the Comte de Pommeraie.

"Is not the waltz simply the most elegant of all dances?" Miss Longworth gushed. "I vow, I felt like a fairy princess."

"And look like one, too," the comte dutifully responded.

"Oh, dear me." She blushed prettily and said, "Monsieur le Comte, you flatter me."

"The truth is never mere flattery," he said smoothly.

"An accomplished partner is helpful, do you not agree?" Allyson asked.

"But of course," Miss Longworth said, "and Monsieur le Comte is the very best." She gave him an adoring look. Then she put on a false expression of shock. "Oh, dear me, now I have insulted the other gentlemen."

"We recognize the comte as our superior in this arena," Lord Braxton said. "He has had far more practice, I think."

The Frenchman acknowledged this compliment by saying, "I have recently been in Brussels, and of course the waltz is all the rage there."

"I shall be so glad when this horrid war is over," Miss Longworth pouted. "I should so like to go to Paris to shop!"

Allyson bit her tongue at this inanity, but blurted out anyway, "I should imagine that not a few wives and mothers in both England and France will also be glad when it is over."

Miss Longworth managed to look hurt, but Allyson detected a glint of anger in her response. "But of *course*. That goes without saying. I just did not think it a proper topic for a *ball*."

Allyson gave the Longworth chit a tight little smile, the comte soothed her with cooing words, and Maryvictoria jogged her elbow so that she smeared a cream cake across her face.

Allyson tried to frown at Maryvictoria but grinned instead. Miss Longworth cried, "Oh!," wiped her face with a serviette, and said in a nasty tone to Allyson, "Do you always find the little misfortunes of others so amusing, Lady Allyson?"

Allyson said contritely, "I am so sorry. I was looking elsewhere."

"Hmphf," Miss Longworth huffed disbelievingly.

The other lady at the table, Miss Prentiss, tactfully changed the subject by asking about the merits of a new play.

Later, in her own chamber after she had dismissed Molly and climbed into bed, Allyson said softly, "All right, you wicked imp, show yourself."

A smiling Maryvictoria materialized on a chair near the bed.

"Did you enjoy the ball?" Allyson asked pointedly.

"Oh, yes—immensely. All those beautiful gowns, the jewels, the music . . ." she said dreamily.

"What prompted you to embarrass Miss Longworth so?"

Maryvictoria looked defensive. "She deserved it—always trying to outdo other ladies. I protect my . . . uh . . . clients."

"Is that what I am? A client?"

"Well, for want of a better term."

"How *can* I convince you that your . . . 'protection' . . . is superfluous?"

"But it is not—not yet," the child said seriously.

"What do you mean 'not yet'?"

"I—I do not *know!*" Maryvictoria wailed. "I am just to wait and watch and they will tell me when it is time, and when I am finished."

"So what is this business of your popping up like a jack-in-the-box every now and then?"

Maryvictoria sighed. "I . . . I get *bored,* you see, just waiting. I mean, I have Caroline and all"—she held up the doll—"but . . . well, *you* know. And do you mind so very, very much?" She ended on a plaintive note.

Allyson thought about this for a moment. "Hmm. No, I suppose not—not yet at least. But if I am carried off to Bedlam, it will be on *your* conscience!"

"Oh, good." With that, Maryvictoria disappeared again.

Allyson lay a long time mulling over this strange phenomenon in her life. Was Maryvictoria real? Or was she some extension of Allyson herself somehow? So far, most of her discourse with Maryvictoria was almost like talking with herself. Of course, there was the cream cake all over Miss Longworth's pretty face. Allyson grinned at the recollection.

The next morning, she made her ride short, but energetic. There were no leisurely chats with other riders. Her conversation with Nathan was rather curtailed, but they did talk briefly about the ball.

"I noticed you with Lord Eastland," she said.

He was strangely quiet for a moment. "Yes, he wanted to see Worthington's jade collection."

"What sort of man is he?" she asked, making conversation. "He rarely comes to town for the Season. Rumor has it that he is looking for a wife this Season."

Nathan smiled. "Is that so?"

"And you should see how some of the mamas' eyes light up at *that* prospect. He is Halstead's heir, you know."

"Yes, as a matter of fact, I did know. Well, with his blunt, he should have little difficulty shopping the marriage mart."

She laughed. "That is rather a cold view of the institution of marriage."

"That *is* what it is among the *ton,* is it not—an *institution?*"

"What about love?" The question was out before she thought to curb it.

"Mostly romantic nonsense. Now lust—that is a different story altogether." He gave her a direct look.

She blushed and looked away. *Infernal man.* They rode in silence for a few moments, then she asked, "Did you see me waltz?" She knew he had.

"Yes, you did magnificently."

"I had a good dancing master."

On that day and the following, Nathan made a point of finding out all he could about Cecil Cranston. He began by tracking Melton down in the butler's pantry and asking him what he knew of Cranston.

A peculiar look came over Melton's face at mention of the name. He leaned against the huge table that dominated the room and hedged with a question of his own. "Why do you ask?"

"He appears to have some interest in the Rutherfords," Nathan said, taking a seat on a nearby stool.

"In *Lady* Rutherford, you mean."

"That was my impression."

"I heard he was back," Melton said grimly. "He's a very rotten apple, that one. I hope he is not planning to make trouble for the earl—or the countess."

"What kind of trouble?"

Melton looked uncomfortable and did not immediately respond.

"Come on, Mr. Melton," Nathan urged. "I know you do not engage in idle gossip about the family, but, believe me, this might be important."

"Whatever I tell you will go no farther?"

"I swear."

Melton gave him a long look, then nodded. "Years ago, before Lady Allyson was born, Cranston was sort of . . . well . . . Lady Rutherford's cicisbeo. I was just a footman at the time."

"Was he a particular friend, or just one of a court who dangled after her? She is a fine looking woman now; she must have been a beauty in her youth."

"She was," the butler said. "And, yes, he was a *very* particular friend. I myself carried notes from her to him several times."

"But Rutherford and his wife seem so . . . close."

"They were not always so. It was an arranged marriage; most *ton* marriages were in those days—still are, I think."

Nathan nodded.

"Anyway, it was all rather discreet, and eventually it sort of blew over. Cranston left the country, and that was the end of it."

Not quite, Nathan thought, but he did not say it aloud. So Cranston was using some old letters as extortion against the countess, but to what purpose? Money? Or information that he might sell?

Some discreet questioning of other servants—grooms in the park when he had ridden out with Lady Allyson—revealed the location of Cranston's dwelling and the fact that he hired only three live-in servants, all men. Later, Nathan sought out the location. Despite his dapper appearance, Cranston lived in a rather run-down area of the city, cheap and barely respectable. Nathan conjectured that the man probably entertained very little.

Nathan also visited Bow Street and engaged two runners to investigate Cranston, and the Fish woman and her male companion. It took the runners less than two days to report back to him. He met them at a little-known tavern.

"Your man was right," the older of the two runners said. "That Cranston fellow is a rotten one—operates on the fringes of respectability. He *might* be mixed up in some smuggling— take us more time to be sure o' that. And for sure he extorts 'protection' money from certain small shopkeepers. One of his house servants does his dirty work. Big bruiser—must weigh sixteen, eighteen stone."

"Cranston *looks* prosperous in company," Nathan observed.

"Looks is deceivin'," the younger runner said. "He owes a bundle o' blunt to clothiers, bootmakers, and the like. His carriage and horses ain't paid for neither."

"Did you perceive any connection between him and the French?" Nathan asked.

They looked at each other and shook their heads. The older one spoke for both of them. "Nothin' out o' the ordinary; smuggling could provide plenty o' truck with the frogs, though."

"True. . . ." Nathan mused. He recalled that in company he had not seen Cranston in groups that included either of Lady Allyson's French suitors. *That could have been deliberate, though.* He shifted the subject. "What about Francis Fish and her man Bart?"

"Them two got no love for anyone associated with the Fairfax women, but it does not appear that they are taking action of any sort," the older one said.

"There are some French émigrés that frequent her brothel, though," the younger man said.

"Well, keep your eyes and ears open," Nathan said in parting.

"Yes, sir," they chorused.

With some subtle investigation of her own—seemingly innocuous, flirtatious questions in several drawing rooms—Allyson, too, had discovered where Mr. Cranston lived. The young footman, Jamie, who would have happily tread burning coals for his Lady Allyson, had been charged with finding out the man's living arrangements. Jamie had reported that another young servant in a neighboring house had said that there were three servants, and that when Cranston was out of an evening, his staff regularly deserted the premises.

"When the cat's away, the mice will play," Jamie said sagely.

"Perhaps they leave a large dog to stand guard," Allyson suggested.

"Nobody said nothin' 'bout no dog."

Nevertheless, she would take along a chunk of bloody beef to distract any canine interference. It was only then that she realized a plan—a real plan—was formulating in her mind. She would simply invade Cranston's house one night and retrieve her mother's letters. The idea was a scary one, but the task should not prove impossible. It was largely a matter of deciding *when* the event should occur. But even that was an easy decision, for of late, Cranston had appeared at the largest parties and soirees of the *ton*. Lady Dashwood's musicale would provide the perfect opportunity.

However, she could hardly roam the streets alone at night as the fashionable Lady Allyson.

"You should not go *alone* at all," Maryvictoria asserted in a remarkably grown-up and disapproving tone. She had, as usual, materialized just after Allyson dismissed Molly one night. "You will need someone to help you search, and someone else to stand guard against anyone's return to that house."

"I can conduct the search myself."

"The whole house?"

"It cannot be so very large," Allyson reasoned. "The man employs only three servants. Hmm . . . You are probably right, though; I will need someone to stand watch. What about *you?* You are always wanting to interfere in my business, and you would make the perfect watchman. Watchgirl."

"Oh, no, not I. *I* am trying to dissuade you from this foolish idea of acting entirely on your own."

"Well, then Molly—or Jamie—"

Maryvictoria silently stamped her foot. "Two babies. Neither of them has more than fifteen years!"

Allyson ignored the child and thought carefully. Jamie was far more levelheaded than Molly, who tended to get excited in a crisis.

"Nathan—" Maryvictoria started.

"No!" Allyson said vehemently. "This is a very private matter. Jamie need not be told of Mama's letters at all, but Nathan would ask a dozen questions and have an opinion on all the answers, some of which he would undoubtedly supply himself."

"Do you not trust him?"

"It is not a matter of trust."

Later, when Maryvictoria had gone, Allyson mulled over the conversation and the plan. No, it was *not* a matter of trust, she affirmed again. It was a matter of pride. Family pride. No one—no one—should know of her mother's indiscretion, if that was what it was. It would kill her father. . . .

Nathan had grown quite fond of Molly, who, in many ways, reminded him of his younger sister Anne—she who had been the Marchioness of Cambden these last several years—the only member of his family with whom he had kept up a sporadic correspondence since entering the army nearly twelve years ago. As he and Molly were often thrown together in serving Lady Allyson, they had developed an easy camaraderie, especially after the visit to Fairfax House. Molly seemed to view him in the role of an older brother, confiding in him about two young men in whom she was interested, a footman and a groom in neighboring houses.

On an unusually quiet evening in early May, Nathan had gone to the stables to visit one of his most reliable friends, the horse Bucephalus.

"I may be in over my head, old boy," he murmured as he patted the horse and fed him the first of the two apples he had brought with him. "I'm no closer to resolving this damned French problem than I ever was, and that infernal woman is driving me mad. I mean, one day she is a haughty lady of the *ton,* and the next, she is treating me as though I were a real person. She has spirit and beauty and compassion. God knows, a man would never be bored with her."

The horse nickered and rubbed its head against Nathan's shoulder.

"And now there's this matter of the countess and that Cranston fellow, who's a dirty dish if there ever was one. I wonder if it would help if I were to pay the man a little visit? Hmm. That would bear some thought."

The horse nickered and shoved at him again.

"Oh, all right. Here's the other one." He gave the horse the second apple and patted his neck. "Good night, my friend."

Nathan made his way back to the house. It was a mild spring night, and in this part of the city the usual stenches elsewhere were absent, or greatly subdued. One might almost imagine himself in the country. Might. Almost.

As he approached the back of the house, he spied Molly sitting on a step looking dejected and pensive.

"Why are you wearing such a picklepuss?" he asked as he lowered himself to the step next to her. "Is it Phillip? Or Thomas? Which one would you like me to challenge in a duel to the death?"

She gave him a weak smile. "No, nothing like that. It's Lady Allyson."

Nathan felt his heart lurch. "What about her?"

"I . . . I'm not sure. She's acting really strange."

"Strange?" He gave her a questioning look. "Explain."

"She had me in the attic with her for hours yesterday looking for men's clothing. Men's clothing! That *she* could wear."

"Did she find some?"

"Oh, yes. Old-fashioned, but she found some that fit."

"Why does she want male clothing?" he asked.

"I do not know, but I do know she plans to go out wearing breeches!"

"Where? And when?"

"I have no idea *where*," Molly said, "but, maybe tomorrow night."

"Tomorrow night? What makes you think so?"

"When I asked her what gown I should press for her to wear to the Dashwoods' musicale, she said she wasn't going."

"From some of the caterwauling one hears at those things, one could hardly blame her," he said lightly.

"You don't understand. Lady Allyson is very fond of music—the whole family is—and Lady Dashwood is said to present only the best."

"Perhaps she does not feel well."

"She feels fine," Molly said shortly. "She also bade me see that this door"—she pointed behind her—"is unlocked tomorrow night. I am to check it at midnight in case someone relocks it."

"Hmm."

"Did . . . Did she mention a plan to you?" Molly asked hopefully. "I mean . . . We all know how you are s'posed to go about with her. . . ."

"No, she did not." Nathan tried to hide his own worry—and his fury. "But I shall take care of it—her. I give you my word."

"I hope I was right to tell you," Molly said.

They sat in silence for a moment.

"Surely she would not go anywhere at night alone," Nathan mused aloud. "And if she were not accompanied by *you,* or me, then who?"

"The rest of the family *are* going to the Dashwood affair." Molly paused. "She might have taken the viscount with her—the two of them are often up to some rig or another—but he's away at school."

"Who?"

"Viscount Sothern. The earl's heir. Lady Allyson's younger brother. The two of them are very close."

"Oh, yes, I had forgot about him."

They again sat in worried, thoughtful silence for a moment. Then Molly suddenly snapped her fingers.

"I know! Jamie! I should have thought of him before."

"Jamie? Jamie! He's only a boy; he would provide little protection for her." Now Nathan truly was worried.

"It has to be Jamie," Molly insisted. "Lady Allyson has sent him on a couple of errands lately, an' he hasn't bragged about them at all."

"Well, that *is* a sure sign," Nathan said ironically. He patted her shoulder. "Don't you worry, now, Molly. I will handle it. And, yes, you did right to tell me."

Chapter 10

"I think someone's followin' us, milady." Jamie sounded worried.

"Don't be silly," Allyson replied. "Who could possibly be following, unless you let slip about our little outing?"

"Oh, no, milady. I swear. Me lips have been sealed real tight."

"Well, then, come along," she said with more confidence than she felt.

Getting out of the house was easier than she had expected. She had managed to cobble together an almost presentable costume of male attire, including dark breeches, a dark coat, and even a pair of boots. She was sure the breeches were meant to be *knee* breeches on a man with more inches than she had, and she had stuffed handkerchiefs in the toes of the boots to make them fit, but in the dark, who would notice? Her plea of not feeling well had caused her mother some concern, but Allyson convinced her it was at worst a minor indisposition.

"I am sorry you will miss the music this evening," her mother said. "I know how fond you are of the folk music especially."

"Please give Lady Dashwood my regrets."

As soon as she was sure the family had gone, Allyson set

about putting on the male clothing. She struggled with some of the strange flaps and closings, but she was glad she had given Molly the evening off, though the maid had been reminded to check the rear door by midnight. She took a long look in the cheval glass, turning this way and that.

Not bad, she thought. *I should do.*

"What you should do is stay home, not go alone—well, virtually alone," Maryvictoria said, materializing on her favorite chair.

"Oh, now don't start haranguing me *again,*" Allyson said. "Just tell me; do you think I can pass as a young man?"

Maryvictoria studied her carefully, motioning for Allyson to turn around. When Allyson turned back, the sprite said, "Um-hmm. So long as no one looks *too* closely. And you must remember to *walk* like a man. You know, long strides and a bit of a swagger. They never worry about skirts or about their legs or hems getting dirty."

"Thank you. I did need that reminder." Allyson stuffed stray ends of hair back into her cap. "Well, I am off. I . . . uh . . . I do not suppose you will be there?"

Allyson could not have said *why,* but she thought she might feel better if Maryvictoria went along, just for moral support, she told herself.

Maryvictoria shrugged. "I do not know if I am allowed. Besides—"

"Besides, *you* disapprove. So be it."

Allyson stopped by the kitchen to collect a sack she had secreted there, and met Jamie at the rear door. She checked to be sure it was unlocked; then the two of them crept through the side shadows to the street in front, where again they tried to keep to shadowed areas.

Nathan watched from the shadows of the stable as a boyish figure emerged from the back door of the house and joined the young footman, Jamie. He grudgingly and silently conceded that, to the undiscerning eye, she might very well pass for a young male. However, Captain Lord Thornton's eye was *very* discerning, and there was something wondrously moving about a woman's sweet curves in male attire. This woman's, anyway.

At the same time, he was sorely annoyed with her. Where in the *hell* was she going? She knew very well her father had assigned him to accompany her on any outings, so what was so important about this one that she would defy Rutherford's wishes? At night, yet, and attended by only a callow youth?

Lady Allyson and Jamie followed a rather circuitous route, but eventually certain buildings, fences, and shrubbery on dimly lit streets began to look familiar to Nathan. Good God! They were in the neighborhood in which the man Cranston had lodgings. His heart skipped a beat. Did Lady Allyson, then, know of Cranston's extortion attempts? As they neared the actual building in which Cranston lived, Nathan came to the conclusion that she *must* know. Lady Allyson and Jamie stopped in shadows on the opposite side of the street from Cranston's lodgings. They conferred urgently with each other. Nathan could not hear what they said, though he could perceive gestures. He eased himself closer.

The boy started to dash across the street, but Lady Allyson stopped him. "Here, take this," she said in a hoarse whisper. She handed him a packet.

"What is it?" Jamie asked.

"A chunk of beef in case there is a dog."

Nathan was impressed with this bit of forethought. The boy dashed across the street into an alley at the side of the house. There was a gate across the alley. Nathan could barely discern motions of the boy, but Lady Allyson, only a few feet away, was very tense indeed. A long moment ensued. Then with a squeak, the gate swung inward.

"All clear," Jamie called softly.

Lady Allyson dashed across the street and let herself in. Doubting that they would relock the gate, Nathan waited a moment before following her. He slid silently inside the gate as she and Jamie paused at the corner of the house.

In this area of town, there were none of the gas street-lamps that illumined wealthier sections of London. However, some moonlight filtered through cloud and fog so that Nathan could clearly follow his quarry. As the other two proceeded, he followed them around the corner. They were huddled on the back stoop, considering a door in front of them.

"Botheration! It *is* locked," Lady Allyson said.

"P'haps we can climb in a window," Jamie said.

Lady Allyson looked up. "They are frightfully high."

"If'n you was to stand on my shoulders—" Jamie said helpfully.

Lady Allyson eyed the boy's slight shoulders.

"Do not even think about it," Nathan said softly, emerging from the deeper shadows.

"Eek!" Lady Allyson squeaked, but she quickly recovered. "You! What are you doing here?"

"Exactly what I am assigned to do—accompany *you*, even on an ill-advised, addlepated, inept burglary."

"Nathan!" Jamie's voice held relief and far more welcome than hers had.

"You shall not interfere," she said to Nathan. "I fully intend to do what I came here to do."

"Jamie," Nathan said, ignoring her protest, "you go and stand near the gate to warn us of anyone coming to this house."

"How?" the boy asked.

"How, what?"

"How should I warn you?"

"Well, can you whistle?" Nathan asked.

"A whistle will alert the whole neighborhood," Lady Allyson whispered contemptuously.

"Well, then," Nathan said, "try meowing like a cat in the throes of-of—you know."

Jamie's teeth flashed in a grin. "Yes, sir."

Nathan himself grinned as the image silenced Lady Allyson—temporarily.

"That was rather vulgar," she said. "And you are *not* stopping me!"

"At this point," he said, "no, I shall not stop you, but I think you will need help finding those letters, in the dark, yet."

She gasped. "How did you know—?"

"I shall explain later. Right now, we must get inside." He reached into his pocket and retrieved some small tools he had equipped himself with earlier.

"What are you doing?" she whispered.

"Picking the lock. Luckily it is not a complicated one," he said as the latch gave and the door swung inward.

"You *are* a man of many talents," she said, but he did not think her tone was admiring.

As they entered, he heard her fumbling in the bag she carried, and then heard the sound of a tinderbox producing a spark, from which she lit a short candle. They were on the ground floor. A dark stairwell led down to what must have been the kitchen. No sound came from there, or anywhere.

"Where to?" he asked softly.

"Upstairs—the first floor. There is a dining room and a drawing room here on this ground floor. A library-study and two bedrooms occupy the first floor. The second floor seems to be servants' quarters."

He was impressed by her knowledge, what his military mind recognized as reconnaissance. "We should try the library-study first."

"That is what I thought, too," she said.

Nevertheless, they looked into the rooms on the ground floor. The dining room seemed to be used, for there were condiment dishes on a sideboard. The other room, however, smelled musty, and what furniture there was in it was encased in Holland covers.

"The man is not given to entertaining," Nathan said.

On the next floor, one of the bedrooms was clearly unoccupied, but the other one had a low-banked fire in the fireplace, and a nightrobe lay casually on the bed. The library-study, across the hall from the bedrooms, was obviously the tenant's favorite room. The entrance was in the middle of the long room, one end of which held a fireplace. Here, too, a small fire was banked. Facing the fireplace was a sofa and two chairs. Decanters and glasses sat on a small side table.

"He may be expecting to bring company back with him," Nathan observed softly. "We'd better hurry."

At the opposite end of the room was a small alcove in which was a large oak desk, the front of which was solid and imposing.

"The desk—" Lady Allyson breathed.

They moved together toward that piece of furniture. An unlit lamp sat on the desk, which also contained a fancy inkwell and blotter pad. As they moved behind the desk, Nathan noted a middle drawer and three deeper drawers on either side. He pulled the desk chair out of the well and tried opening drawers. Only the bottom-right one was locked. It took some time to manage unlocking it. Nathan could sense Lady Allyson becoming increasingly nervous.

"Hurry," she said, even as she examined the contents of the middle drawer.

"I must take care. Don't want to leave telltale scratches, do we? Anything there?"

"Nothing."

He heard the lock give. "Ah." He pulled the drawer open and looked through the papers there. "Bills. And bills. And bills. Here, you look. See if any of the handwriting is familiar to you."

They exchanged places, and he held the candle as she carefully looked through the papers. "Nothing," she said in an anguished tone.

Despite her male attire, Nathan was very aware of the *woman* standing so near, and that his need to protect her went beyond her father's orders to him. She had wisely left off her usual flowery perfume, but she still smelled of soap and something else. Ah! Lemon. She must rinse her hair in lemon water just as he remembered his sister doing. He wanted to kiss her, here and now. *Remember your place, Thornton! And that this is neither the time nor the place!*

He put a reassuring hand on her shoulder. "He must have them in the bedroom. We'll check there."

Suddenly, the loud exaggerated *meow* of a cat pierced the silence of the night. Nathan handed her the candle, pushed the drawer shut, and managed to relock it.

They could hear footsteps coming up the main stairway of the house—at least two people, a heavier tread, and a lighter one.

"In here, and kill the light," Nathan said, shoving Lady Allyson into the well of the desk and quickly crawling in with her. She wet her fingers and pinched the flame as he drew the chair toward the desk as far as possible.

It was a big desk, a man's desk. The knee well was large, but two adult people were nevertheless a close fit. They sat with knees drawn up, facing each other. Allyson tried to hold her breath so as to listen harder. Nathan gripped her hand.

"Relax," he whispered as they heard the door open and saw a very faint illumination of the room; one of the newcomers probably held a small candle.

"In here, sweet thing," a coarse male voice said.

A female responded. "Oh, Ralph. Do you really think we should be here, in 'is private quarters?"

"He won't mind." Ralph's laugh was a mixture of disgust and triumph. "He can't mind. He owes me three months' back wages. Besides, I know where his skeletons are hid, so to speak."

"Oh." The woman giggled nervously.

Allyson and Nathan heard the other two move in the direction of the fireplace. Ralph said, "Here you go, Edna. Just sit here while I get us some better light and some drinks. It *was* Edna, wasn't it?"

"Yes, you silly boy," she cooed. "Hurry back, now."

Ralph came toward the desk. Allyson drew in her breath as he fumbled with the lamp chimney. Light flooded the room from above where she and Nathan sat. They looked at each other. She knew he was as chagrined and frustrated, though perhaps not so frightened, as she was at their predicament, yet both also found it amusing, for they grinned nervously at each other. They heard Ralph clattering a decanter and glasses; then he moved toward the sofa.

"Thank you," Edna said.

Allyson and Nathan heard Ralph lower his bulk to the sofa. From this sound and his footsteps earlier, she conjectured he was a big man.

"This is quite good," Edna said.

"Only the best for Mr. Cranston," Ralph replied.

There was a rustle of cloth, then a long silence.

"You taste like brandy." Ralph's voice was husky.

Edna giggled again. "Imagine that."

They must have drained the glasses because now there were soft murmurs and an occasional moan and a good deal of rustling of cloth.

"Do you like that?" Ralph asked.

"Oh, yes. Don't stop. It's *so* good."

Allyson was profoundly embarrassed and keenly aware of the man who sat close to her. Unable to meet Nathan's gaze, she leaned her head back and glanced at the bottom of the center drawer of the desk. She drew in a sharp breath. There, glued to the bottom, was an envelope! She touched Nathan's knee and pointed.

His eyes glowed in shared triumph. Carefully, silently, he loosened the envelope and withdrew its contents. He handed the sheets to Allyson. Even in the dim light, she recognized her mother's distinctive script. She looked at Nathan.

"Is that it?" he mouthed.

She nodded.

They became aware of the others in the room again.

"Ralphie, dear," Edna said, "this sofa ain't goin' to work for us—you're too big. An' I am not doin' it on the floor! Ain't you got a bed in this house?"

"We'll use one across the hall," Ralph said.

"His own bed?"

"No. No. The other one."

"What if he comes home?" she asked.

Fine time to think of that, Allyson thought sourly. An amused glint in Nathan's gaze told her he was thinking the same thing.

"He won't," Ralph replied. "After that music thing, he'll go find a game. Won't come home 'til four or five at the earliest."

"Good," she purred. "I like it slow an' easy."

There was more rustling of cloth against cloth as they apparently stood up.

"Bring that brandy," Edna said.

"Righto." Ralph moved toward the desk and picked up the lamp. They left, plunging the room into darkness.

Allyson would have crawled from under the desk immediately.

Nathan put up his hand and whispered, "Wait."

She settled back, puzzled. The door opened again. It was Ralph's heavy footsteps. He must have carried a candle, for the light was faint and flickering. He muttered to himself. "Damned woman! Nothin' but a doxy, but her ladyship has to have a proper glass for 'er brandy!"

Allyson glanced at Nathan and saw his eyes glinting with amusement. She put both hands over her mouth to stifle her laughter. They waited only a moment more after Ralph left the room the second time.

"How did you know he would return?" Allyson whispered, taking the hand Nathan offered to help her out of the desk well.

"I didn't. It just seemed like a good idea."

"The letters?"

"Right here." He lifted the lapel of his coat slightly.

They were standing very close together and, for a moment, neither of them seemed inclined to move. A shiver of anticipation and growing awareness coursed through her body, and Allyson knew instinctively that it stemmed from more than shared danger. He stepped away to find a spill near the fire and to relight their candle.

"I . . . I am sorry, my lady, that you were . . . subjected to that scene," he said very softly.

"I found it rather . . . uh . . . amusing. Perhaps I am not so much of a lady, after all." She chuckled ruefully but kept her voice barely above a whisper. "I doubt I would have insisted on proper glassware."

He grinned broadly and spoke in the same tone. "*Don't* make me laugh. We still have to get out of here."

"Back the way we came?"

"Yes, but we daren't use the candle this time." He lifted it high to examine the top of the desk. "Except for the lamp, it looks the same. We are leaving no tracks."

"Good."

He went to the door, opened it a crack, and listened intently. "Ready?"

She nodded, her apprehension returning in full force.

He extinguished the candle. "Give me your hand. We don't want to get separated in the dark."

She complied and immediately felt comforted, protected by his very presence. They slipped out the door and crept along the wall toward the rear stairway leading down to the ground floor.

"Careful," she whispered, "there was a table in this hall."

Her warning came an instant too late as he jostled the table, sending a large porcelain vase crashing to the floor.

"What the hell?" Ralph came rushing into the hallway holding a lamp and wearing only his trousers. "Who are you? What are you doin' here?" He set the lamp on the table and advanced toward them. Nathan quickly shoved Allyson behind him.

"Go!" he said to her.

"No. You might need help."

Ralph grimaced wickedly. "He'll need a lot more help than a whey-faced addle-cove like you can supply!" With that, he dove at Nathan, punching him hard in the stomach and knocking the air out of him.

Allyson looked in vain for something to use as a weapon.

Finding nothing, she launched herself at the brute. Only later did she think how foolish that was. Ralph outweighed Nathan by three or four stone, and he weighed *twice* as much as she did.

"Stay outa this, pup," Ralph growled, easily pushing her away, but in the process she lost her cap. "Good God! A mort!"

Nevertheless, her action, and Ralph's stupefaction at seeing her hair come cascading down, gave Nathan a chance to regain some of his breath.

"He's right. Stay back," Nathan ordered sharply, and swung at the giant, aiming for a rather oversized midriff.

Edna, emerging from the bedroom doorway, clad only in a shift, screamed.

Ralph landed another telling blow that Allyson was sure would give Nathan a headache for a week. At the same time, the giant managed to hook a foot around Nathan's ankle, and they both went tumbling to the floor, Ralph in the superior position. Before he could strike another blow, however, Ralph was himself struck down from behind by a copper pan for warming beds.

"Edna! For God's sake, what'd you do *that* for?" Ralph bellowed.

Edna had no chance to declare her innocence before the warming pan struck again and Ralph was out cold.

"Maryvictoria!" Allyson said, but the child did not show herself, and Allyson immediately found the warming pan thrust into her own hand.

Edna looked bewildered. Nathan rolled Ralph off him and rose to his feet. He moved his head around, seemingly checking that all the parts were in working order.

"Are you all right?" Allyson asked.

"I think so. Come on, let's get out of here."

Edna was bent over the still-prone Ralph, sobbing now. "You said it would be all right, you big oaf!" She looked up at Allyson, and her eyes widened in surprise. "I *know* you— I mean, I know who you be."

"No, you do not! You just think you do," Nathan said as a warning. He grabbed Allyson's hand and rushed her out of the house.

They let themselves out through the gate and found Jamie waiting for them.

"I heard that racket and was about to come in."

"Thanks." Nathan patted his shoulder. "Perhaps you could be persuaded to loan Lady Allyson your cap? She seems to have lost hers."

"Oh, yes!" Jamie quickly snatched off his cap, and Allyson tucked as much of her hair into it as she could.

As they started off, Nathan asked, "What was that you said about 'victory' back there, my lady?"

"Uh . . . 'Carry on to victory,' perhaps?"

"And wherever did you find that warming pan? That was a godsend."

"Umm. Yes. It was, was it not?"

They said nothing more as the three of them hastened on their way. Following some of the back route Robert had once shown him, Nathan had them returned to the back entrance of Rutherford House in far less time than the excursion out had taken.

The door was unlocked, and a nervous Molly sat in the kitchen waiting for them.

"Oh, my stars! I have been that worried, I have!"

"You needn't have been," Allyson said gently. "But since you have waited up despite my orders to the contrary, you may help me out of this . . . this costume in a few moments." She turned to Jamie. "Thank you, Jamie. You were a great help, and there will be a little extra for you on quarter day."

"Thank *you*, my lady. I . . . I am always happy to serve you." The boy blushed and went off to his own quarters.

"Nathan, you and I have something to discuss," she said in a no-nonsense tone. "I shall meet you in the morning room in, say, fifteen minutes?"

"Very well, my lady."

Chapter 11

Nathan quickly changed into his usual livery and splashed cold water on his bruised face before reporting to the morning room. He arrived first and thought surely that fifteen minutes probably meant half or three-quarters of an hour to a lady of the *ton*. He was surprised when she arrived promptly.

She had exchanged her male attire for a light blue muslin day dress. She had obviously hastily pinned up her hair, for stray wisps floated enticingly about her face. He rose as she entered. She looked keenly at his face, stepped closer, and lifted her hand, then abruptly dropped it. She wore a confused expression, and he noted with a fleeting sense of triumph that she had taken time to splash on some of the familiar flowery perfume.

"That . . . looks painful," she said.

"I have survived far worse, my lady."

"Yes, I suppose you have, as a soldier." She held his gaze for a moment.

He merely nodded, waiting for her to open the subject uppermost in her mind.

"Please be seated," she said, dropping her gaze and placing herself in a white wicker chair with a colorful cushion.

He took a similar seat opposite her. "Did you bring the letters?"

"There." He gestured to where they lay on the table.

"I want to know how you knew of them," she demanded.

He told her, ending with, "I assure you I had no intention of eavesdropping on Lady Rutherford's private conversation."

She gave him another direct look. "It never once occurred to me to suppose that you had."

"I cannot believe Her Ladyship would set *you* the task of retrieving those letters, though," he said.

"She did not." She explained how she had come by her information, adding, "Unlike you, I *did* intentionally listen in on a private conversation."

"Even now your mother has no idea that you know of them? You have not discussed their existence with her?"

"No."

"Why? If I may be so bold as to ask?"

"She . . . She would find the situation extremely embarrassing. As a matter of fact, I might also."

Nathan sat in thought for a moment, studying the woman before him. She was beautiful, and courageous, and loyal—and oh-so-foolish. If she had been caught in that house—and she very nearly was—the scandal would have reverberated throughout the city. And that could still happen. Had not Edna said she knew the woman dressed as a boy? He wondered if he could find Edna and buy her off? Or *scare* her off? He came back to the issue at hand.

"The letters. I presume you intend to return them to Lady Rutherford."

"Well, no. I . . . I thought merely to burn them."

"Without telling Lady Rutherford you had done so?"

"No-o-o . . . She would have to know; would she not?" Lady Allyson was uncharacteristically unsure of herself.

"How?"

"What do you mean 'how'?"

"I *mean*," he said patiently, "had you planned to march into her chamber and say, 'Oh, by the way, Mama, I have taken care of an unpleasant matter for you'?"

"No! Of course not. She does not know I know."

"I gather your father knows nothing of them?"

"I think not. I hope not."

"I hope not, too." In working with Lord Rutherford, Nathan had come to respect the man more and more. He would hate to see Rutherford unnecessarily hurt. Any credible hint of infidelity on the part of his wife would surely kill the earl.

"It would kill Papa." Lady Allyson echoed his thoughts.

"So, do you have a plan?" he asked. "Lady Rutherford needs to know these no longer pose a threat to her." The envelope containing the letters lay on the table between them like a snake with a terrible potential of striking.

"N-no. Frankly, I had not really thought beyond retrieving them."

He grinned. "Now, why does that not surprise me?"

"You are being impertinent, yet again."

"Pardon me, my lady. But it may interest you to know that I have a possible solution."

"Tell me."

"I think it best that I request an audience with the countess and tell her frankly how *I* came upon knowledge of their existence, that I retrieved them, and then simply give them to her."

"How very heroic of you."

He grinned. "I know, I am such a good fellow, am I not?" His voice turned serious. "But it is the only thing I can think of that will keep you or your father out of it, and save face for Lady Rutherford as well. Unless *you* have a better idea . . . ?"

She sat silent for a moment, then sighed. "No, I have none. Actually, this does not put you in the best of light, eavesdropping on other people's business and burglarizing other people's homes."

He shrugged. "I shall live with it, and she need not know *all* the details. This will work. I know it will."

"Yes, I think it will." She rose and extended her hand. "And I do thank you, Nathan."

"My pleasure, my lady." Instead of taking her hand in a friendly handshake as she apparently intended, he gripped her fingers and bent his head to brush his lips across her knuckles.

She gave him a startled look, pulled back, and hurried from the room, leaving behind a trace of flowers.

Overstepped the bounds again, Thornton, he admonished himself, but he refused to be sorry about having done so.

Allyson was engaged in what she was coming to view as her nightly chat with Maryvictoria.

"I thought you were going to stay away from Cranston's house. And did you not say you are not 'allowed' to interfere? If that is true, what was that business with the warming pan? Or even with Miss Longworth's cake-smeared face?"

"I *think* I said I am not allowed to *change* how events will turn *out*. What will be will be." Maryvictoria fidgeted with Caroline for a moment, stroking the doll's yellow yarn braid. "Eventually, *you* would have found and used that warming pan, or something else."

"Eventually. . . ." Allyson conceded.

"So, you see? I merely saved some time."

"Not to mention more injuries to poor Nathan."

" 'Poor' Nathan? You are softening toward him, then?" Maryvictoria's tone was eager, hopeful.

"I . . . He was very helpful tonight. And . . . And I suppose it *is* possible to develop a certain sort of friendship with a servant. . . ." Allyson verbalized her musings.

"People are people," Maryvictoria said rather ponderously.

"Even little-girl ghosts?" Allyson teased, largely to shift from a subject she was finding discomfiting.

"Even us."

"We."

"We—what?"

"It should be 'even we,' " Allyson said.

"Oh, Saint Peter! And Paul and Michael, too!" Maryvictoria said impatiently. Then she clapped her hand over her mouth. "I forgot."

"Forgot what?"

"He doesn't like us to use their names like that. He says it is too much like swearing and we have no business swearing, not even if a client is 'specially expirating—I mean exas-exasperating."

Allyson laughed softly. "I am sure He will forgive you. You *were* provoked."

"Oh, yes, He will. He tries to be gruff sometimes, but He is really very kind."

"In any event," Allyson said with a yawn, "I must admit I *was* glad of your . . . uh . . . presence tonight."

"You see? I can be quite useful." Maryvictoria rose. "I shall bid you good night now."

Allyson snuggled into the bedcovers and considered the physical sensation she had experienced as Nathan brushed his lips across her hand. "You really must gain better control of yourself," she muttered into her pillow. Her last thought before sleep overtook her was that she would like to be a fly on the wall when Nathan returned her mother's letters.

Nathan stood up straighter and took a deep breath before rapping on the countess's sitting room door.

"Come," her voice called. She sat at her desk, but seemed to be ignoring a pile of papers in front of her. She twisted on her chair. "Oh, Nathan, what is it? Am I needed?" She started to rise.

"No. No." Nathan gestured for her to stay seated. "There is no crisis in the house, my lady."

"Good." She sank back into her chair and gave him a questioning look.

He had thought long of this moment. Now that it was upon him, he fell back on simple phrasing such as he had suggested to Lady Allyson the night before. "I have something of yours, my lady." He pulled the envelope from his jacket and placed it in the hand she extended.

"What on earth . . . ?" She looked at the contents, and the color left her face. "Oh! Oh, my heavens!"

"Are you all right, my lady? Shall I get you a glass of water? A dish of tea?"

She took two deep breaths, then said shakily, "I . . . uh . . . No, thank you. I . . . just need a moment." She fingered through the contents of the envelope again. Her mind seemed to be working furiously behind those lovely eyes so like her daughter's. "I . . . think you had better take a seat and . . . and explain. . . ." She gestured to a chair placed at an angle to face her own. "Did Mr. Cranston send you? Is this his way of tormenting me further?" Anger was replacing her initial shock.

"No, ma'am. He did not—"

"You are acting on your own?"

"In a manner speaking, my lady."

"And how much do *you* want? Surely, a footman's price will be less than that of a so-called 'gentleman' of the *ton*." Her voice was hard and bitter.

"You misunderstand the situation entirely, my lady—"

Her eyes looked startled for a moment; then she buried her face in her hands. "Oh, my heavens . . . my husband . . . This is why he insisted on hiring you." The words ended on a restrained sob.

"So far as I know, Lord Rutherford knows nothing of this business, my lady." Nathan hoped his own matter-of-fact tone would help calm her. He was pleased when it appeared to do so.

"Then what . . . ? Do, please, explain." She sat back in

her chair, her arms folded across her chest, suspicion still in her voice.

"I apologize for eavesdropping on a personal conversation, my lady." He then explained the circumstances of his overhearing Cranston's threatening her at the Worthington ball.

"And on the basis of that conversation alone, you took it upon yourself to . . ." She sounded skeptical.

"I might have done so," he said, "but I also admit to bringing the matter up with Mr. Melton, who is, by the way, extremely loyal and extremely discreet."

She nodded. "Melton is a dear. But, go on."

"That is it. I found where Cranston lives and retrieved the letters."

"Just like that?" She snapped her fingers. "I find it hard to believe he just turned them over to you."

"Nor did he do so. I stole them."

"Stole them?"

"Burgled his house."

She still looked skeptical. "For a footman, you are a man of varied talents."

"Possibly."

"And you did this alone?" she challenged.

"No, ma'am. I had help, but I assure you my help is very reliable."

"Did you or your help read the letters?" She seemed embarrassed now.

"No, ma'am."

"Then how did you know—?"

Nathan was ready for this question. "I looked at them only enough to identify the script."

"I see." She sat in thought for a moment. "And now? Now what do you expect in exchange for your silence?"

Nathan clenched his teeth, then said, "Again, madam, you misunderstand. I return them to you. As far as I am concerned, they never existed."

"Truly?"

He nodded. "Truly."

"And my husband? I would not have him hurt."

"He is not involved."

She held his gaze for a long moment. "I apologize, Nathan. I misjudged you."

"Yes, ma'am. Will that be all, my lady?" He rose.

"Yes. Oh, my yes. And thank you, Nathan. Thank you very much."

"I was glad to be of service," he said, letting himself out the door. He wished there were some way she could know that her gratitude should go in equal or greater measure to her daughter.

Confident that "all's well that ends well," Allyson had gone about her usual rounds of social calls in the next couple of days. On a morning ride, Nathan had told her of his interview with Lady Rutherford.

"Thank goodness it is over," she said.

"We may hope so," he said.

"Well, what can Mr. Cranston do, without the letters as proof?" she asked brightly.

"I do not know, but the man is determined and somewhat resourceful. You must be cautious, my lady."

"You think he was behind the kidnapping attempt?"

"I do not know; I just say, be careful."

"Perhaps you worry too much."

"Perhaps." He sounded glum.

She kicked her heels into the mare's side, thus ending the conversation.

However, she was reminded of it rather abruptly and unpleasantly at Almack's weekly assembly. During an interval between dances, Allyson chanced to be standing somewhat apart from others, when Lady Morton approached her with the man Cranston in tow.

"Lady Allyson, you have won over another heart. Mr. Cranston begs to be presented to you."

"Oh?" Allyson tried to cover her uneasiness. "H-how do you do, sir?" She did not offer her hand.

He bowed formally. "Indeed, yes. I have so looked forward to this moment." He turned to the older woman, and in a dismissive tone said, "Thank you, Lady Morton." Then, "Will you take a turn about the room with me, Lady Allyson?"

"Well . . . I . . . uh . . ."

But he gave her no chance to demur further. He gripped her elbow and propelled her forward.

"Sir!" She protested firmly, but softly, so as not to attract attention.

"Be quiet and listen," he ordered. "Since you have seen fit to poke your lovely nose into my business, you and I shall have to come to some arrangement."

She tried unobtrusively to free herself from his grip. "I have no idea what you are talking about."

"Oh, do you not?" He smiled maliciously and held his grip. "Is not this the girl who likes to prowl around at night with servants?"

"Now *you* have no idea of what you are talking about," she said in the haughtiest tone she could muster.

Again he flashed a mirthless smile. "I must admit you have spirit. You would have made me proud."

Allyson began to think the man was drunk or slightly deranged. She wanted to escape, but she certainly did not want to cause a scene in the midst of society's most exclusive assembly.

"Your mother and I were very close once," he said silkily. "You might have been my daughter, you know."

"Perhaps Mama was *very* young and *very* foolish once," she said lightly. "Most of us are at some time." She saw his lips tighten in anger.

"You have a wicked tongue, my lady. Now—let me tell you what you are going to do. Having stolen something that does not belong to you—"

"Nor to you," she shot back.

"You are going to have to pay proper restitution."

"You are clearly out of your mind," she said.

"Not another word," he said menacingly. "Think on this: I can produce the doxy who saw you in my quarters. Lady Allyson in a bachelor's household, unchaperoned, in the dead of night. That would play well in *ton* drawing rooms, would it not? Not to mention the halls of government?"

Allyson felt a cold chill course through her, but she held on to her defiance. "No one would believe—"

"Oh, they will believe, all right, just as they will happily resurrect the old stories about the lovely Lady Rutherford who may or may not have cuckolded her new husband some—let me see—twenty-four years ago?"

"You despicable worm!" She finally released herself just as they made it back to where he had approached her.

"Tut! Tut! You just think on it. I shall contact you again in a week or so."

Utterly shaken, Allyson looked around the assembly room for her sister and Lord Lawton, who had accompanied her this evening. As Clara left the dance floor, Allyson caught her attention.

"Clara, I am feeling decidedly unwell. I must leave—now."

"Now? But there are three more sets," Clara whined, completely oblivious to her sister's distress.

"I shall send the carriage back for you."

"Oh, well, in that case, I hope you will be feeling better."

"I am sure I shall." In truth, Allyson was glad she would not be sharing the tight confines of a town coach with the Lawtons. Not after that encounter with Mr. Cranston.

When her coach had been summoned, she retrieved her evening wrap and hurried out to the waiting vehicle. Nathan was holding the door for her. Her first inclination was to throw herself into his arms and spill out all that had happened. She was startled by this unorthodox idea.

His tone was one of sharp concern. "What happened?"

"Why . . . Nothing."

"Oh, yes, there *was* something," he insisted, examining

her face. "I saw that Cranston fellow; he almost had the door shut on him, he was that late."

"Would that he had."

"What did he do?" There was a fierce quality to his tone.

She looked around at other coaches with drivers and footmen idling about. "I will tell you at home."

As she sat alone in the carriage, she had second thoughts about telling him, though. After all, what right did she have to drag a servant into this rather personal mess? But had he not already been involved?

In the end, she did tell him. As they entered Rutherford House, she gave Melton her cloak and accompanied Nathan to an anteroom off the main entrance where important visitors were sometimes asked to wait to see the earl or the countess. Allyson was only mildly surprised to see that the room already held a visitor, of sorts. Maryvictoria sat on the window seat looking lively and alert. Allyson and Nathan stood in the middle of the small room, and she quickly told him of the encounter with Cranston.

When she had finished, she said, "There, now you know. Instead of extorting money from Mama, he has apparently turned to me." She felt a great sense of comfort in being able to share the burden of this terrible secret.

"Vicious," Nathan said. "It is particularly vicious that he will 'get back to you.' Meanwhile, he wants you to fret and worry."

"I suppose you are right."

"And I seriously doubt he will have given up on Lady Rutherford. I was afraid of something like this after Edna said she recognized you."

She felt so thoroughly dejected that she gave a small moan. "I seem only to have made matters worse." She gazed into Nathan's eyes and felt a strong urge to move closer.

He lifted his arms, then lowered them and stepped back. "Perhaps . . . But perhaps not. If I can get to the saucy Edna, she might be persuaded to see that her interests could be better served elsewhere."

"Pay *her* off, you mean? I fail to see how that would solve anything, trading him for her."

"Being a party to extortion is a rather serious offense, and she surely knows Cranston would never stand up for her. I doubt our Edna would like the accommodations in Newgate Prison."

Allyson merely sighed heavily.

"Without her corroboration, his story will not stand up," Nathan said in a reasoning tone.

"What about the threat regarding my mother and father?"

"Without this new tale to add fuel, gossip that is over twenty years old will have little chance to catch hold."

"I hope you are right," she said.

As Nathan left the room, he heard Lady Allyson say something to the effect that "Eavesdropping is never a very attractive trait, my dear."

Lord, the woman is talking to herself, he thought.

He had come so close to taking her in his arms. So close. Perhaps he should have. He had sensed that she might have welcomed the comfort, but that would hardly have been the behavior of a footman, would it?

He set himself to finding and reasoning with Edna.

Chapter 12

Nathan found his chat with Edna to be even more interesting than he had anticipated. Tracking her down had taken some doing. Edna was an "independent," working her business out of at least three taverns that catered to men of the so-called "lower orders."

Approaching Nathan at a worn, stained table, she jerked a thumb at the publican serving up a drink. "Tommy says you been lookin' for me." She looked Nathan over carefully. "Hey! I know you. You're the one what got into it with Ralphie. What you want with me?"

"Please have a seat, Miss . . . Renwood, I think it is." Despite being dressed as a common London worker, Nathan addressed her as he might have a raw military recruit.

"You'll have to buy me a drink. Tommy likes his share o' the business."

"I have already done so." Nathan gestured to the harried and unkempt Tommy, who immediately brought a glass of gin.

"I ain't had nothin' to do with anything Ralph mighta done," she said defensively.

"That is not why I am here," Nathan said.

"You want some of what Ralph's been gettin', maybe?" she suggested. "We can probably arrange that."

"You are a very attractive woman, Miss Renwood, but that is not why I am here, either."

"Call me Edna. Maybe I can change your mind." She leaned closer to the table, showing a great deal of cleavage. She *was* attractive in a rather hardened way. She had dark hair and eyes, and she seemed to be reasonably clean, unlike many of her kind working the streets. Nathan conjectured, with a tinge of regret, that in five years' time she would have lost what looks she had, though.

"I want to discuss the events of that night with Ralph," Nathan said.

"My time is valuable, you know."

"I shall pay for your time." He put a small purse on the table, which she eyed greedily.

"So, what do you want to know?"

"You said at the time that you recognized my . . . companion."

"The woman dressed as a boy. I did. She's one o' them hoity-toity ladies what gives things to the Fairfax women. I seen her around."

"And you so informed Mr. Cranston?" Nathan asked.

"Yeah, I told 'im. He was right furious, he was. Tore into Ralph somethin' fierce, especially when he found somethin' missin' in his desk. Called Ralph all sorts o' names."

"So you were still there when Cranston returned?"

Edna shrugged. "I like Ralph. He's a good un most o' the time. I sort of nursed his wounds, you might say."

"And when you identified the woman to Cranston . . . ?" Nathan prompted.

"He like to woke the dead with his rantin' and ravin'."

"Did he offer you money to say you recognized her?"

A crafty look came over her face. "Well, what if he did?"

"If he did, and if you agreed, you could find yourself in a very messy situation."

"Look, mister—what's your name, anyway?"

"Nathan."

"Well, look, Nathan. Cranston may *seem* the fine gentleman, but he's one tough customer. I ain't crossin' *him*. End up floatin' in the Thames, I would."

"You might, but if you continue your present association with him," Nathan said in an even tone, "I can promise that you *will* end up in Newgate Prison, and either hanged or transported."

"Wha—?"

"Extortion is a serious crime, Miss Renwood. In this case, it is against the family of an earl. You would not stand a chance, my girl."

"Extortion? I don't know nothin'—I think you better pay for my time now and be gone." She started to rise and extended her hand.

"Sit down!" he ordered quietly.

She sat. She seemed both frightened and defiant. "What do you want?"

"I want you to forget that you can identify my companion of the other night. You must have made a mistake."

"Like I said, if I did that—" She made a slashing motion across her neck.

"What is he paying you?" Nathan asked.

"Not enough for what you've just said!" She named a sum.

"You are not from London, are you?"

"I'm from York, but what's that to you?"

"Perhaps you would like to return there? Or maybe go somewhere else for three or four months? I will give you twice what Cranston is paying you, *and* I will see that you get a monthly allowance so long as you stay out of London for four months."

"How much?" she asked grudgingly, though her eyes had widened at the offer.

He named a sum he was sure exceeded her erratic earnings on the street.

Again, she eyed the purse on the table. "What's to keep me from takin' your money an' stayin' here?"

"You do not *get* the initial money until you are safely in

York, or wherever you wish to go. Then someone will deliver the rest at regular intervals at whatever direction you will give."

"Hmm. I'll have to think on this. Mr. Cranston—"

"Will not take kindly to your trying to squeeze more money from him, will he?" Nathan watched as a spark of fear flashed in her eyes. "And if you refuse me, I will have you arrested immediately."

"On what charge?" she asked defiantly. "And who gives *you* the authority—?" She cast a contemptuous glance over his clothing.

"Never mind *who,* just understand that I *can* do it, and the charge will not matter. You would spend a good, long while in Newgate. And who knows what would happen when they were filling the next ship for Botany Bay?" His calm voice and measured words were effective.

She gave him a steady look. Clearly she was frightened and just as clearly she believed him. Her shoulders slumped in defeat. "How am I to get out of London?"

Nathan breathed an inward sigh of relief. He hated bullying this vulnerable young woman, but he also knew that she would be safer doing as he wanted her to do. Cranston was not the sort to leave loose ends lying about later.

After that, dealing with Edna had been relatively easy. Nathan had accompanied her to her quarters, a pitifully small room she shared with another female above a cobbler's shop. Luckily, the other girl was out. Edna collected her few belongings and shoved them into a small, battered valise and a cloth sack. She left a message for her friend, saying she was leaving for a few weeks. The cobbler stood in the door of his shop and watched her leave.

Nathan had hired a hackney and gave loud instructions for the driver to take them to an address near Covent Garden. Once there, he dismissed this hack and hired another to take them to Spitalsfield, where he ensconced Edna in the house of the Fairfax sisters. These two ladies were only too glad to assist when they learned of a possible threat to Lady Allyson.

The two hackney rides had left Nathan and Edna with

considerable time together. As her initial apprehension dissipated, Edna began to chat more freely. Actually, she would not mind leaving London for a while, maybe forever. Who knew what the future would bring? And it would surely be nice not to have to worry about funds, at least for a while. And not to have to deal with the Ralphs of the world, though as she had said, he was all right, really.

She giggled. "He was not very happy when he came 'round that night."

"Is that so?" Nathan asked absently.

"He accused *me* of hitting him with that warming pan!"

"He must have been quite angry when he found out it was my . . . uh . . . friend."

"Oh, he was. But, you know? I don't see *how* she managed that! It *still* seems impossible to me."

"What do you mean?" Nathan asked, his interest piqued now.

"That pan was on the hearth in Mr. Cranston's room; I seen it earlier, you see. Big, fancy one, it was."

"So?"

"Well, you an' Ralph was rollin' around on the floor in front of the doorway to Mr. Cranston's room. Arms and legs flashin' all over. . . ."

"So?"

"So how did the lady get past you two to get that pan and crown Ralph with it? She was on the other side of the hall."

"Hmm. I don't know," Nathan said. "But I am glad she did."

"I tell you, it was *real* strange, like that big pan just come flyin' out on its own."

"You seem to have a vivid imagination, Edna."

The next day, Edna was on her way to York in a nondescript carriage driven by a man who performed odd duties for the Foreign Office. Nathan thought only fleetingly of Edna's account of his fight with Ralph at Cranston's quarters.

* * *

By late June, many of the notables of society had already retreated from the city as summer drew on. Still, the residents of Rutherford House found themselves with full social calendars. Allyson was particularly thrilled to receive Lady Melbourne's invitation to Holland House to meet Madame Germaine de Stael, who had recently found it expedient to leave Napoleon's empire.

"I, for one, do not understand all the fuss about this French woman," Clara said when Allyson mentioned her invitation as the family enjoyed tea in the drawing room after dinner.

"Actually, she is Swiss," Allyson said calmly. "She is one of the most influential women of our day. She has written several books and essays. She speaks several languages, too."

Clara visibly shuddered. "A bluestocking! Really, Allyson, you should curb certain tendencies you exhibit. Gentlemen do not find such women attractive."

"Perhaps that is why her salons were so very popular in Paris."

Clara sniffed. "All the same, she is mostly French."

Allyson knew her sarcasm was lost on her sister; her father looked at her over the rims of his glasses with one of those "be-nice-to-your-little-sister" looks she had received repeatedly in their childhood days.

In the event, Allyson found the famous exile as charming and interesting as she had anticipated. She left the Melbourne salon feeling rather privileged to have been included. As it happened, Allyson was leaving at the same time as Madame de Stael and her male companion. The de Stael carriage stood directly behind the Rutherford vehicle. Nathan, resplendent in Lord Rutherford's livery, stood as usual at the door of the Rutherford coach to hand Allyson in.

Madame had made an innocuous comment about the English weather; then she stopped in midsentence and gasped. Allyson saw her staring at Nathan.

"But I know you!" Madame de Stael said. "You attended

my salon in Paris. You were very young. On the grand tour, I think. Oh! I am usually so good with names."

Nathan bowed formally to the woman. "Nathan Christopher, Madame."

"Hmm. Was that the name? It does not fit, somehow. We discussed Rousseau; I remember that. . . ."

"Germaine," her companion prompted.

"Oh, dear, I am always rushed in this country, but it was nice to see you, Mr.—"

Allyson simply stared, dumbfounded, at Nathan.

"My lady?" he invited, as he once again held the door.

She allowed him to hand her in, but shot him a questioning look. "A salon in Paris?" she asked, but he had already closed the door and taken his place on the back of the coach.

Allyson turned the incident over and over in her mind. Was Madame de Stael mistaken? Had she taken Nathan for someone else? But, no, Nathan had acknowledged her. A grand tour? He had been an aristocrat then? Or at least gentry? And he was now a *footman?* That made no sense at all.

She intended to confront him the instant they arrived home. Unfortunately, she had no chance to do so. As they entered, Melton's first words were, "Nathan, His Lordship wishes to see you immediately."

Well! There was always tomorrow morning's ride.

Nathan was glad to postpone trying to dance around Lady Allyson's curiosity about his acquaintance with Madame de Stael. It simply had not occurred to him that the French woman would remember a young man she had met briefly a decade earlier. Why, she had even remembered the subject of their conversation!

He had, indeed, been on a grand tour, that custom of the previous century that sent young men off to the Continent to gain some worldly polish. It was a custom that had been curtailed by the rise of Napoleon Bonaparte. After the fiasco with the squire's daughter, Nathan had been involved in a scrape at school. As a boarding student, he had been one of the leaders in a student strike for better food.

"A strike!" his father ranted. "Where in the *hell* did you get such a harebrained idea?" The Duke of Halstead raised a hand when Nathan would have responded. "Never mind. I know. It is those damned Luddites, I am sure. Spreading their poison, from smashing machinery to fomenting rebellion even among our own children. Well, I will not have *my son* involved in such."

"It was about food—" Nathan protested.

"Hah!" his father said. "Well, see how you like the *food* on the Continent. I am sending you on a grand tour. You will be accompanied by Tellson and William and one servant each." Tellson, who had been tutor to the Halstead sons, had stayed on as the duke's secretary. William was Halstead's ward, Nathan's cousin.

"But—" young Nathan started.

"No 'buts,' " the duke ordered. "It is done. I will not have you making mischief here, at least not for a few months. And if I hear so much as a *whisper* of your creating havoc abroad, I will make you very, very, sorry indeed. Have I stated this clearly enough even for you?"

"Yes, Your Grace," Nathan answered stiffly.

Thus had sixteen-year-old Nathan gone off to the Continent with Henry Tellson and William Thornton. Tellson, in his thirties, was a stuffy man, all prim and proper. But he was knowledgeable, and Nathan had soaked up much under his tutelage. William, two years older than Nathan, was personable, but a youngster of somewhat limited intelligence. Nathan recalled always having to explain their jokes to him.

All in all, it had been a good trip and it had, indeed, served to give both young men some worldly polish. Had it come back to haunt him?

"You wished to see me, my lord?" he now asked of the Earl of Rutherford, who sat at his desk.

"Yes, Nathan. Close the door and have a seat." When Nathan had done so, the earl went on. "I have had a message that will especially interest you. It will be in broadsides within the hour, and in all the newspapers tomorrow. Wellington has achieved a decisive victory at Vitoria. Caught the puppet King Joseph and his entire entourage as they tried to flee Spain!"

"Yes! Oh, yes!" Nathan exulted. "That is fine news, indeed, my lord. Would that I had been there." He could not help the note of regret in his voice.

"Never mind, my lad. You are doing a fine job right here."

Nathan bit his tongue to keep from saying anything harsher than, "But we have no real leads on our spies here yet, do we?"

"No, but perhaps it is time we did something to flush those birds out of the bush."

"Past time, I should think."

"You are right, and this victory makes it even more imperative. Wellington was unable to pursue the fleeing enemy."

"Unable to—?"

"Seems our British soldiers were caught up in the richest plunder they had ever seen. Too busy looting to listen to orders."

"That happened at Badajoz, too," Nathan said.

"So, now sources tell us Napoleon has sent Soult back to the Peninsula to try to ward off our advance into France."

"*That* is not such good news. Soult is a very capable general; Napoleon was a fool to withdraw him from Spain earlier." Nathan paused. "With all due respect, my lord, what does this mean to *us* here at home?"

"With Napoleon on the defensive in both Spain and in the east, activity has increased here. French agents are desperate to know what their troops will face—numbers, and supplies, and plans. *And* they are particularly interested in knowing what we know of *them*."

"But that has always been true." Nathan leaned back and crossed his knees. "We want to know the same of them."

Rutherford chuckled. "So we do. But Vitoria has escalated matters."

Nathan waited for Rutherford to get to his real point.

"We have come up with a plan to, as I said, flush out our birds."

"Am I right in assuming I have a specific role in this plan?"

Again Rutherford chuckled. "You are. We are putting out the word that I am holding a house party at my estate near the coast in Sussex, and that I will be meeting with one of our top agents in France. He will be giving me vital information, or so the story goes."

"Will there even be an agent?"

"Oh, yes. Two of them. I will meet with one who will be bringing and receiving information we are planting. *You* will deliver and receive the genuine articles at a different location."

"Sounds rather dangerous—for you and your family, I mean," Nathan said.

"A little, perhaps. But I am to make the false information available—but not *too* available—for our culprits to steal, or copy. They will not want us to find it missing."

"A house party," Nathan mused aloud.

"A *large* house party. My wife loves to entertain. I have had something to say about her guest list, so many of our guests will have some sort of connection with French interests."

"I see. . . ."

"You will leave tomorrow morning, ostensibly to help prepare the house for arrival. Actually, the steward and housekeeper will handle those matters, and you will have a few days to nose around the countryside and so on, you know?"

"Yes, sir. But . . . But what about Lady Allyson?"

Lord Rutherford gave his young servant an intense look. "She will simply have to curb some of her activities, maybe develop a minor indisposition."

"She will not like that."

"I will handle my daughter," Lord Rutherford said firmly.

* * *

Allyson was pleased by her father's announcement that evening. She, like all England, welcomed the news of the victory at Vitoria. Already it was being seen as a vital turning point in the war. As for the house party, Allyson loved the Sussex estate—the earldom's principal seat—where she had spent most of her childhood.

She was a little mystified when her father said after dinner, "I would have a word with you in the library, Allyson."

Once there, he sat her down near the fireplace and took another chair near her.

"Papa, you seem so serious."

"You will not like what I have to say," he said. "First of all, there will be no morning rides until we arrive in Sussex."

"No morning rides?" she wailed softly. "But why?"

The earl did not directly answer her. "You may join your mother and sister for drives in the park, so long as Lawton or some responsible male accompanies you."

"Papa—"

"Moreover, you will curtail any shopping trips or social calls. If you need something, send a footman or a maid. Your mother will put out the word that you have sprained your ankle and the doctor insists you not move about overly much. You may join her in receiving callers."

"Am I allowed to know why my life is to be so restricted? I thought you intended Nathan to—"

"Nathan will not be here."

Allyson felt a sudden emptiness, a sense of panic at this news. "You have dismissed him? But, why?"

Her father sighed. "Nathan works for me."

"Well, of course he does. All our servants do."

"You do not understand. He also works for me in the Foreign Office. I tell you this only because I need your full cooperation in the next few weeks. I am sending him to Sussex ahead of us, but I will not have you exposed to danger in the meantime."

"Danger?" she asked, not quite taking all this in.

"Allyson, that attempted abduction was probably no accident, and no attempt at simple robbery, either. Nathan managed to foil that one, but I am not taking a chance on another. With this business at Vitoria, we are sure the French will be ever more desperate for the kind of information I possess."

Allyson was intrigued by the earlier comment. "Nathan foiled—what do you mean?"

"He was the worker on the scene."

"Those eyes. Why did I not realize . . . ?" Then she found her hackles rising. "You mean to tell me you had him *following* me? Why was I not informed?"

"It did not seem necessary to alarm you unduly, and, actually, that day he was substituting for a Bow Street Runner. The incident did, however, show us a need for more concerted efforts."

"Still, I think—"

"I recognize that stubborn look," her father said. "I did what I thought to be the prudent thing to do, and I am still doing so. You must accept that fact."

"This house party—it is part of your Foreign Office business?"

"Partly. Not entirely. I want your mother to have a good time. You know how she enjoys entertaining."

"Yes."

"I tell you all this in strictest confidence, Daughter. And I have done so only to keep you from defying my orders and trying to go your own way. Do you understand?" There was almost a pleading note in his voice.

"Yes, Papa," she said contritely.

"You are to discuss this with no one. *No one.* Not even your mother and sister, and certainly not with anyone who will be our guest in Sussex."

Allyson frowned. "Mama—"

"Knows as much as she needs to know. And you are *not* to plague her with questions. Her job as hostess will be demanding enough. Is that clear?"

"Y-yes."

There was a moment of silence, then Allyson said, almost shyly, "He is not what he seems, is he?"

"Who?"

"Nathan."

"Well, he *is* a footman, but he is also a very capable soldier."

Allyson thought this a rather cryptic answer, but knew she would learn no more at this point.

"You *will* comply with my wishes, will you not?"

"Yes, Papa."

Chapter 13

Since the Worthington Ball, Allyson had attended several social affairs at which the Marquis of Eastland was also a guest. When the marquis made a point of seeking an introduction to her, Allyson fleetingly recalled the widespread rumor that he had come to town—however late in the Season—to seek a wife. She had smiled at her own foolishness in thinking, even for an instant, that the heir to a dukedom would seriously consider *her*. What? Direct his attentions to one seen as "long in the tooth" and "on the shelf" when there were all those nubile young women at Almack's and elsewhere? Not likely.

Still, he never failed to ask her to dance when dancing was part of the entertainment. He had partnered her in card games, and he occasionally sought her out for casual conversation. Now that Allyson had become "house bound," he called almost daily. She welcomed his visits, for he was amiable and interesting, if a bit austere. She thought his social and political position weighed heavily with him. However, he was handsome and entertaining, and she enjoyed teasing him out of that austerity.

The growing friendship had not gone unnoticed by Allyson's mother and sister. Lady Rutherford was delighted and sought to encourage the relationship. Thus, it came as no surprise to

Allyson that Lord Eastland was to be included among her
mother's house guests in Sussex. Lady Lawton, on the other
hand, seemed torn. Poor Clara, Allyson thought, did not
know whether to welcome a possible tie with such a powerful family, or to be jealous that her sadly unsuitable sister
might one day outrank a mere baron's wife.

For her part, Allyson viewed the marquis as a friend, much
in the way of her friendship with Lord Braxton. She had always enjoyed her friendships with *men*. She enjoyed their
discussions more than those of women. She thought the marquis sought her out partly as an escape from the simpering
misses and desperate mamas who saw him as a tasty morsel.

"Are you throwing me over for Eastland?" Braxton teased,
leaning over the back of her chair in the Rutherford drawing
room.

"Are you suggesting one may cultivate only one friendship at a time?" she countered.

He raised an arched brow. "Friendship?"

"Yes, friendship," she said firmly. "Now, perhaps you
would be so kind as to fetch me a glass of lemonade?"

"Anything for our invalid," he replied, with a glance at her
shapely ankle resting on a footstool.

When Braxton returned, Eastland was occupying the
chair next to Allyson. Braxton gave her that arch look again
and silently handed her the glass.

"Thank you," she murmured, not daring to catch his gaze
directly for fear she would burst into laughter. "You were
saying, Lord Eastland—"

"How very pleased I am to accept your parents' kind invitation to visit Sussex."

The growing friendship between Lord Eastland and Lady
Allyson also occupied the mind of the marquis's younger
brother. The *ton*'s rumors were rampant among the servants,
too. Nathan had seen Eastland dance with her, and, though
he himself had tried to play least seen when Eastland called

at Rutherford House, Nathan was fully aware of Eastland's seeking out the earl's daughter. Somehow, that did not sit well with Nathan; He told himself he simply did not think they would suit.

He had made the trip to Rutherford Hall in Sussex in record time on Bucephalus. Having turned over his letters of introduction and instructions to the steward and the house-keeper, he was given a room in the servants' wing. For the next few days, as the hall was aired and shined to pristine perfection, Nathan familiarized himself with the countryside.

Using the password and countersigns given him by Lord Rutherford, he made brief contact with two men who were part of the network established by the Foreign Office for passing information back and forth across the English Channel. One was an innkeeper on the outskirts of a village near the sea. Farther east along the coast was another village whose blacksmith dealt in more than broken wagon wheels and farmers' tools.

Nathan enjoyed the freedom of these days, but he recognized them as an interlude only. He sensed that matters were heading toward a critical point, on more than one front in his life. There was, of course, this business of ferreting out a French spy. Once that was done, could he—would he—return to his regiment in the Peninsula? There was also the matter of his family. That meeting with his brother in the Worthington library had prompted him to think it might be time to mend those fences, or at least acknowledge that they were overgrown with moss.

And then there was Allyson. Allyson? When had he dropped the "Lady" in his mind? Not since that Portuguese contessa had he been so attracted to a woman, and this time was different. Not only was there a strong physical attraction, but he also felt a need to cherish and protect. *That is your job, Thornton,* he told himself. But he knew it was more than that.

Maryvictoria had not appeared in several days. Allyson rather missed the little imp. Whether she was "real" or not, she seemed to help Allyson sort things out. So where had she gone? *Not that I really* need *her, of course.*

The trip to Sussex involved logistical matters that might have challenged a military strategist, but Lady Rutherford marshaled her forces as well as any general. The caravan included both the Rutherford and Lawton travel coaches; a carriage for servants, including Molly and Melton, the French chef, and other personal servants; and a baggage wagon. Four footmen served as armed outriders. Miss Pringle traveled with the earl and countess; Allyson, with the Lawtons. Initially, Lawton graciously took the backward-facing seat, allowing Allyson and Clara the more desirable one.

When they had been on the road for some time, suddenly there she was. Maryvictoria, clutching Caroline, perched in a corner of Lawton's seat. "I am coming, too," she chirped.

"Where have you been?" Allyson challenged.

"I beg your pardon?" Lord Lawton looked curiously from his wife to his sister-in-law. Clara, too, was looking at Allyson strangely. "I have been right here for the last hour or so." He sounded defensive and confused.

"What is the matter with you, Allyson?" Clara was annoyed.

"Uh . . . Nothing," Allyson said. "I do apologize . . . I . . . was just thinking. . . ."

"Strange question," Clara said.

Maryvictoria giggled. "You forgot."

Yes, I forgot. Allyson remembered to *think* rather than verbalize aloud. *So, where have you been and why are you here, now?*

"I have other clients, too, you know," Maryvictoria said with an air of self-importance.

Oh. No, I did not know. And here I thought I was the only one being driven mad.

Maryvictoria ignored this barb. "I *do* love the country. Besides, you might need me."

"Good Lord, I hope not," Allyson blurted aloud.

"You hope not *what?*" Clara asked, giving her that look again.

"Oh . . . uh . . . I hope we do not have inclement weather," Allyson improvised.

"This is England, and we are going very near the coast; we will undoubtedly have our share of bad weather," Lawton said ponderously.

Having departed London in the early morning, the Rutherford-Lawton caravan arrived at the hall in late afternoon. Stiff and tired from the journey despite stops at posting inns, Allyson was glad to be home. She was also relieved to escape the confines of the coach with Clara and Edmund. Clara, ever mindful of her "interesting condition," had complained much of the trip, making small demands upon her husband, whose response was invariably, "Yes, dear."

At one point, Maryvictoria shook her head. "It would seem no other woman in the world was ever so put upon as to have a baby!"

Allyson smiled at this echo of her own thoughts.

Clara, now sitting with her husband, said grumpily, "How *can* you be so unfeeling as to smile at my misery, Allyson?"

Her husband patted her hand and gave his sister-in-law an accusing look. "I am sure she meant no offense, my love."

"No, of course not," Allyson placated. "Actually, I was thinking that tomorrow I may ride again." Then she addressed the sprite beside her. *Young girls are not supposed to know about babies.*

"Nor are young unmarried women," Maryvictoria shot back. "Besides, you forget—I might have been your grandmother."

When they arrived at the hall, Lawton jumped out to hand his wife out, leaving Allyson to be attended by a footman. A tremor went through her as she gazed into Nathan's eyes and then took his hand.

"Nathan," she managed by way of greeting.

"My lady, welcome home."

She could not account for how inordinately glad she was to see him. And then she remembered the questions she wanted to put to him, but this was neither the time nor place.

She looked around for Maryvictoria, but the sprite was gone. Allyson followed the others into the house.

Nathan reported that evening to Lord Rutherford all that he had learned—which was not much—in the days he had already been in Sussex. It was very late; all the other travelers had retired when the earl summoned Nathan to the library and offered him brandy. They sat sipping their drinks and comparing information.

"There are a number of fishing boats that ply the channel—several that return with cargoes of more than just fish," Nathan said.

"That has been going on since the time of William the Conqueror, and probably even before then," the earl said. "You have met Thomas?"

"The innkeeper. Yes."

"His brother operates one of those fishing vessels. Fellow named Gibbons has another that we use from time to time."

Nathan frowned thoughtfully. "So, we are dealing with two contacts, the blacksmith and the innkeeper; two men arriving from and returning to France; two fishing boats and their crews. That is too many people, in my view."

"And perhaps a spy among my guests," Rutherford said. "Do not overlook him."

"Or her."

"Or her. But if the ruse is to work, we must make it appear that we are using normal procedures, and we have used all these before, of which the enemy agent or agents may well be aware." The earl sipped at his drink. "There are a couple of other matters you should know about. I hope they will not compromise your position here."

Nathan waited for the earl to continue.

"Allyson knows you work for the Foreign Office."

"Lady Allyson knows about me?"

"Only that you were a soldier and you now have another

assignment. Nothing else, though she does know you were the man who foiled her kidnapping."

Nathan felt a twinge of apprehension. "I assume you felt it necessary to reveal this information to her, but does it not put her in some jeopardy? What if she lets something slip?"

"She won't. Allyson knows very well what is at stake. I told her only enough to persuade her to follow my orders in London." The earl gave his footman a chagrined look. "My daughter is a very headstrong young woman."

"Yes, I know."

"And the other matter. Eastland will be among our guests."

"Here?" Nathan asked dumbly.

Rutherford smiled. "Yes, here."

"Hmm. That may pose a problem."

"I thought you said, after that encounter at the Worthingtons', that he was wholly trustworthy."

"I did, and he is. But what if we are seen together by someone with a long memory?"

"Let us hope that does not happen. Most people will see only Eastland and a footman."

"Probably."

Allyson had looked forward to the sort of solitary ride she had been wont to enjoy on Rutherford property in Sussex. When she arrived at the stable the next morning, she was surprised to find Nathan waiting for her with two saddled horses. The fact that she was more pleased than annoyed to see him also surprised her. Still, she would not admit that to him.

"I should not have thought your presence necessary on my rides here in the country," she said.

"Good morning to you, too, my lady." He offered her a hand up to the sidesaddle. "Your father thought we should continue to exercise caution. I agreed with him."

"So he told me. I just did not think his caution went quite this far."

"Do you object to sharing your ride with me?" he asked.

"This morning? No. As a matter of fact, I have a few questions to ask of you."

"Aha. I somehow thought you might."

They rode along at an easy pace. She glanced over to find his eyes twinkling in amusement.

"I suppose I should begin by thanking you for rescuing me from an abduction."

"I was merely doing a job."

She found this comment somewhat deflating. "I . . . see. What I do *not* see is why it had to be such a secret, why I was not aware that I was being spied upon."

"Protected," he corrected.

She grimaced. "Protected, then."

"Did your father not explain that he—we—did not want to alarm you or curtail your activities unduly until it might become necessary?"

"Yes, but—"

"But you wanted to be in charge," he finished.

"Of my own life, yes."

"Tell me, my lady, until the last few days, have you not done exactly as you wished?"

Put that way, her objections did seem somewhat petty, but she was not ready to concede. "Still, I should have been informed."

"Of what?"

"Of your association with Papa's government work, for one thing. I do not like discovering that you are not what you pretend to be." She gazed at him directly, but he refused to meet her eyes.

"We all do what we think we must at any given time," he said quietly.

There seemed little reply to be made to this. They rode for several minutes with only the creaking of leather and an occasional horse hoof hitting a stone to break the silence. They were heading toward her favorite spot on the estate, a place where a high cliff overlooked the river and allowed a panoramic view that was breathtaking.

"And how does it happen that a *footman* has had a grand tour?" she challenged, hoping to catch him off guard.

He chuckled. "I knew that one was coming."

"Well?"

"I accompanied a duke's ward to the Continent."

"Your father must have been quite close to the duke for you to be included in such a venture." She knew the situation was unusual, but not unheard of. There were many ways to reward good servants.

"Yes, you might say they were close."

Something in his tone told her he did not want to share any personal information about his past. So, she diverted the subject by asking about places he had seen on the tour. He readily talked about his impressions of castles on the Rhine, cathedrals in Cologne and Paris and Chartres, and the canals of Amsterdam.

She sighed enviously. "I have been no farther in this world than the Highlands of Scotland."

"You will one day," he said lightly. "I promise. This war will not last forever."

They arrived on the edge of the cliff.

"There!" she said with a sweeping gesture. "Is this not worth the ride?"

The stream below meandered in a blue ribbon through green fields dotted with sheep. Copses of trees stood out here and there, with an occasional wisp of smoke arising from a cottage.

" 'Earth has not anything to show more fair,' " he quoted.

She smiled. "You are right; though Wordsworth was writing of the city, not the country."

"It is beautiful," he said simply. "Thank you for sharing it with me."

She pointed up the river. "If we walk that way a few yards, we have an even better view, but it is not safe for the horses."

He dismounted and helped her do so. There was an easy camaraderie between them that had never been there before, though she still felt excitement surge through her veins as he touched her. They walked to an outcropping of large boulders from which the view, if possible, was even broader and richer.

"Is it not the most gorgeous sight you have seen?" Having brought him to this place, she wanted desperately for him to share her enthusiasm.

He glanced at the view, and then his gaze locked with hers. "Yes, most gorgeous," he said.

Afterward, neither could have said who moved first, but suddenly she was in his arms, his lips moving hungrily over hers. Her arms slid upward around his neck, pulling him closer. As his hands tightened about her waist, she molded her body to his. The kiss deepened. Hearing a low moan, she realized it came from her own throat.

She came to her senses and stepped back, appalled at what had happened.

Allyson had been kissed before, but never like this. Never had she so forgotten herself with a man. Even now she would like nothing better than to lose herself in Nathan's kiss again—but no! She was *not* one of those aristocrats who used their servants as amorous playthings, and there could be nothing else for an earl's daughter and a footman. She felt herself blushing furiously, unable to meet his gaze.

"I apologize, my lady." He released his hold on her. "That should never have happened."

"No, it should not have," she said brusquely to cover her embarrassment. "But in truth, it was as much my fault as yours. We must simply forget it happened."

"As you wish, my lady."

She wondered if it would be as hard for him to forget as she knew it was going to be for her.

On the return ride, they both tried rather unsuccessfully to engage in small talk. Finally, Allyson suggested a vigorous gallop, thinking that might help release the tension. It worked. They arrived back at the stable laughing and gasping for breath.

Chapter 14

That was surely not the smartest thing you have ever done, Nathan groused at himself as he changed into proper livery. Smart or not, he could not bring himself to be sorry about that kiss. For a moment, there, everything had seemed absolutely right in his world. Perhaps when this spy business was over . . .

Then what? Did he think it likely Allyson—Lady Allyson—would forgive his deception? Well . . . Perhaps she would. Her response had not exactly been cold. Or even cool. He smiled at remembering her shy blushes. Still, a woman did not figure into his future plans, and that was that. It was just as well she had drawn a line when she had.

That afternoon, as carriage after carriage began arriving at the hall, Nathan was as busy as any of the other footmen, hauling valises and trunks to various guest chambers. He made a point of being the man to transport the Marquis of Eastland's luggage to his room. When he had deposited the last two bags, Nathan turned to the man in a chair near the window.

"May I get you anything else, my lord?"

Eastland grinned. "Yes, I should like some water for a bath."

Nathan gritted his teeth. He accepted his duties readily enough as they pertained to other guests, but Eastland was obviously going to enjoy rubbing Nathan's nose in his servant's role. He dared not tell his brother what he thought, for Eastland's valet was hovering in the dressing room. Luckily, this was not the man who had served his brother in their youth, but Nathan was taken aback when he heard his brother address the man as André. A Frenchman?

When Nathan returned with two large buckets of hot water, André was nowhere to be seen.

"What did you do with your man?" Nathan asked.

"I sent him down to press my clothes for dinner so I could speak to you."

"What about?"

"This little game of charades you continue to play, for one thing."

"It is not a game, Eastland," Nathan said tightly. "Surely, even you—member of the indolent aristocracy that you are—know that the war is reaching a critical point."

"Yes, even I know. But if you are discovered— Are you aware that Lady Eggoner is among the guests here? She has remained close to our father since her husband's death. Your being exposed as a servant would be as devastating to the family name as your being a spy."

"I am not a spy. I am trying to help *catch* a spy."

Eastland waved his hand disparagingly. "I doubt *ton* gossips would make that distinction."

"So be it. I will not allow gossip to control my life, nor my work. Now, did you have anything else on your mind?"

"As a matter of fact, I did." Eastland tapped his fingers nervously on the arm of his chair. "I am thinking of making an offer for Lady Allyson, and since you have known the family more intimately than I, I am wondering if you know of anything about her that would make such a match unsuitable."

Nathan felt he had just been dealt a devastating blow to his gut. "Lady Allyson? You want to *marry* Lady Allyson?"

"I must marry *someone*—the succession, you know—and

she seems to have the looks and bearing that would eventually become a duchess."

The thought of Allyson in Eastland's bed, attempting to secure the succession, made Nathan slightly ill. "She . . . uh . . . She is very independent," he finally said.

"I *have* noticed that about her; her parents have been far too indulgent, I believe. She can be trained to overcome that unseemly streak. She would also need to be more circumspect in her friendships."

"More circumspect in—"

"You *do* know of her association with a pair of sisters named Fairfax?" Eastland asked.

"Yes. But . . . Are you telling me you have had her *investigated?* A woman you are thinking of taking to wife?"

"Of course, it is the prudent thing to do. And that association would definitely have to stop. I am just wondering if there are other unacceptable associations of which I should be aware."

"I know of none," Nathan said tersely. He was damned if he would aid in Eastland's "investigation."

"Good, I shall proceed then."

Nathan took his leave and then slipped away for a long while. He needed to think. He was angry and frustrated. His brother—his own brother—was going to marry the woman he himself loved? Loved? Where had *that* idea come from? But he realized it was true. He also realized that Captain Lord Nathan Christopher Thornton did not *want* to be in love. Perhaps in a few years . . .

He remembered saying something to that effect to his sister when she had once asked just when he might eventually settle down. Her reply came back to him now.

"It just does not work that way, Nate. One is not allowed to *choose* when and with whom one will fall in love. It just happens."

"I shall take your word for it," he had said lightly, not believing her for a moment.

Now he believed.

It had happened. Really happened.

And she would marry his brother. So much for ever mending those fences.

She *could* refuse the marquis, but of course this thought was born of foolish schoolboy hope. What woman would give up a chance to become a duchess?

Eastland would smother her spirit, turn her into one of those windup toys, one that would make the correct duchess movements and express all the correct duchess sentiments. Nathan could not stand the idea of that happening.

Allyson enjoyed entertaining, though perhaps not to the extent that her mother did. Nevertheless, she had agreed to help her mother host this affair. She was expected particularly to look after the younger set. This included many of the young women and men she regularly saw in town. Allyson might have left the spiteful Loretta Longworth and Caroline Dawson off the guest list, but Miss Longworth's mother was a particular friend of the countess, and Miss Dawson's father was very close to the prime minister. The Worthingtons were also among the guests, and despite her youth, their daughter quickly became one of Allyson's favorites.

Among the younger men, only Lord Eastland's was a new face. Allyson knew there had been much speculation about his presence. She also knew that several mamas—and their daughters—had their eyes on his every move. She adopted an attitude of tolerant amusement at their behavior, and even teased the marquis about it. He shrugged off her teasing, but took few pains to discourage the attentions he received.

Among the older guests were the Longworth, Dawson, and Worthington parents; Lady Eggoner, another particular friend of the countess; and Allyson's Uncle Percival, her mother's brother, whom Allyson adored. Altogether, it was rather an eclectic group of people who had been invited to this extended house party, and entertaining them would challenge even the countess's strategic prowess.

She planned excursions to historic sites, a shopping trip for the ladies, and a pugilistic contest and shooting expedition for the men, but for rabbits only, as grouse and pheasant were not yet in season. Evening offerings included cards, charades, music, or billiards. Breakfast and lunch were informal affairs, with food served from chafing dishes on a sideboard; but dinner was formal, served by a small army of footmen. The seating arrangements were varied as much as protocol allowed.

The climax of the party would be a ball to which local gentry were also invited, as well as some of the holiday guests in nearby Brighton.

All this activity and preparation often forced Allyson to forgo her morning rides. When she did ride, often as not she was accompanied by one or more of the male guests— Braxton, Pommeraie, or Arnaud, and now, Eastland. Thus, she saw little of Nathan, except in passing as he served at evening meals or in the drawing room. She told herself this was just as well, though she thought often of that kiss, and her heart quickened whenever she *did* see him.

Maryvictoria, of course, had much to say about this. "I do not understand why you insist on making yourself miserable over a man, especially a man who has such excellent qualities."

Since they were alone in Allyson's chamber, there was no need to communicate silently. "I am *not* miserable," Allyson insisted. "You forget, the man is a *footman*."

"People are people," Maryvictoria said for perhaps the third time. "Give him a chance. You might be surprised."

"I have already been 'surprised,' " Allyson muttered. "But you know very well that England is not ready for the level of democracy you are suggesting."

"Perhaps she should be."

Allyson's tone dripped sarcasm. "Oh, yes, and one insignificant earl's daughter is going to change hundreds of years of social history! I think not."

"She might." But Maryvictoria did not sound very convincing.

Allyson changed the subject. "Where do you go when you are not badgering me?"

"Oh, around."

"Do you sleep?"

"Sometimes."

"Where?"

"There is a very comfortable sofa in the attic. I spend time in the stables, too. Bucephalus is not very happy. He feels he is being ignored."

"Good heavens! You talk to animals, too?"

"Well, of course. They are living beings, too," Maryvictoria said scornfully. "And sometimes far more interesting than people."

"I do not doubt that," Allyson said, but Maryvictoria had already faded away.

Allyson lay in her bed thinking of Maryvictoria's oft-repeated phrase, "People are people." Of course they were, and Nathan Christopher seemed as fine as any she had ever known. But he was a *footman*. She must keep her distance, no matter how much she—I . . . uh . . . *cared* for him . . . was attracted to him . . .

She groaned and buried her face in her pillow.

Since his presence was not needed to accompany Lady Allyson in the mornings, Nathan spent much of his time in the countryside, trying out alternate routes from probable meeting sites with the agents from France. He wore nondescript clothing and rode an ordinary hack, for the magnificent Bucephalus would attract far too much attention.

He stopped one midmorning at an inn on the outskirts of Lewes for a tankard of ale. Two old men played cards near a window. He engaged in some chitchat with the innkeeper about the weather, then took his tankard to a corner table on which a newspaper lay. He was engrossed in yet another story of the battle of Vitoria when two other men came in.

They, too, bought tankards of ale and then put their heads together at a table on the other side of the room.

Surprised that he recognized both of them, Nathan pulled his cap lower on his head and raised the newspaper higher. One was the valet to the Frenchman, Arnaud, and the other was Cecil Cranston. Cranston appeared to be questioning the servant. Cranston's presence in this part of England likely boded ill for Lady Rutherford, or her daughter. Nathan saw Cranston take a folded paper from his pocket and shove it across the table to the valet. Cranston said something, and the valet nodded. Cranston then passed the man some money. Soon, both finished their drinks and left.

The dressing bell for guests had already rung when Lady Rutherford's maid informed Nathan that Her Ladyship wanted to see him in the morning room, a room little used with so many people in the house. Nathan had expected the summons. He found Lady Rutherford already dressed for dinner in a dark blue silk gown and wearing a fortune in diamonds. She paced about the relatively small morning room.

"My lady?"

Without preamble, she thrust a paper at him. "Read this."

It was a note signed only "C," demanding that she meet him in the choir stalls of the cathedral in Lewes when she took her female guests on a shopping excursion two days hence.

"What is he even doing here?" she fumed. "And how did he come to know of our shopping expedition?"

"They wasted no time," Nathan said calmly, and told her of seeing Cranston with Arnaud's valet at the inn.

"Why did you not tell me earlier?" she challenged, with a pause in her pacing.

"I intended to warn you, my lady, but it was only today that I saw them. Um . . . When did you receive this note?"

"Someone slipped it under my door. My maid found it when she came to dress me for dinner."

"But she did not read it?"

"No, she did not."

"What do you intend to do?"

"Do? I have no idea. To start with, ask Monsieur Arnaud to send his valet packing, perhaps."

"That might occasion some talk."

"Oh, you are right. . . . I just hate the idea of a traitor in our midst," she said.

"I will personally see to Arnaud's valet this very night," Nathan promised, "but I think you should consider meeting with Cranston."

"Meet with him? I never want to see the blackguard again! Besides, I would be afraid to meet him alone. He has a violent temper."

"So I have heard, but you need not be alone, my lady. I will make a point of being there ahead of both of you. At any sign of danger, I shall intervene. But I think we should learn what we can. . . ."

Again the countess paused, a thoughtful look on her face. "You think he might have something to do with this French spy business?"

"I think we cannot dismiss that possibility until we know more; the man spent several years on the Continent, after all."

"All right. I *had* thought of canceling the shopping trip, but if you will be there—"

"I will be there."

And, two days later, he was.

Dressed as a beggar, with lamp blacking smeared on his face to simulate a beard, he slouched in a back pew of the church, trying to look disconsolate and inconspicuous. There were four other worshipers spread among the pews— an elderly man and three middle-aged women. One of the women had sniffed and given him a harsh look when she came in.

Earlier at the hall, Nathan had seen the ladies of the party off on their shopping expedition. Although a few of the females had chosen to remain behind, it took three carriages to accommodate the chattering group, dressed in their colorful summer plumage.

As he waited to hand her into a carriage, Lady Allyson gave him a questioning look. "Are you not accompanying us?"

He gestured to the entourage. "Three coachmen, three grooms, and three outriders for a journey of only ten miles seems sufficient."

She smiled. "You have a point."

"Don't tell me you have been missing me," he said softly.

"Impertinent wretch," she said equally softly, but she smiled all the same.

He had taken an alternate, shorter route across the countryside to the town, and now—after reconnoitering the whole church—he sat awaiting the arrival of the countess and her tormentor. The countess arrived first. Dressed in a maroon walking dress, she pretended to be a tourist, interested in the architecture and artifacts of the church. She kept a leisurely pace as she made her way forward, up the altar steps, and into the choir space.

Cranston arrived a good ten minutes and more past the appointed time. *The bastard,* Nathan thought. *He wants her nervous and apprehensive.* Cranston looked around, but apparently saw nothing untoward, and went directly to the choir. Nathan waited only a moment before moving up near the carved stone screen separating the choir from the altar. He wedged himself in between a pillar and a corner of the screen. The excellent acoustics of the choir allowed him to hear every word, though neither party spoke loudly.

Cranston spoke first in an affable tone. "Well, my love, you were more resourceful than I gave you credit for being."

He apparently reached toward her, for she said, "I am *not* your 'love'—and, please, do not touch me. Just tell me what this meeting is about."

"Very well." His tone was harder. "Money, of course. It is ever about money."

"Without the letters, your scurrilous tales of non-events a quarter of a century ago will carry little weight. I think my reputation can withstand the onslaught."

"Oh? And what about the somewhat . . . uh . . . colorful . . . figure your daughter cuts in society?"

"Allyson?" The countess's voice sounded strained.

"The same."

"Leave my daughter out of this."

His chuckle was malicious. "I am afraid I cannot do so. That meddlesome wench should learn to exercise more restraint. I am surprised you allow her such free rein."

"I have no idea what you are talking about. Allyson simply has nothing to do with—"

"Ah, but she does." His voice was now hard, flat, and vicious. "I can produce two witnesses who can swear to her being unchaperoned in the company of a man in a bachelor household."

Nathan thought Cranston was either bluffing or did not yet know of Edna's defection.

"What utter nonsense," Lady Rutherford said.

"It *could* be. But it is not. And, with two witnesses, how do you think the story will play with the *ton?* I hear the Marquis of Eastland is quite interested in the incomparable Lady Allyson. He is known to be quite a stickler for the proprieties."

"You despicable snake."

"Tut. Tut. No name-calling," he said. There was silence for a long moment; then Cranston spoke again. "By the by, my price has gone up. I want *twice* my original figure now."

She gasped. "Twice—"

"Your daughter will pay the consequences should you fail me, my love."

"What fustian!" she replied, but Nathan detected a tremor of fear in her voice. "You lost your hold on me when you lost those letters, so now you threaten to ruin Allyson."

"I shall do whatever it takes, my own love. Call it 'the sins of the mother,' or some such. But, *get me that money.*" He ground out the last words in a menacing tone.

"I can get such a sum only in the city," she said. "It will take time."

"No, you will not put me off again. You have two days after your return to the city. Not a moment more." With that, he abruptly left the choir and swept through the nave without a backward look.

Nathan peered around the pillar to watch until Cranston was out of the church; then he slipped into the choir. Lady Rutherford sat in one of the stalls, her head on her hands on the railing in front of her.

"My lady?"

She looked up, tears in her eyes. "Oh! Nathan, I hardly recognized you." She wiped at her eyes with a small, lacy handkerchief.

"That *was* the plan," he said lightly, hoping to help her regain her composure. He leaned against the railing and waited for her to do so. "Are you all right, now?"

"No," she said ruefully, "but I shall survive. . . . You heard?"

"All of it."

"He—he threatened Allyson. I shall have to pay."

"I am sure you know that if you do so, you will be paying forever."

She nodded. "But what choice have I?"

"Perhaps . . ." he offered slowly, "you should talk it over with your husband."

Her response was instant and sharp. "No! I will not have Duncan distressed by this mess of my making!"

"You may have been at fault all those years ago, but certainly not now."

"I can*not* involve my husband." She added in a resigned tone, "I will pay—somehow—to protect Allyson. I have a great deal of jewelry—"

"Please, my lady, do *not* do it. His demands will never end."

"But Allyson—"

"I will protect Lady Allyson," he said fiercely.

She gave him a long, penetrating look. "You know? I rather think you will." She rose. "Come, I must get back to my guests."

Nathan smiled. "My lady, you cannot be seen leaving here with a beggar."

She returned his smile and patted his hand. "You are right, of course. Thank you, Nathan."

Upon their return to Rutherford Hall, many of the ladies chose to retire to their rooms. Having missed her ride that morning, Allyson chose to take a walk through the gardens, of which there were several acres. She took a book with her, intending to enjoy the warm summer sun so long as it lasted this day. After a brisk walk, she returned to the bench where she had left the book. She had read only a few pages when she heard the crunch of footsteps on the graveled path.

The Marquis of Eastland soon emerged. Dressed in fawn-colored breeches, a dark green jacket, and a lighter green waistcoat, he was every inch the gentleman. He removed his hat on seeing her, and a slight breeze ruffled his hair, giving him a less austere look than he usually had.

"Lady Allyson," he greeted her, "well met! However, I must confess a footman told me where I might find you."

She wondered fleetingly if that footman had been Nathan. Somehow, the very word *footman* always evoked his image. "You were looking for me?" she asked curiously.

"Yes, do you mind if I join you?"

She moved to one end of the bench and gestured for him to sit. He sat and craned his head at an odd angle to read the title of her book.

"What are you reading?" he asked, though she doubted that was what was really on his mind.

"A novel. It is new, but quite delightful. *Pride and Prejudice* is the title."

"Oh, yes, I have heard of it. A woman writer, I believe."
He sat in silence for a moment, his hands on his knees.

"My lord?" she prompted.

"The thing is, I am somewhat nervous. I have never done
this before, you see."

"I am not sure I understand."

"I . . . uh . . . spoke with your father. He has given me
permission to pay my addresses to you." His voice became
increasingly stronger.

Now she understood perfectly, and she felt a flurry of
panic. Should she have foreseen this? Why had her father
said nothing to her?

"When did you speak with him?" she asked, to give herself some time to consider this turn of events.

"Why, only this morning. After the ladies had gone."

"Oh." Well, then, her father could hardly be blamed for
not warning her. Nor would he have turned away a man of
Eastland's social and political stature while his daughter was
so clearly free.

The marquis turned on the bench to face her directly. He
took the book from her and laid it aside so he could avail
himself of her hands. The actions seemed methodical and
ritualistic, and she observed them as happening to someone
else, certainly not to her.

"Lady Allyson, my dear Lady Allyson, please say you will
make me the happiest of men and consent to be my wife."

"But, my lord, this is so sudden," she said, recognizing
even as the words slipped out how melodramatic and fatuous
they sounded. Heavens! She was resorting to clichés.

"It is true we have known each other only a few weeks,
but it is time I married, and, I believe that, with a very little
direction, you will one day make a fine duchess."

"I . . . see. You are seeking a future duchess."

"Precisely. Though of course my father still holds the title
and I've no wish to succeed him anytime soon. But you do
have many of the qualities such a position will require when
the time comes."

Allyson wanted to laugh. This was not so much a marriage proposal as an interview for an upper servant's position. "I . . . I cannot—"

"You need not give me your answer this very instant," he assured her, "but it did occur to me that we might make the announcement at your mother's ball next week and have the wedding in late autumn. That would allow you sufficient time, would it not?"

"Sufficient time?" she repeated dumbly. "Oh, yes. I . . . I suppose it would, but—"

"Good. Once I make up my mind about something, I see no reason for inordinate delay."

Allyson was feeling overwhelmed. She *had* to gain control of this conversation.

"You do me great honor, my lord, but—"

"There is no need for such gratitude between a husband and wife," he said magnanimously, as he rose and pulled her to her feet.

He lowered his head to hers and kissed her fully on the lips. The kiss was not unpleasant, but there was none of the sizzling sensation or urgent *need* to respond that she had felt with Nathan's kiss.

"I . . . I . . . hardly know what to say, my lord, but—"

"You need say nothing at all now, my dear. We shall make our plans later. Shall I escort you into the house now? It will soon be time to dress for dinner."

"You go ahead," she urged him. "I need a few minutes to gather my wits."

"I quite understand, my dear." He smiled indulgently and left.

Allyson plopped herself on the bench and bent double in silent laughter, lest he hear her behind him. She found his arrogance and presumption more amusing than appalling, but how on earth could she respond to such a proposal?

Chapter 15

Things had not gone well for Nathan in the last few days. Lady Rutherford still refused to confide in her husband, nor would she agree to withhold the extortion money from Cranston once she returned to London.

"If it will help keep Allyson safe, I shall simply have to do it."

"It probably will not do so, though, if the man's threat is genuine and he wants yet more money. And he will," Nathan argued.

"But it *might*."

He did persuade her to delay as much as possible and to use *him* as her courier in delivering the extortion money.

Secondly, the scheme for foiling French agents, a plan that had seemed foolproof in London, had reached a stalemate. The decoy documents had been locked in the earl's desk, but not so secretly, and not so securely, that a miscreant would not be tempted by them. A watch had been set on the library, but there was no suspicious activity about the desk. The closest anyone had come to that piece of furniture was when a maid had taken two lazy swipes across it with a feather duster.

Nathan strongly suspected that he was being watched whenever he ventured out into the countryside on Bucephalus.

He had sensed someone following him on more than one occasion, though he took evasive measures. When he decided to allow the "someone" to catch up with him, the other rider disappeared. Apparently, a member of the armies of servants and guests currently at Rutherford Hall had developed a particular interest in the activities of one of the footmen.

Lord Rutherford summoned Nathan and Lord Worthington for a hasty meeting in his wine cellar. He lit a lantern to give off a weak light.

"These walls are so thick, no one could possibly overhear us," the earl explained, closing the equally thick door. He then stood with his arms crossed.

Worthington took a seat on a small barrel. "Do we have anything new?" Worthington was a stocky man in his fifties, a man Nathan knew to be much lighter on his feet than his girth and demeanor suggested.

"Nothing," the earl said glumly. "No one is taking our bait, and Thomas says if the fishing is going well, his brother is likely to be late coming in."

"On the other hand, anything could have happened out there in the channel," Worthington said.

"It could have," Rutherford agreed, then addressed Nathan, "What do you think, Captain?"

"A change of plan might be in order."

The earl frowned. "A change in plan?"

"The point is, or was, that we wanted them—whoever 'they' are—to take this bait. They must be on to its being false. Therefore, we must make them think they can still achieve their goal."

Worthington snorted. "Oh, that sounds easy enough."

"Hear him out," Rutherford said.

Nathan went on. "If Thomas does not get word to us soon, I will meet with him anyway. I will bring *something* back with me, and Rutherford can seem to exchange it for what is in the desk, and I can then speed the packet to London."

"Of false papers?" Worthington asked. "Why?"

"So that *you* can take the genuine article the next day—if

we have it—at a leisurely pace in a carriage. I heard you say, did I not, that you had to return to London before the ball?"

"Yes, I do. I am leaving my wife and daughter here, though."

"This will make you an open target, Thornton," Rutherford said to Nathan.

"That is, of course, the point, sir," Nathan replied.

"Could be dangerous," Rutherford warned.

"Well, I shall give them a run; I have a good horse." He winked at the earl. "Then to save my own hide, I give up the dispatch case. Worthington will do the real work."

"I and three or four armed men," Lord Worthington said mildly.

"I cannot like it"—Rutherford paused, then added—"but I haven't a better idea."

"This should work," Nathan said.

Finally, in these last few days, Nathan had seen little of Lady Allyson except for that brief exchange on the day of the shopping trip, though he thought of her constantly, of how the sun caught reddish glints in her brown hair, and of how her eyes revealed her emotions so perfectly. And of how she had felt in his arms. No matter how he tried, those images stayed with him, even after his brother had dealt that most devastating of blows.

Nathan had delivered hot shaving water to the male guests the morning after the shopping expedition. Eastland himself answered the footman's knock.

"Thank you," the marquis said, and pointed to the dressing room. The valet was not in either room, so Eastland apparently felt free to talk. "Well, brother, you may wish me happy. Finally, at the ripe old age of nearly six and thirty, I have popped the question!"

"Lady Allyson?" Nathan asked dully.

"Of course. With a husband's firm hand, she will one day make a good duchess."

"She accepted, did she?"

"Not in so many words," Eastland admitted, "but you know how women are—they do not want to seem too eager."

Memory of Allyson's eager response to his kiss flashed into Nathan's mind. Had she responded like that to Eastland's embrace?

Eastland went on, "We shall make the announcement at Lady Rutherford's ball, and have the wedding in the autumn."

"Sounds rather firm," Nathan said.

"Just need to work out the details, but women love things like that."

Nathan extended his hand. "I do wish you happy."

Eastland took it in a firm clasp. "You will come to the wedding, will you not? I know we have had our differences, but this will be an important family affair. It would not look good if you were not there to stand up with me."

"If I am not back on the Peninsula, I will," Nathan said, and swore that, short of Boney's surrender in the next month, he damned well *would* be back on the Peninsula before he attended *this* wedding!

He finally escaped his brother's room, but he was in such a hurry to do so that he failed to check the hallway before leaving. Lady Eggoner was coming toward him, not fifteen feet away. She paused and glanced at the door from which he had emerged, then back at him, a thoughtful look about her.

"May I help you, madam?" he asked in his best servant manner.

"No-o. No, thank you," she said and hurried on.

Later, as he served in the dining room, he noted that Lady Eggoner kept glancing from him to Eastland. He also saw her nod her head in some secret discussion with herself. *Well, she knows,* he thought.

He also noted that Allyson was Eastland's dinner partner. So it really was true.

Maryvictoria stood in the middle of Allyson's chamber with her hands on her hips. "You are *not* thinking of accepting that proposal, are you?"

Allyson turned from her writing desk to observe this indignant apparition. "Good evening to you, too, Maryvictoria Elizabeth. Have you had a pleasant day?"

Maryvictoria stamped her foot. "Well, *are* you?"

"How did you know? I've told no one; were you there?" Allyson accused. "I thought you said you did not eavesdrop on really private matters."

"Nor do I, but you have thought of little else all evening; you have been virtually shouting in your head."

"I suppose if I want any privacy, I must stop thinking." A hurt look came over Maryvictoria's face, so Allyson softened her tone. "In any event, it scarcely concerns you. Are you not the one who recently commented on my advanced age?"

Maryvictoria sighed and perched on the edge of Allyson's bed. "Truly, my lady, you are making my job *so* difficult."

"Your job. And what might that be?"

"I am to *try* to ensure your happiness. Please believe me," the child said earnestly, "this man is not right for you."

"And the right one is all wrong," Allyson muttered. "You would have me leading apes in hell."

"I doubt you will end a spinster."

"Oh? You mean I have a choice?" Allyson did not bother to hide her sarcasm.

"Of course, everyone has choices. That is what life is, a series of choices that each of us makes. Well, most people do, at least. Those that are allowed to grow up."

The wistful note in Maryvictoria's tone touched Allyson's heart. "I'm sorry, Maryvictoria." The girl nodded, and both were quiet for a long moment; then Allyson spoke. "I am curious. What *is* your objection to the Marquis of Eastland?"

"As a person? Nothing. He *is* a trifle pompous, but he takes his responsibilities very seriously. He is also overzealous in protecting his position in society."

"But so are many people of such rank," Allyson said.

"He would bore *you* to flinders within a fortnight."

"Perhaps. . . ." Allyson was not ready to concede the point fully.

Later, after Maryvictoria had gone, Allyson lay in bed thinking over her conversation with the marquis, and this one with the opinionated sprite. The truth was, she did not know Eastland very well. He had sought her company at parties and routs, had danced with her, and had called on her, but their conversations, until this last one, had always been rather superficial. The weather, a new collection at the British museum, an opera or a play—these had been the topics of their discussions. She surmised he was a Tory, but she had no idea how strong his political views might be. She could not imagine *him* on a mission to retrieve incriminating letters.

This thought brought forth the image of the man who *had* accompanied her, and had handled the aftermath with discretion and understanding. She was quite sure the woman, Edna, would even now be languishing in jail, and Allyson's own reputation would be in shreds, had the Marquis of Eastland been involved. He certainly would never have considered her "proper" enough to become a duchess!

And then there were those kisses. What was it that made one man's kiss no more moving than a handshake with the bishop, and another's evoke wild, unbridled desire?

Maryvictoria was right, but the child had jumped too hastily to her conclusion. Allyson was not seriously tempted by the Marquis of Eastland's offer. Flattered, yes, but not tempted. Why, the man would probably never allow his wife an opinion! Look how he had simply brushed off her attempts to respond to his proposal.

Now, if she could just penetrate that massive sense of self enough to refuse him without making an enemy of him.

Another day went by during which there was not even a peep about a footman and a marquis being related. Lady Eggoner had said nothing to Nathan, though he had been one of those serving tea in the drawing room that evening and she had had ample opportunity to accost him. The next morning, Nathan followed his brother to the stable where they held a brief tête-à-tête prior to the marquis's riding out with Lady Allyson.

"Did I not tell you this was an impossible situation?" Eastland snapped.

"Why has she said nothing to either of us? Or to the other guests? It would be a juicy bit of gossip."

"Perhaps you were mistaken." Eastland's tone suggested, *You usually are.* "Or perhaps she simply chooses to let what will be, be."

"What do you mean?"

"If she had recognized you as a Thornton, she may well have surmised you are working on some sort of government scheme and, as a loyal Englishwoman, she has chosen to let it be."

"That is possible," Nathan agreed, but it nagged at him all the same.

As a groom brought out two saddled horses, Nathan hastily departed. It would not do for others to speculate about what a Rutherford footman might have to do with a marquis. Approaching the house, Nathan encountered Lady Allyson on her way to the stable.

"Good morning, my lady."

"Good morning, Nathan. Is this not just the most glorious day?"

" 'Tis a beauty," he said tersely, and kept on going. He heard her pause behind him, but he did not look back.

Feeding an army of guests, in addition to the family and an even bigger army of servants—what with personal servants who accompanied the guests—required careful planning on the part of the chef and his enormous staff. It also involved a great deal of shopping, and sending servants to collect the raw materials for these meals.

Nathan was frequently the footman sent in a small one-horse cart to collect seafood. This duty was, of course, a perfect cover for meetings with the innkeeper Thomas, who on this day finally had a small packet for Nathan. After carefully putting it inside his jacket, Nathan went on to the fish-monger's and picked up the chef's standing order. Were he riding, he might have worried a great deal about carrying the packet. He had suspected he was followed and watched only when he was riding. Nor had any of the other footmen mentioned anything untoward when such delivery duty had fallen to them.

Nevertheless, he took the precaution of always going armed, with a small pistol tucked into his clothing, and another into the seat of the cart. On this day, as on previous occasions, he was relieved not to have to use them. His return to the hall went without incident, and, as planned, he was discreet, but not secretive, in handing the documents over to Lord Rutherford, who locked them in his desk.

"Thank you, Nathan. It is too late now, and too little moon these nights for you to start immediately, but first thing in the morning, you are off, my lad."

"Yes, my lord."

As Nathan left the library, he carefully closed the door, which had been left slightly ajar. There were three people in the vast entry hall off which the library was located. Two maids were polishing furniture and the stair newels; the third person, walking away, was Monsieur Arnaud's valet, who appeared to have picked up a letter from a table where the post for guests regularly lay.

The maids giggled and exchanged disparaging remarks about the valet's manhood. On seeing Nathan, they greeted him with flirtatious smiles.

Had the valet been deliberately eavesdropping? Or was he merely anxious to avoid a confrontation? Nathan's "chat" with the man following Lady Rutherford's receipt of the note from Cranston had been firm and to the point. Any further incident would result in Arnaud's being asked to leave, and a probable consequence of that would be the valet's losing his job. The man had seemed suitably cowed. Nathan knew the valet spent much of his free time with other French servants. The Comte de Pommeraie's valet and coachman

were also French, as were the maids of Lady Eggoner and
Miss Dawson. So far, there had been no cause to single any
of them out as a likely spy.

Since he would be leaving at dawn—and dawn came very
early in summer—Nathan was excused from ordinary serving duties that night. He wondered if anyone would note his
absence.

He would have been pleased to know that one person, at
least, noted that there had been a change in dining room duties for the footmen. Allyson was surprised at the degree of
her curiosity about why he was not there. Melton simply had
something else for him to do, but why should she care? Of
course, there was that matter her father had discussed in
London. Surely he was not in some danger, was he? She
tried to put such thoughts aside. Her main concern this
evening was to get that interview with Lord Eastland behind
her. Her opportunity came when the entire party had returned to the drawing room after dinner. As some chose to
play cards, and others joined small groups in conversation,
Allyson approached the marquis.

"May I speak with you privately, my lord?" Her voice was
soft and steady, despite her nervousness. After all, one did
not refuse a future duke's offer every day.

"Of course, my lady. We have plans to make, have we
not?" His tone was soft enough, but Allyson was sure several
ears nearby had been attuned to his comment.

He followed her into another, smaller drawing room that
the family used when there were fewer guests in the house.
She took a winged back chair, and he took another, with a
sidelong glance at a settee.

"Yes, my dear?" he said.

"My lord—"

"Under the circumstances, surely we can use our Christian
names, can we not, dear Allyson? Mine is Malcolm."

"My lord," she began again and saw him frown, "I asked

to speak to you so that I could give you my answer to your . . . your question of the other day."

"I see." He crossed his legs and put his laced hands on his knee. "You like to have everything in proper order, is that it?"

"I . . . You might say that." She paused. "My lord, you have honored me greatly with your offer"—he nodded magnanimously—"but I find that I cannot accept it."

He straightened upright, both feet on the floor. "I beg your pardon?"

"I cannot marry you."

"Is this a joke? Or are you simply being extraordinarily coy?"

"Neither, my lord," she said softly. "I am very sorry."

"You cannot be holding out for a better offer; therefore, I assume you fancy your affections to be engaged elsewhere."

"Yes, I believe they are," she admitted to him and to herself.

"Have you considered that in our circles marriage is a very serious business?"

"I should think it a serious concern in *any* circles," she said tartly.

"Yes, of course. But I have offered you a social position that few women in England could equal."

"I am very aware of the honor you do me, Lord Eastland. Would that I could give you the answer you wish, but I simply cannot."

"Well, then, so be it. You are not some green girl, so I take you at your word. I shall *not* renew my offer."

"Thank you, my lord."

He rose and offered his arm. "Shall we return to the company?"

"Yes," she said, though she really wished to flee to her room and mull over what had happened.

Neither spoke as they returned to the formal drawing room. There were speculative looks directed their way, but no one said anything until much later in the evening when Lord Braxton managed to corner Allyson in a window alcove for a private moment.

"Am I to wish you happy, or is there hope for me yet?"

"I have no idea what you mean," she stalled.

"Come, my dear, doing it too brown. That little tête-à-tête with Eastland was not about trading on the 'change."

"It *could* have been."

"There have been bets on the books for three weeks and more that you will be the next Duchess of Halstead."

"Is that so?" She was genuinely surprised.

"Yes, that is so," he mocked. "So, will you?"

"Will I what?"

"Be the next Duchess of Halstead?" he asked with exaggerated patience.

"As a matter of fact, no."

"But he did offer for you?"

"Lord Braxton! You know I cannot respond to such a question. It would be unseemly."

"Then he did! And I'm dashed if you didn't refuse him!" There was a note of triumph in his tone.

She put her hand on his arm. "Lord Braxton—Richard—please . . . You must say nothing. Nothing, mind you." She waited until he nodded his acquiescence; then she said, "I hope you will not lose a great deal."

He leaned closer and whispered. "I won. I bet on *you*."

"How—?"

"I have seen no signs that your interest is seriously engaged, and I doubted any title alone would be sufficient inducement."

"You know me too well," she said.

Nathan arose before dawn, met Lord Rutherford in the library, and, at the first sign of light, was on his way to London. The packet of documents containing half-truths and lies was in his saddlebag. Later, at a more civilized hour, Worthington would set out in all the pomp and glory befitting a fastidious member of the *ton*.

The entire adventure went precisely as Nathan had outlined it to Worthington and Rutherford. Nathan had even foreseen exactly the copse of trees in which he would be accosted. Bucephalus had been skittish for some while, sensing Nathan's heightened nerves, or some unusual movement in the trees.

Suddenly there appeared on the road before Nathan two masked riders blocking his way.

"Halt!" one of them yelled, his voice muffled by the mask.

Instead, Nathan signaled his well-trained warhorse to turn instantly, and he pulled his pistol, but there behind him were two more masked riders emerging from the trees.

"Give it up," one of these called out. "You cannot take four of us—all armed."

"What do you want?" Nathan demanded, forcing a strained note into his voice. "I've very little money."

One of the foursome—the one who had told him to "give it up"—dismounted, keeping his pistol trained on Nathan, as were the other three. "Hand over the weapon," he demanded in cultivated tones. "I strongly suspect that you know very well it is not money we seek from you."

Nathan tossed his pistol to the ground and tried to appear as if he might make a run for it.

"Please, spare us any heroics," the same man ordered in a reasoning tone. "A few papers are not worth your life. Just hand over that dispatch packet."

Using his knees to signal his mount, Nathan backed Bucephalus a few steps away. "Who's to say I have any papers?" Nathan wanted to hear more of this voice, which so far he had not recognized.

"You hand over the packet, and I give you my word, *you* may ride free."

"Your word," Nathan said contemptuously.

"But I wanted that horse," another, younger voice whined.

"*You* couldn't ride that horse," one of his companions said.

The man who had dismounted had never taken his eyes from Nathan. "My word is good," he assured in the same reasoning tone. "Our orders are to obtain that dispatch packet. We will kill to get it, if we must. It is your choice."

Nathan and the man spent a long moment taking each other's measure. Pale gray eyes, average height, and excellent boots were the only distinguishing features Nathan noted. The rest of his attire was neat, but nondescript, much like Nathan's own.

"Your choice," the man repeated, "but we will not wait all day."

Nathan heaved a sigh and reached toward the saddlebag.

"No tricks," the man barked. "You would be dead before you fell to the ground."

"No tricks," Nathan muttered in apparent defeat. He retrieved the packet and reached down to hand it over. Four sets of eyes were on the packet, and Nathan knew that if he *were* to make a run for it, this would be the moment.

Finally, the man who had dismounted put the packet into his own saddlebag and remounted. "We thank you, and the emperor thanks you," he said, signaling the others to ride out. They left at a gallop, and suddenly Nathan was alone in the copse of trees.

"Mission accomplished," he murmured aloud, and turned his horse in the direction from which he had come.

Chapter 16

Nathan returned to Rutherford Hall late in the afternoon. The kitchen was chaotic in preparation for the evening meal. Catching Jamie's attention, he sent the young footman for Melton, who would at this hour be busy in the dining room. When Melton arrived, Nathan asked him to inform His Lordship that he, Nathan, would be waiting in the wine cellar. Melton then made a show of ordering Nathan to the cellar for a particular wine.

Twenty minutes later, Lord Rutherford appeared, shouting angrily that of course there were several bottles of his special Bordeaux, and why must he do the work for which he hired servants? An apparently flustered Melton was at his heels, but the butler remained in the kitchen to vent his own "frustration" on a hapless footman.

"Good show, sir," Nathan said, chuckling.

Rutherford smiled sheepishly. "Had to have some reason to be down here at this hour. So, I assume you had a good day?"

"Very good. Exactly as planned. And Worthington?"

"He got off well. Made a big show of being worried about highwaymen, and I—ever so accommodating—offered him two additional outriders."

Nathan nodded his approval, then proceeded to give Rutherford a detailed account, including the information that one of his "interceptors" had worn fine boots and spoke with a cultured accent.

"French?" Rutherford asked.

"No, English, but I did not recognize the voice."

"We *must* be getting closer."

"I think so, my lord."

"Good work, Captain."

Rutherford then returned to his guests, carrying to the kitchen two bottles of an especially fine wine. Nathan followed a few minutes later with three more and explained to no one in particular, "His Lordship said he wanted these, too."

Nathan then disappeared up the back stairs to the servants' quarters and fell exhausted into his own bed.

The next morning, he was prepared to accompany Lady Allyson on her ride, but once again she was surrounded by younger male guests, as well as his brother. *A gaggle of ganders,* Nathan thought sourly and went about other duties.

There were plenty of those, for this was the night Lady Rutherford had chosen for her ball. She and Melton directed footmen in moving furniture and huge potted plants all morning. There was a brief respite at noon; then they began arranging garlands of greenery, ribbon streamers, and fresh flowers.

Nathan served at the elaborate dinner preceding the ball and cursed his luck at being stationed across from Lady Allyson, who once again was partnered by Lord Eastland. She was dressed in a cream-colored silk gown with a deliciously low neckline and a scandalously low back. It was trimmed in soft yellow embroidered roses. In her hair she wore small real roses of the same shade. Nathan felt his body tighten at just looking at her. She carried on polite conversation with her dinner companions, Eastland on one side of her and the ubiquitous Lord Braxton on the other. Once or twice she caught Nathan's eye and gave him a small, brief smile. *Triumphant at catching the heir to a dukedom,* Nathan thought. On the other hand, his brother did not seem overly triumphant. *Probably thinks she is merely what he deserves.*

Nathan was also to serve at the ball later. Well, perhaps once the engagement was announced, he could put Lady Allyson Crossleigh out of his mind. At the ball, he did not make a cake of himself, but he watched her dance every dance.

Just before the supper dance late in the evening, the earl stood near the musicians and called for everyone's attention. *Here it comes,* Nathan thought, trying to steel himself against pain.

To Nathan's immense surprise and utter consternation, there was no engagement announcement. The earl thanked his friends and neighbors for attending and told the assembled group how much he and the countess, who stood beside him, had enjoyed the house party, and he sincerely hoped their guests had had a good time.

There were calls of "Hear! Hear!" and the earl signaled the musicians, then led his wife to the dance floor. Those not dancing were abuzz with gossip, much of which Nathan could not help overhearing.

"I fully expected an 'interesting announcement,' " one dowager said.

Another shrugged. "Apparently Eastland did not come up to scratch."

"It would be a good match," another woman offered tentatively.

"Perhaps Lady Allyson refused his offer," the third woman's husband said. "Lord knows she has refused other good matches."

"Refuse a future duke?" The first woman was appalled at the very idea. "Oh, not likely. Not likely at all."

And those were Nathan's sentiments, as well. So what had happened? Had Eastland changed his mind and argued for postponing the announcement so that the whole idea might fade away? Yet he *had* offered, and a gentleman could not honorably renege on such a proposal. Had her father objected? No. Eastland would perforce have spoken with the earl first. It simply made no sense.

Finally, in the wee hours of the morning, the servants were dismissed, and one very perplexed footman found it difficult to sleep.

Allyson had had a grand time at the ball. She loved to dance, and her partners had been interesting and amiable. So what if there had not been the excitement of that first waltz in the music room weeks earlier? Lord Eastland had been all that was proper, never outwardly showing any lessening of his regard for her. He had also shown a good deal of attention to other young women, including the daughters of Longworth, Dawson, and Worthington.

Allyson knew many of the Rutherford guests had expected a betrothal announcement. She was also aware of and slightly amused by the gleeful looks of false pity or of triumph in the expressions of certain young women or their mamas when such an announcement was not forthcoming.

Her mother had been disappointed when she sought her parents in their private sitting room and told them she had refused the marquis. The countess had risen from her chair to sit beside her daughter on a sofa.

"You are *sure*, my dear? It would be a very good match, you know."

"Yes, Mama, I do know, but I think Lord Eastland wants a future duchess more than a wife. In the end, we might both be unhappy. I am quite sure that I would be."

"What is it that you want from marriage?" her mother asked gently.

Allyson looked from her mother to her father seated across from them and softly wailed, "I want what *you* have, someone who will love and support and defend me, no matter what."

There was a long pause as her parents stared deeply into each other's eyes. Then her father cleared his throat.

"I should like to see you wed," he said. "There is much happiness to be found in the institution of marriage. However, if you do not marry, you will always have a place with us, and you will certainly be able to manage when we are gone."

"Thank you, Papa. I—I think I knew that."

Her mother put an arm around her shoulder and tried to lighten the mood. "You are not quite a spinster, yet, my dear. The right man may still turn up."

Allyson wanted to bury her head in her mother's lap and cry, "He already has." Instead, she refused to meet her mother's gaze lest she reveal her pain.

Maryvictoria had not appeared for several days, but when Allyson finally dismissed an exhausted Molly and climbed into bed after the ball, there she was. Allyson had lain with her eyes closed, her mind reeling.

"I know you are not asleep."

Allyson jerked her eyes open and raised herself to a half-sitting position. "No, I am not. I suppose you are here with marvelous words of wisdom."

"No, I just like to drop in now and then, especially when you might need to talk." Maryvictoria sat cross-legged at the foot of the bed.

"How thoughtful," Allyson said sincerely. "Were you there? At the ball?"

"Oh, yes. And at the dinner, too. It was all so beautiful, the ladies all dressed like royalty. But the men these days! Why do they insist on that somber black?"

"To allow the women to look smarter?"

"Well, they resemble nothing so much as a bunch of crows," Maryvictoria said sourly. "And some of them could be quite handsome, too." Then she brightened. "But the music and the dancing were wonderful."

"And not one spilled drink or squashed cake," Allyson said. "You must have been on very good behavior indeed."

"Well . . ." The child looked a bit chagrined.

"Maryvictoria Elizabeth?"

"Did you see Miss Longworth stumble as she waltzed with Lord Eastland?"

"*You* did that?"

"Well, she was just so smug, you see. . . . But then he did the gentlemanly thing and blamed himself. All she did was tighten her hold on him."

Allyson grinned. "Foiled your plan, did she?"

"Perhaps. You know, I think those two might deserve each other. . . ."

"Are you playing matchmaker?"

"Not very well, it seems." Maryvictoria was quiet a moment; then she said, "You were right to refuse the marquis. I was really afraid you were going to make a mess of things."

"Make a mess—!" Allyson pretended stronger outrage than she felt.

Maryvictoria went on as though there had been no interruption. "You really must not worry about the future. It will take care of itself."

"Easy for *you* to say," Allyson said peevishly.

"I know, but it will. Sleep well."

Then she was gone and Allyson did sleep well.

By mid August, all the guests at Rutherford Hall had departed. Most, like the Lord and Lady Lawton, had journeyed to their own estates, but a few, including the earl's entourage, were braving the heat and foul air in returning to London. Parliament had not yet opened its autumn session, but government work forged ahead. Facts and rumors, secrets, and lies flew around the Foreign Office with the speed and aimlessness of bullets on a battlefield. In the end, though, one fact remained: despite his debacle in Russia and new alliances against him, the Corsican monster retained a good deal of strength and continued to win battles.

Nathan's footman duties had undergone some subtle changes. Aside from Melton, who knew everything anyway, other members of the staff seemed to take their cues from the master and mistress. Both the earl and his wife seemed to have a particular respect for Nathan and to want him available for special duties. Nathan was relieved that this new status seemed to breed no resentment among the rest of the staff.

His primary "service" was still to protect the earl's eldest daughter, and to that end she was still forbidden to go abroad without him. Not that she seemed to mind terribly. She had long ceased carping at his presence. Nathan thought that most of the time she actually enjoyed his company.

She had not mentioned Eastland's offer, nor had Nathan asked. Prior to leaving Rutherford Hall in Sussex, Eastland had managed to inform his brother tersely that there would be no union of the Halstead and Rutherford Houses.

"What happened?" Nathan asked.

"Like most women, Lady Allyson hasn't the sense God gave a goose," Eastland said. "Here, she had a chance at one of the highest social positions in England, and she just tossed it away. Why, she might have rivaled the Duchess of Devonshire in that one's prime."

Nathan fought to keep his voice even. "She refused you, I take it?"

"She did. Me. Heir to a duke. I sincerely hope she lives to regret it, too."

"Will you offer again, then?"

"No, absolutely not. You know me better than that."

"Did she say why?"

Eastland paused. "I think the chit fancies herself in l-o-o-ove. Schoolgirl nonsense, of course—and at her age!"

Nathan smiled. "I doubt it has an age limit."

Eastland merely snorted.

Nathan now spent a good deal of thought on just whom Lady Allyson might be in love with. If it was an unsuitable party, he would, by damn, find some way to warn the fellow off. The trouble was, the only ones for whom she showed any partiality were Lord Braxton and the Comte de Pommeraie, and both of these were eminently suitable.

* * *

Accompanied by Molly, John Coachman, and the ever-present Nathan, Allyson had gone shopping early one afternoon. She lingered over choosing gloves and a new bonnet. At both shops, Nathan had stood waiting for her on the pavement outside the shop door. She tried on a straw bonnet with a profusion of pink silk roses that she seriously considered buying. Molly and the milliner *oohed* and *aahed* over it. Then she noticed another, plainer bonnet in the window. As she pointed toward it, she caught sight of Nathan outside the window. She smiled at him and pointed at the hat on her head. He regarded it for a moment, then shook his head. She pointed to the plainer one trimmed in green ribbons. He nodded.

"I shall take this one," she said as she tried on the plainer one.

"Yes, madam." The milliner wore a rather knowing look that puzzled Allyson.

After a lengthy stop at Hatchard's bookshop, they returned to Rutherford House, where Allyson noticed a crested coach parked in front with a groom attending the horses. She instructed her driver to proceed to the back. As Nathan handed her and Molly from the Rutherford carriage, he wore a rather tight expression.

"Did you see that coach in front?" she asked. "I did not recognize the crest."

"It is the Duke of Halstead's," he said.

"The Duke of—"

"Halstead."

"Why on earth—? Do you suppose—?" She left these thoughts unfinished and hurried into the house with Molly at her heels. The Duke of Halstead had never, to her knowledge, been more than a casual acquaintance of her father, and then only in Parliament.

Was he here to plead Eastland's case? No, surely not.

She changed quickly into a muslin day dress in case she was called to meet with the duke. She found her mother in her sitting room, but the countess knew nothing of this visit.

"He arrived only a few moments ago and asked to speak with your father. That is all I know."

They waited together, but no summons came for either of the Rutherford women.

Melton had been hovering in the back, waiting for Nathan's return.

"You are wanted in the library, Nathan. Immediately."

Nathan sighed. "I should have foreseen this."

Melton obviously did not understand, but Nathan had neither time nor inclination to explain. He proceeded to the library and knocked.

"Come," the earl called. "Ah, Nathan. We were just talking about you. I think you know the Duke of Halstead." He gestured to the man in a chair in front of the desk.

Nathan nodded and bowed slightly. "Your Grace."

The Duke of Halstead was a tall, thin man whose hair was more gray than brown. The dark blue eyes, which he had passed on to this son, sparkled with interest—and anger. *Some things never change,* Nathan thought, even as he noted more stoop to the older man's shoulders and more lines in his face than he remembered. *What is he? Nearly seventy!*

"Is that all you have to say to your own father?" the duke barked. "After all these years?"

"You may remember that my *father* all but disowned me several years ago. What more would you have me say?"

"I never disowned a child of mine!" Halstead raged. "And you might begin by explaining why you are here."

Rutherford rose. "Perhaps I should leave the two of you to—"

"That will not be necessary," father and son said simultaneously, though the son added, "my lord."

Rutherford slowly sat back down.

"Well?" the duke demanded.

"Here in England? It is my native land."

"Here in England, when I thought you to be on the Peninsula! I have combed casualty lists repeatedly, and you were in England all the while! And you never once thought to disabuse me of my mistaken impression. No, that filial duty was left to your brother!"

Nathan, who had never before sat in his father's presence without permission or instructions to do so, sank into the other chair facing Rutherford's desk. This time the diatribe could not end in a beating or banishment. He would just let the invective roll over him. One of the duke's comments echoed in Nathan's mind. He had combed the casualty lists. Perhaps the old man cared after all.

The duke went on accusingly. "Now I find you have not been on the Peninsula for months. Moreover, you were *wounded*. Wounded, for God's sake, and I did not know!"

"One might almost think you cared," Nathan said, unable to overcome years of pain that welled behind his sarcasm.

"Of course I care, you misbegotten whelp! You're my son. And why are you here? In this household? Why are you not at home where you belong?"

"You mean where I never did quite belong, do you not?" Nathan asked quietly.

He saw that this was a palpable hit. His father wiped a hand across his face and said, his tone more subdued now, "If that was your perception, there is nothing I can do about it"—his voice rose in strident tones—"but I will not have my son tied to this household—"

Rutherford coughed significantly.

Nathan said urgently, "Please, Your Grace, keep your voice down."

"As a lowly servant," the duke finished in a softer but firm tone. "You will assume your place in society as a member of my family and cease making your way as a . . . a *footman*." The last word was uttered with profound contempt. "I doubt not you are doing this to embarrass me; God knows your grandmother left you fixed well enough."

Nathan looked questioningly at Lord Rutherford, who said, "I had not yet explained when you arrived. We had just got beyond polite pleasantries."

"Explained *what?*" The duke was back to barking.

"Did Eastland not tell you—" Nathan started.

"He told me you were in London—not on some god-forsaken battlefield—and that you were working as a servant. My son—a servant!"

"Of the king," Rutherford said. "And a very valued one at that." He proceeded to explain fully Nathan's role in the Rutherford household and with the Foreign Office. The earl spoke softly and calmly. His very tone was taking some of the bluster out of the duke. Rutherford finished by saying, "We are nearing our goal, we think. It would be disastrous were Nathan to be exposed now."

"Well, I'll be damned," Halstead said in surprise. "Why was I not informed?"

"Actually, I thought Eastland *had* informed you," Nathan said.

"Well, he did not."

Suddenly, Nathan knew why Eastland had kept back that information. In a continuation of childhood rivalries, Eastland wanted Nathan to appear in the worst possible light. Nathan had always been smarter, more athletic, and more popular with other young people—of both sexes—than his brother. Naive and trusting, a young Nathan had confided in his brother when he found himself in some contretemps or another. Eastland had always reported such to their father and subtly exaggerated Nathan's infractions. Eastland was the heir. Their father doted on him, and believed him implicitly.

"He did not," the duke repeated in a pensive tone. Nathan thought perhaps his father had figured it out, too.

"May we assume you will keep this information confidential, Your Grace?" Rutherford asked. "There is a great deal of clandestine activity both here and on the Continent that must be protected."

"Yes, of course," the duke replied. "I hope I have not compromised your work by appearing here today."

"We can explain your visit some way," Rutherford said.

By merely allowing the servants to speculate, Nathan thought, but he did not say this aloud. So what if it appeared Eastland wanted his papa to run interference for him?

"I, too, am a loyal Englishman," Halstead said gruffly. "Is there anything I might do to aid the cause, as it were?"

Rutherford looked to Nathan and gestured for him to answer.

"No, I think not—at least not at this time. But we do thank you for offering, Your Grace."

"Will you *stop* 'Your Gracing' me?" the duke growled at Nathan. "I am your damned *father,* and there is not a damned thing you can do about it!"

Nathan gave him a long, hard look, then grinned. "Yes, Father."

He offered his father his hand. The duke's hand was thin and fragile looking, but he clasped his son's hand strongly for a long time before taking his leave.

"You will come home, will you not, when this is all over?"

"Yes, Father, at least for a visit."

Chapter 17

In some ways, Allyson felt her life was returning to normal. She did not question when it had become "normal" for her to be accompanied by the same footman every time she left the house. Nor did she wonder any longer at the fact that she enjoyed talking with him on their morning rides far more than she enjoyed most of what passed for conversation in *ton* drawing rooms.

With fewer people in town these days, their rides tended to be interrupted less often. It occurred to her that perhaps she really knew Nathan better than she did any of her suitors—ever. Conversations with the footman had few limits as to topics. They discussed the weather, soldiering in the Peninsula, the prince regent's spending habits, her school-day escapades, fashions, books, even farming and animal husbandry. She was rather surprised at the depth of his apparent knowledge of the last two topics, of which she readily admitted ignorance.

She found that he evaded questions about his youth and his family, though he had admitted to having an older brother and a younger sister. She suspected his father had been a stern man.

There had been no more kisses, but she knew that, on her

part—and she suspected on his, as well—such lack was due to rigid self-control, certainly not to absence of desire. Every time he touched her, in such things as handing her into or out of a carriage, or giving her a boost into the saddle, she felt a tremor of physical awareness. On occasion, their gazes would meet momentarily, and she was sure he felt it, too.

Still, Lady Allyson was very pragmatic. She would simply enjoy what she could of this interlude in her life. After all, her own father had suggested the soldier's assignment as a footman was strictly temporary. Furthermore, there was simply no getting around the gulf that existed—or *should* exist—between a footman and an earl's daughter.

"You worry too much about unimportant matters," Maryvictoria said.

"They are not unimportant to *me*," Allyson replied. "My friends and my family are very important to me."

"Your parents would support you, no matter what."

"They would. But Clara would have the vapors, and Lawton might insist she cut me. Sometimes she is a silly goose, but, ninnyhammer or no, she *is* my sister. I want to know my niece or nephew."

"And your brother?"

"I will not have Oliver be plagued by his schoolmates. Just look at the awful things said of Lady Ferrington. Oliver would have perpetual black eyes!"

"Real friends—" Maryvictoria began.

"Would feel sorry for me. They might not drop me, but they could not invite me to their affairs, nor could I entertain them in kind. Eventually we would drift apart, and I, and my unsuitable husband, would be outcasts."

"Being in love is important," Maryvictoria argued.

"True. But I am not some hen-witted heroine in a novel, willing to give up everything—willy-nilly—all in the cause of love. The Minerva Press novels end with the lovers riding off into a rosy cloud. Those stories never deal with the storms and trials of real life afterward, when the cloud turns gray."

"That is not a very romantic outlook."

"No, I don't suppose it is, but it *is* practical," Allyson said. "Someday I would like to have children. I want my children to have such opportunities as I have had, not have their lives overshadowed by limitations and a scandal involving their parents."

"Hmphf!" Maryvictoria huffed. "At this rate, perhaps you *will* end an ape-leader!"

"Perhaps," Allyson agreed glumly.

A few days after this unsettling discussion, Allyson sat at a late breakfast with her mother when Melton entered to say that Lady Paxton was calling and insisted on seeing Allyson.

Allyson excused herself and met her friend in the library. "What is it, Sydney? You look distressed."

"Oh, Allyson, I am. I apologize for calling at such an hour, but I hardly know *what* to do."

"Come, sit. And tell me about it; then we shall have a dish of tea."

Lady Paxton laughed weakly. "Your solution to everything—a dish of tea." She sat on a sofa; Allyson gave the order to a servant, then closed the door and sat next to her friend.

"All right. What is it?"

"That horrible Francis Fish has pulled in another minnow for her brothel."

"No, do not say so."

"Unfortunately, yes. Betty Lou heard it on the street, and the Fairfax sisters sent me a note."

Allyson patted Sydney's hand and said sadly, "You know we cannot save them all. We had the element of surprise when we helped Betty Lou and Molly."

"I know. And some even *seek* that life, but this girl is different; I know she is."

"How do you know?"

"Betty Lou knows her from her home village, saw her in an open carriage with the Fish woman, and then learned what that monstrous female plans. And then *I* saw them out one day, too."

"Go on," Allyson urged.

"Allyson, the girl is beautiful. Her name is Helen, and the name is fitting. Golden blond hair, alabaster skin, and thoroughly innocent, unless I miss my guess."

"How did Mrs. Fish get hold of her?"

"The usual way. Whenever she needs a new girl, she meets the stages coming in from the country and singles out young women traveling alone. You know, tells them she has a respectable boarding house for young ladies. They fall for it, and then they are trapped, as were Betty Lou and Molly."

"You mentioned a plan?"

"As you know, the girls are usually drugged or plied with alcohol and 'initiated' the first night. But Mrs. Fish has kept this one more or less isolated. Helen really believes she is being protected and befriended. Instead, the Fish woman is showing her off to drive up interest—and the price—and she plans to *auction her off* tonight!"

"How old is Helen?"

"I doubt she has more than thirteen years, perhaps only twelve. I think she looks older than she is."

"Oh, good grief!" Allyson muttered.

A knock on the door signaled the arrival of the tea, and the conversation was delayed as both women waited for the footman, Jamie, to leave. Allyson poured the tea and offered her friend a biscuit, which Sydney nibbled absently.

Lady Paxton sipped the tea, then said, "We must *do* something before it is too late."

"I agree, but *what?* Our just marching in as we did before would not work a second time. Mrs. Fish has hired another unsavory sort to help Bart."

"If only we were men, it would be easy enough to gain entry," Lady Paxton lamented. "Perhaps if we disguised ourselves as men . . ."

Allyson shook her head. "It would not work in a well-lit room."

"You are right. A foolish idea."

They sat in silence several moments sipping their tea and thinking hard.

"I have it!" Allyson said. "Nathan."

"Nathan? You mean your footman?"

"The very one. He is quite reliable in devious activities." Allyson rose to ring for a servant, who answered immediately, and she sent him for Nathan.

"Someday you must tell me how you learned of this peculiar talent in your Nathan," Lady Paxton said.

"Perhaps I will—someday," Allyson replied, foolishly liking the sound of "*your* Nathan."

When Nathan appeared, Allyson introduced him to Lady Paxton. He bowed and waited expectantly.

"You had better have a seat, Nathan," Allyson said.

When he was seated, she explained with occasional interruptions from Lady Paxton the problem and their tentative plan.

"Now, let me be sure I understand this," he said. "You ladies want me to march into a brothel that will be crowded with drunk and disorderly men, and guarded by Lord knows how many bully boys like Bart, and rescue a young girl who may or may not wish to be rescued. Do I have it right?"

"Well . . . Yes. More or less," Allyson said.

"Not dressed as a footman, of course," Lady Paxton said. "I shall provide you the clothing of a gentleman."

"Oh, that makes all the difference in the world," he quipped.

"It will get you in the door," Allyson retorted.

"But how will it get me *out?*"

"We will also supply you with enough money to buy the girl's services," Lady Paxton said.

"How am I then to get out of the Fish place with the girl? What if she does not want to come?"

"That probably will not be a problem—her not wanting to leave." Allyson felt herself blushing. "The girls are usually drunk or drugged for their first time."

As he sat thinking it all over—at least that was what Allyson thought he was doing—she added in a helpful tone, "Molly and I will be able to draw you a plan of the place."

"Never mind. I have been there," he said absently.

"You *have?*" both women responded.

He looked up and seemed distinctly uncomfortable. "Not what you think," he mumbled. "I had to rescue one of my m—uh, one of my mates—who thought he could handle Bart. He could not."

"Oh. They—they will not recognize you, will they?" Allyson asked.

"They probably *wouldn't,*" he said, his choice of verb indicating continuing doubt about the plan. "I was in an army uniform at the time. With soldiers, as with servants, people tend to see the clothing and not the person in it."

There was a little pause; then Lady Paxton said, "Well. It should be all right, then. And Lady Allyson and I will be there to help."

"Be there? Oh, no. No." His tone was adamant.

"Not *in* the place, but we will take you there in a coach and remain available for when you bring her out," Lady Paxton explained.

"Frankly, ladies, you have no business being within ten miles of that place. John Coachman—"

"Will drive, of course, but we *will* be there," Allyson insisted.

Nathan took the seat opposite Lady Allyson and signaled the coachman to start. They were using the same plain coach Allyson regularly used in visiting the Fairfax sisters.

"I still do not like the idea of you and Lady Paxton coming along," he said. "I am not overly fond of *my* being involved in this escapade."

"Methinks the gentleman doth protest too much—I saw your reaction when we told you of Helen. You were shocked, too."

"Well . . . Yes, but that sort of thing goes on all the time, you know."

"I do know, but one child saved is one child saved."

"I cannot argue with that profound bit of logic," he said.

Suddenly, Lady Allyson looked startled. She stared into the corner of the coach, and Nathan felt impelled to move over. It was almost as though a small elbow had touched his ribs, but so softly that he was not actually sure he had felt anything.

"No, you cannot be—" Lady Allyson leaned forward, still regarding the empty seat beside him.

"Be *what?*" he asked.

She shifted her gaze to him. "B-be so callous as you try to sound." Her gaze slid back to his side. "Yes, I forgot—again." She sounded testy.

"What did you forget?" Nathan asked.

She looked directly at him again. "I . . . uh . . . forgot to ask if you were carrying a firearm."

"Yes, of course. I doubt any sane man goes into that part of the city at night without protection."

She settled back into her seat and said no more to him until they arrived at Lady Paxton's residence. Nathan wondered briefly if Lady Allyson was given to falling into short trances. He had heard of such. A person would seem oblivious to his or her surroundings for a few minutes, then snap back to reality. Perhaps she suffered from that condition, which so far as he knew—and certainly in her case—posed no danger to the sufferer, nor to others.

In a spare bedchamber, Lady Paxton had laid out a complete set of outer clothing for a gentleman's evening on the town. He assumed the garments had belonged to her late husband.

"I have included two pairs of shoes," she said. "I hope one of them will come close to fitting. If you need help arranging the neckcloth, either Lady Allyson or I can help." She smiled. "We both have younger brothers, you know."

"I think I shall manage." The thought of Lady Allyson

close enough to perform such an intimate duty did sound enticing, though.

A short while later, he entered the small drawing room in which the two women waited.

"Not a perfect fit, but close," he said.

"Ver-ry nice," Lady Paxton said approvingly, but it was the silent admiration he saw in Lady Allyson's eyes that warmed his heart—and other aspects of his anatomy.

"Here, you will need this." Lady Allyson handed him a thick wallet to put inside his jacket, along with the pistol that was already there.

"How much is in it?"

"Something over fifty pounds," she replied. "It was all we could scrape together in such a short time."

"Fifty pounds! The girl would have to be Aphrodite herself to command such a price!"

"No one said you have to spend it all." Lady Allyson was obviously striving for a light note.

She is nervous, he thought, *but—hell!—so am I.* "Have you any brandy?" he asked of Lady Paxton.

"Of course." She gave him a questioning look, but rose to pour a generous amount of the amber liquid.

"Not too much," he cautioned. "If I am going to appear foxed, I should smell that way, too."

"Then sprinkle a bit beneath your collar," Lady Paxton advised. "That is what some ladies do with perfume."

"Good idea."

In the carriage a few minutes later, Lady Allyson wrinkled her nose and said, "Well, yes, you *do* smell foxed." They all laughed nervously, but were then silent until they neared the Fish establishment.

As he stepped out of the coach, he heard Lady Allyson say sharply, "No, this is no place for a young lady."

He turned back briefly. "I *tried* to tell you that earlier."

She shifted her gaze to hold his for a long moment. "Be careful, Nathan," she said softly. "Please be very careful."

He swallowed. "I will." He wanted to kiss her right there

and then. Instead, he turned to make his way along the pavement to the door of the brothel. He had the strangest feeling that he was not alone, but of course he was.

He entered the establishment easily enough. Bart was not at the door, but his counterpart, a big, square-looking man, gave Nathan a piercing look.

"You been here before?" he asked.

"No, I don't shrink—think—so." Nathan deliberately slurred his speech. "Might have done, though. Heard there was some special fun to be had here tonight."

There was a great deal of boisterous noise coming from the first floor above. Loud male voices were punctuated with shrill feminine shrieks.

"Yes, it ain't started yet, though," the big man said. "You still got time, if you got money."

"Th-that I have. Good English money." He patted his coat and looked around him rather foolishly. "Right now I need another drink."

"Right upstairs, sir. Our girls will take good care of you. Real good care of you."

Nathan felt the man watching him as he went above stairs, deliberately stumbling twice. The room above was furnished in elegant, comfortable, deep blue furniture. Scantily clad young women hung on the arms of several men. Musicians occupied a small dais at one end of the room. Servants attired like the musicians in light blue livery served drinks freely. Apparently, Francis Fish was using alcohol to lubricate the wheels of anticipation.

A crowd of forty or fifty clients in the room represented a wide range of ages. A few might be students on holiday from university, and a few were on the nether side of their seventh decade. Most were somewhere in between. The men were becoming louder and more boisterous. *Like schoolboys on an outing,* Nathan thought.

He walked around sipping a glass of wine and pretending to have had far more drink than he had.

Impatience emerged as the dominant emotion in the room. "Where's the gel?" someone shouted.

"Bring 'er out," another demanded.

Francis Fish was a tall woman of ample proportions. Her red hair undoubtedly had a good deal of help, for her skin betrayed her age—late forties, early fifties, Nathan concluded. She was dressed in a tight red satin dress, which revealed a generous amount of bosom. When she apparently judged her audience ready, she had one of the musicians burst forth with a loud fanfare. The room became quiet.

"Gentlemen," she called, "the moment you have been waiting for. I give you"—more fanfare—"Helen!"

A young girl was pushed up beside the madam. A collective intake of breath sounded through the room. Helen was dressed to suit the image suggested by her name, in a sheer toga-like garment that covered all and revealed all. The fabric was draped enticingly over firm young breasts and lithe legs. There was a hint of shadow at the juncture of her legs. Her arms were bare. She was feminine perfection. But it was her face that took the breath away. It was a classic oval with finely arched brows set off by golden blond hair. She was an artist's dream of an untouched Venus.

Francis Fish waited for her clients to start salivating, then called out, "Now, was she not worth waiting for?" She leaned close to the girl. "Smile, sweetheart." The girl did, revealing perfect white teeth behind rosebud lips, but it was the smile of an automaton.

Men bellowed their approval.

"Who will start the bidding?" Mrs. Fish asked.

"Three guineas," a voice called from the rear. Nathan suspected it came from one of Mrs. Fish's minions, and it occurred to him that three guineas was more than a month's pay for many men on the Peninsula.

The price edged up, a few shillings at a time, to five guineas, then seven, eight, nine, and finally, ten. The bidding leveled off at ten.

Mrs. Fish raised Helen's arm and twirled the girl around to urge her customers on. "A virgin, gentlemen. As sweet as they come. And all yours—perhaps."

"Ain't no whore in London worth more'n ten guineas," a portly, well-dressed man muttered.

"I will bid twelve guineas," shouted an old man in a querulous voice. He might have been the girl's great-grandfather.

"Sure you are capable, Gramps?" asked one of the younger men who had dropped out of the bidding early on.

"I am slow, but I am good," the old man retorted to general laughter.

Nathan had placed a bid earlier, but then waited. Now, he bid thirteen guineas in a voice used to conveying orders across areas of a battlefield.

"Fifteen," the old man said in a triumphant tone.

"Twenty," Nathan said in the same steady tone.

The old man gave up. "You have bested me, sir. I agree with Hedley—ain't no whore in London worth so much."

Nathan counted out the money into Mrs. Fish's outstretched hand.

"Enjoy yourself, lovey," she said. She looked harder at Nathan, and her brow creased in a small frown. "You know, I feel I should know you."

"Unlikely, ma'am," Nathan lied glibly. "I have been in India with the company for the last ten years."

"A nabob," someone muttered. "No wonder he went so high."

Nathan ignored the sour note and reached for the girl's hand. Helen looked at Mrs. Fish questioningly.

"You go on, now, Helen. Be nice to the gentleman."

As a path parted for them in the crowd, there were several bawdy comments, which Nathan ignored, and he doubted Helen understood them. When they exited the room, a servant pointed up the stairs.

"Second door on the right."

He took the girl to the room indicated and shut the door. She seated herself on the edge of the bed.

"Helen!" he said sharply. "Do you *know* what is going on here?" He wanted to know how alert she was, or how deeply she was under the influence of whatever drug she had been given.

"N-not exactly," she said. Her eyes seemed a little more focused than they had earlier.

Rage and pity stormed through Nathan. He willed himself to be calm. That anyone should be allowed to treat a child so! He knelt in front of her.

"Mrs. Fish is not a nice person," he said. *There's the understatement of the century.*

"She isn't?" Curiosity rather than disbelief colored her tone. "She let me play with her cat." She seemed to look right through Nathan. "What's *your* name?"

"My name is Nathan, and I am going to help you."

"No, I mean *her* name." She pointed behind Nathan.

Nathan, with a fleeting image of Allyson's taking it upon herself to follow him, looked behind him. "Who? There's no one there."

"Oh." She nodded profoundly. "Yes, all right."

Suddenly it struck him. It was not merely drugs that accounted for the rather dull look in Helen's eyes. This beautiful human being with an abundance of physical attributes had been shorted when it came to mental abilities. *And damn her hide, that Fish woman knows it!*

"Helen, listen to me. I am going to take you away from here."

"Can she come, too?" Again she pointed into thin air.

"Of course she can," he said, placating her. "Two very nice ladies will take care of you for a while."

"Do they have pets? I like animals."

"I am sure they do. Now listen carefully. We are going to walk down the front stairs—"

"I'm not allowed in the front yet."

"Tonight you are, but you must stay very close to me— hold on to the waistband of my trousers—and *don't* let go, no matter what. Can you do that?"

She nodded. "Are we having an adventure?"

"You might say that. All right—shall we go?"

The hallway was empty, but when they reached the first floor, the flunky who had given directions before stood in front of the drawing room door.

"That was quick." He leered. "You sure you got your money's worth?"

"Don't take all day if you know what you're about." Nathan lurched drunkenly toward the young man; Helen held tight. Nathan had his pistol flat in the palm of his hand, and he slapped it against the side of the flunky's head. The youngster sank to the floor like a sack of grain.

"Come on." Nathan urged Helen down the next flight of stairs where the same bully boy stood guard at the entrance.

"Hey! Where you think you're goin'?" The man reached for a bellpull.

"Out," Nathan said airily.

"No, you ain't." The big, barrel-chested man with arms the size of hams moved to block the door.

"No!" a female voice screamed behind Nathan. It was Mrs. Fish. "You paid for her services this night, not her person. She's mine!"

Nathan stepped to the side, keeping Helen behind him as the Fish woman came on down the stairs.

"You cannot take her from the premises, sir. Now go on back upstairs and enjoy yourself." The woman was reasoning with a drunk. "I'll have a bottle brought to your room. Come, Helen." She reached a hand for the girl, who cowered next to Nathan, clearly not understanding what was going on. "Mack!" Mrs. Fish gestured to the bully.

"I think not," Nathan said in a clear, sober tone. He leveled the pistol at Mrs. Fish's left breast. "We are leaving, and you, madam, will call off Mack here and see us safely out. Is that clear?"

Her eyes sparked with anger and fear. Fear won out. "Stay back, Mack." She looked at the sober, determined man before her. "Now I recognize you. You made trouble for me before."

"Then you also know I mean business. Now open the door carefully and walk out before us. If you scream or make a move, or if Mack here fails to behave, you, madam, are a dead woman." He hoped she would have no inkling of his reluctance to pull that trigger.

As she started down the front steps, the Rutherford coach drove up. Suddenly, Mrs. Fish stepped on a round stone about the size of an apple, fell down the rest of the steps, and sprawled ignominiously in the dirt. Nathan would have sworn the steps had been swept clean when he entered.

"Hurry!" Allyson called from the open door of the coach.

He bundled Helen in and followed her, reaching to close the door even as John Coachman whipped up the horses.

Chapter 18

Allyson knew her comment earlier about the Fish establishment not being a place for young ladies had puzzled Lady Paxton.

"Did you change your mind about our being here?"

"Oh, no." Allyson fell back on her standard explanation when caught out about Maryvictoria. "I was just thinking aloud."

Now, as Nathan and Helen clambered into the coach, Maryvictoria reappeared, squeezing herself in beside Helen, who was terrified.

"You will be all right," Maryvictoria assured Helen. "These are good people."

"Are you sure?" Helen whispered.

She can see you? Allyson asked, remembering this time to communicate silently.

"Yes," the ghost child said. "People like Helen have special powers. I 'spect it is God's way of evening things out a little for them."

Maryvictoria continued to reassure Helen, who responded in barely audible whispers. Allyson knew that to Nathan and Lady Paxton Helen appeared to be talking to herself.

"I have heard of children creating imaginary playmates," Lady Paxton said, "but Helen appears a bit old for such."

Nathan said quietly, "*Appears* is the key word, my lady."

"Are you suggesting what I think you are?" Lady Paxton asked, putting a finger discreetly to her head.

"Yes."

Lady Paxton clenched her gloved hands in her lap. "Oh, that monstrous, monstrous woman! How could anyone be so depraved as to—"

"The Fish woman deserves every foul name one might attach to her," Nathan said, "but I doubt she is the only guilty party."

"Her family?" Allyson asked, appalled.

Nathan nodded. "*Someone* put the girl on a London stage. I doubt she came up with the idea herself."

They took Helen to the Fairfax sisters, who gladly welcomed her. Their man Boskins was in the room when Allyson and her companions were preparing to leave.

"Are you quite positive you do not want us to send extra help to guard against any retaliation?" Allyson asked.

"I do not think it will be necessary, Lady Allyson," Priscilla Fairfax said. "We employ two men besides Boskins, who is himself quite, quite capable."

"Besides," Penelope said, "our neighbors like us and what we do. I believe they have made it very clear to Francis Fish and her Bart that they will be tolerated only so long as they leave *us* alone."

Boskins nodded at this.

A few days later, Lady Paxton reported that she had sent someone to Helen's home parish to inquire about the girl. An older brother had put Helen on the stage, but he apparently had the tacit, if not overt, approval of her parents. Allyson and Lady Paxton agreed that Helen was undoubtedly safe where she was, and eventually a suitable home might be found for her.

"I doubt not the 'suitable home' may remain Fairfax House itself," Allyson said when she explained all this to Nathan during a morning ride. "Mr. and Mrs. Boskins are quite taken with Helen."

* * *

Those morning rides were a continuing source of enjoyment—and worry—to Nathan. Such a predictable routine in activities made one vulnerable. He tried to avoid this hazard by varying their route to and from the park. Yet, the park in early morning was nearly always their destination. He had become intensely aware of other riders and vehicles in the park.

Since the return from Sussex, there were three rather smart-looking male riders who made little secret of their interest in the lovely Lady Allyson, but none had approached her. As for vehicles, there was often an assortment. Some obviously used the park at that hour as a shortcut from one part of town to another. Some were older people in open or closed carriages who, he surmised, wanted to be out but could no longer ride.

He tried to observe these especially, but they changed on a daily basis. He did notice one in particular. It was a closed coach, but the single occupant—a heavily veiled woman in black—kept the windows open. The coach appeared two or three times a week. The driver seemed a taciturn type who never returned the tipped hat or raised whip greeting of other "regulars."

To add to Nathan's worries, there was Lady Rutherford's unfinished business with Cranston. She had arranged to meet the man between certain shelves in Hatchard's bookshop, with Nathan placed on the other side. She had insisted on delivering what money she could and pleading for more time.

"A hundred pounds?" Cranston growled. "A hundred pounds? Do you take me for a fool, madam?"

"It is a start," she said. "Besides, that is a fortune to many people."

"Not to me, and you must know that. Are you all about in the head? Did I not tell you that my price was ten times this amount?"

"You did, but I cannot—"

"You wore more than that in jewels at the last ball you attended!"

"Most of the jewels are not mine; they are part of the Rutherford entail. Others are personal gifts that Rutherford would surely miss."

"That, my love, is not my concern."

"I cannot—"

"You *can,* and you will." His voice was icy. "It is still early in the day; you can take some of those baubles to a moneylender now and meet me here *tomorrow* with a thousand pounds."

"Nine hundred," she said.

"A thousand," he replied. "You owe me this much for the trouble you have given me. A thousand—tomorrow."

"Tomorrow is impossible," she insisted in a weak voice.

"Tomorrow—or you know the consequences."

He stalked away, leaving her "Please—" hanging in the air.

"You heard," the countess said to Nathan.

"Yes, and obviously he sees that you are willing to pay, and that he can bleed you completely dry in a matter of time."

"But—"

"My lady, you simply must consider informing His Lordship and letting him help you handle this situation. I doubt not *he* would make short work of Cranston."

"O-oh," she moaned.

Fearing she might have attracted attention from others browsing in the shop, Nathan stepped in front of her to hide her from view. "Yes, my lady," he said in a loud voice, "I shall take you to the carriage immediately. Just take my arm."

Later, he managed to convince her not to deliver the money the next day. He reasoned—and she reluctantly agreed—that Cranston would hold off so long as he thought he would eventually receive the money. The next day, Nathan stood by unseen as Jamie delivered the countess's note to Cranston, who swore and ranted. Jamie knew nothing of its contents, which Nathan knew merely repeated her need for more time.

The following morning, all Nathan's worries and fears came crashing in on him.

The ride had started well enough, with Nathan's being especially vigilant as he and Lady Allyson traversed the streets to the park. Once inside the gates, he relaxed a bit, and they rode at a leisurely pace, passing the veiled woman in her coach, as they continued a mild disagreement over a newly published work of the poet Byron.

"Women see more in him than men do," Nathan argued.

"I challenge that rather narrow view," she countered with a laugh.

Just then, a single rider came bounding toward them, head down, intent on driving his mount between theirs. Neither Nathan nor Lady Allyson had any choice but to allow the division. As the rider came barreling forward, he raised an arm on Nathan's side and had in his hand what appeared to be an ice pick. Nathan grabbed the man's arm, throwing him off balance, but the man maintained enough control that he used the momentum of the movement to knock Nathan to the ground, though the attacker followed him.

Occupied as he was in trying to avoid the ice pick, Nathan had no chance to grab his pistol. However, he was aware of a second intruder on the other side of Lady Allyson, and her scream sent chills piercing his heart. He swung hard at the brute on the ground with him. The man grunted and let go of the weapon, but as Nathan rose to his feet, the man managed to trip him. Nathan heard a team approaching at a fast clip. Both he and Allyson screamed "No-o!" as the veiled woman's coach door opened and Allyson, kicking and screaming, was thrust inside.

The coach thundered on.

The second rider, still mounted, came to his companion's aid. With the handle of his riding crop, he dealt Nathan a resounding blow on the head. As Nathan fought against the blackness threatening to overcome him, he was aware of his attacker's remounting and the two of them galloping off.

Nathan dragged himself to an upright position by grabbing at a stirrup of his saddle. He merely hung on for a few seconds, still unsure whether he was going to remain conscious. Finally, he was in the saddle, but of course there was no sign of the riders or the coach. Muttering every obscenity in his vast vocabulary of such, he gathered up the reins of Allyson's horse and followed in the direction the coach had taken, but it had been swallowed up in traffic.

A man occupied the coach along with the veiled woman. He grabbed at Allyson's arms and pinned them to her side. He also managed to wrap his legs around hers to immobilize her.

"Let me go!" she screamed, but then the woman clapped a cloth over her nose and mouth and held it there. Allyson was aware of a strong, pungent odor.

Then she was aware of nothing at all.

The ache in Nathan's head was minor in comparison to the one in his heart. He had failed in what he had come to view as his most important official duty: protecting Lady Allyson. But it had become more than a duty; it was a sacred trust. He was not sure exactly when the once onerous duty had become so vital to his own life, but it had. And he had failed. As many of those obscenities were directed at himself as at the miscreants who had succeeded in abducting her.

On arriving at Rutherford House, Nathan left his precious Bucephalus in the care of a groom and immediately sought an audience with Lady Rutherford, Lord Rutherford being occupied at Whitehall this day.

"Nathan!" she said in alarm. "There is blood on your head! What has happened? Allyson?"

He told the story quickly, not sparing himself in leveling blame.

"I *knew* these rides were unwise," he said with all the wisdom of hindsight. "I should have had Lord Rutherford put a stop to them."

"No, this is my fault." There were tears in her eyes and in her voice. "I should have paid the money."

"We do not know of a certainty that Cranston is behind this," Nathan said. "There are two other possibilities."

"The French. And who else?"

Nathan explained about the rescue of Helen and Allyson's role in foiling the brothel madam a second time.

"Oh, good heavens. Why did she not tell me?"

"Probably to spare you worry. Still, Cranston is a strong possibility." He sighed and looked at the floor, then directly at the countess. "Allyson knew about the letters," he confessed. "She was my accomplice—rather, I was *her* accomplice—in retrieving them." At Her Ladyship's prompting, he gave her a brief account of that particular adventure.

"Oh, my poor, headstrong darling! It *must* be Cranston then. I *should* have paid him. I could have managed it somehow."

"We cannot worry about that now," Nathan said, taking charge. Only later did either he or the countess consider this breech in decorum for a footman. "We must act fast to get her back."

"How?"

"First, find out for certain who has her. I intend to go immediately to the Fish woman and find out what she knows, if I have to strangle her! While I am gone, my lady, I suggest you send a note to His Lordship and explain to him what happened. How much you tell him of your involvement with Cranston is up to you. I will try to respect your privacy."

"I shall do so immediately." She was apparently heartened by having *something* to do.

It was still midmorning when Nathan arrived at the brothel. He pounded on the door repeatedly until someone finally answered.

"What the hell do *you* want?" a sleepy-eyed Mack asked. A young woman in a dressing gown appeared behind him.

"I wish to speak with Mrs. Fish immediately," Nathan said.

"Well, she ain't wantin' to speak with you." Mack started to close the door.

"I have brought my friend with me." Nathan pulled his pistol and pointed it at the man. "Be a good fellow and send this young woman for the madam, and do it *now!*"

Mack gestured to the girl, who quickly disappeared up the stairs. Fifteen minutes later a furious Francis Fish came down the stairs, her hair barely combed. She wore a garish oriental garb of some sort.

"*What* is going on? You!" She recognized Nathan. "You get out of my house this very instant. What's the idea of intruding on the only chance we have to sleep?"

"I am not leaving until I get the information I came for."

"Information?" She sneered. "I wouldn't give you the price of a pound of tea in China—if I knew it! Now you just put that silly toy away and get out of here."

Nathan lowered the gun, but kept it in his hand. He heard Mack breathe deeply. "I think I should introduce myself. I am Captain Lord Nathan Thornton. I work with the government."

"Well, la-di-da. Am I supposed to be impressed?"

"My immediate superior is the Earl of Rutherford. His daughter is Lady Allyson Crossleigh."

"The busybody. I recognized her coach the other night, and you can tell her so. Wonder how she'd like it if I was to drop a hint in certain circles of her coming to a brothel in the dead of night?"

"Perhaps you can run upstairs and ask her yourself," Nathan suggested, but he already thought he might be fishing in the wrong sea.

"And just what do you mean by that?"

"Lady Allyson was kidnapped this morning."

"And you suspect me, or Bart?"

Nathan shrugged. "It occurred to me that you might want to frighten her to stop her work in this part of town."

"I'd like nothing better, but I ain't so stupid as to be messing with a peer's daughter." She glared at him. "You woke me from a sound sleep for *this,* when I didn't get to bed 'til after five this morning?"

"Look, woman—"

"Mrs. Fish to you."

"Mrs. Fish. If it turns out you had anything at all to do with Lady Allyson's abduction, I shall personally hire Bow Street Runners to follow your clients and broadcast to their families their association with you. I daresay your business would slack off considerably."

The look she gave him told him she knew the threat was real.

He went on. "And this promise applies equally if there is ever a repeat of that affair with the girl Helen. If you want to stay in business, you stick to females who know what they are getting into."

"Are you quite finished?" she asked in a haughty tone, but it had a false ring. "I know nothing of the lady's disappearance, but you are welcome to search the premises, if you so desire. Mack, show him around. I am going back to bed."

Nathan rather admired the old harridan's spirit, and somewhat to his surprise, he believed her.

"I'll come back if I need to," he threatened, and left.

Allyson drifted in and out of consciousness, finally becoming aware of her surroundings. She was lying on a makeshift pallet on a cold stone floor. A blanket had been tossed over her. She looked around. The room was small and had one window with bars on it.

"Thank goodness you have finally waked up."

Maryvictoria materialized, sitting cross-legged in the middle of the floor, her skirt spread modestly over her knees.

"Maryvictoria! What are you doing here? And . . . Where is *here?* Where are we?"

"An empty warehouse near the docks."

"I am thirsty," Allyson said crossly.

"There is a jug of water and a cup over by the door. And a chamber pot in that corner." She pointed to the corner opposite Allyson.

"All the necessities of genteel living," Allyson said. She rose, felt slightly dizzy, then righted herself. She tried the door. Locked. She pounded on it. "Release me at once!" she shouted.

"There is no one out there," Maryvictoria said. "Well, no human."

Allyson bent down to peek through the keyhole. What she could see of the other room was nearly as bare as this one, but there was a small stove with a kettle on it. Steam rose from its spout. Someone had been here a short while ago. She could also see the corner of a table and a chair. Then she sensed movement, and a large black dog loped into her range of vision. He came over and sniffed curiously at the door.

"How long have I been here?" she asked, returning to the pallet.

"A few hours. 'Tis after noon now."

"You were there, when they . . . uh . . . snatched me?"

"I have been accompanying your rides for some time."

"Without telling me? Maryvictoria, that is outrageous."

"Well, to be truthful, I usually just hover in the vicinity, but when I saw what was happening, I decided to come along to keep you company." Maryvictoria giggled. "They had no idea they had an extra passenger."

"Did you happen to see? Was Nathan badly injured?"

"He is all right," Maryvictoria assured her.

"Good. . . . Who are these people who grabbed me? What do they want?"

Before Maryvictoria could respond, Allyson heard a door open and close, then the voices of two men.

She jumped up and peered through the keyhole. She could see a dark-haired portly young man place some odd-shaped packets on the table. He began to unwrap them as the other man, perhaps five years his senior and more finely dressed, poked at the fire in the stove. She recognized the second one as the man in the coach with the veiled woman.

The dog raised its nose toward the table. "No, Rex. Down, boy," the younger one said. The dog obeyed reluctantly, it seemed.

"Food." Allyson realized that, having missed her breakfast, she was hungry. "I do hope they mean to share." She pounded on the door. "Let me out of here!" she yelled.

"Ah, sleeping beauty awakes," the older of the two said. "Calm down, my lady," he called. "You will be here some time yet. No sense wasting your energy."

Recognizing the sense of this, Allyson returned to the pallet. "Who are they, Maryvictoria? You must have had some hint."

Maryvictoria looked sad. "They did not say anything on the way here that would identify them. They talked about sending your papa a note."

"They could be French," Allyson mused aloud. "But these two do not sound French. They are definitely English, and perhaps traitors."

Soon the lock on the door rattled, the door opened, and the taller and older of the two men handed her a piece of paper on which were meat and cheese and bread. When she had placed it on the pallet beside her, he reached through the door for the kettle his companion handed him and poured from it into her cup. The dog had followed him in and approached Allyson. She held out her hand to him and then patted him.

The man used his foot to push the dog out of the way. "Some watchdog you are. Call your dog, Willard."

"Rex!" The dog returned to the other room.

The man with the kettle handed her the cup. She placed her gloved hands around it, savoring the warmth.

"This is far from the elegance to which you are accustomed, Lady Allyson, but people hungry enough and desperate enough make do with what they have." He spoke in the refined tones of one educated at a public school.

"Is that why you are willing to be a criminal—perhaps a traitor?"

"Oh, dear. Such vulgar terms—but in a word, yes. It is either that or *work* for a living. Bastard sons have fewer choices in life, you see."

Allyson sniffed contemptuously. "There is always the church, the army, the law; an honorable man would—"

"Work. Yes, I know. However, I was born to be one of the idle rich, but, unfortunately, on the wrong side of the English blanket."

"I think someone must have troubled himself enough to provide you a decent education," Allyson observed.

He bowed mockingly. "Clever lady."

"My father will have you hanged for this outrage."

"Ah, but first he must find us. Before that, he will deal with us, give us what we want, and then we shall be gone."

"He will not give you anything," she said defiantly.

"I rather think he will, when the alternative is to have his daughter's lovely body found floating in the Thames." He paused. "He should be getting our note within the hour."

A combination of steel and mockery in his tone sent chills down Allyson's spine.

"I see we understand each other," he said as he closed the door and turned the lock from the other side.

"Well!" Maryvictoria stood in the middle of the room in her characteristic stance of hands on her hips. "That one is what we might have called 'a dirty dish' in my day."

"In any day." Allyson turned her attention to the food and very weak tea.

"While you quell that growling beast in your innards, I shall see what *I* can do to make life interesting for those two."

With that, Maryvictoria, unencumbered by gravity or

closed doors, wafted into the next room. Allyson took a last sip of tea and scooted across to peer through the keyhole again.

Both men were seated at the table now. She could see the younger one clearly, and the lower legs and occasionally the hands of the other. The dog Rex lay under the table, and the younger man slipped him a bite from time to time. Maryvictoria began to float around the younger man's head. He batted his hands around his ears. The dog was alerted and began to bark vigorously.

"Damned mosquitoes! They weren't this pesky earlier."

"Must be that wonderful cologne you wear. They are not bothering me, Willard. And *what* is wrong with that beast?"

"Well, they are of a certainty attacking me!" Willard slapped around his head even harder and yelled at the dog.

The other man rose to get the kettle from the stove. "Do you want more tea? Can you not shut that dog up?"

Willard slapped again, shoved his cup over, and told the dog to "Be quiet!" The dog was running in furious circles now, more agitated than ever.

As the one with the elegant accent began to pour, the dog jostled his legs, putting him slightly off balance so that the hot liquid splashed on the table and into Willard's lap.

"Holy Christ, Fitz!" Willard jumped up and danced around in pain. "Watch what you're doing."

"Terribly sorry, old boy. It's that damned dog of yours." Fitz poured his own cup full and returned the kettle to the stove, by which time Willard had reseated himself, still muttering. The dog continued to run around the table and to bark and jump at Maryvictoria. Then suddenly his barks turned into pitiful whines and he slunk out of Allyson's view, his tail between his legs.

As Fitz sought to take his own seat, the chair mysteriously moved, and he banged his bottom soundly on the stone floor.

"Did you move my chair?" he accused.

"I didn't touch your damned chair."

"Well, it did not just move on its own, now, did it?"

"Must have done, or else *you* moved it."

Fitz, muttering under his breath, resituated his chair and sat down. A ghostly feather appeared in Maryvictoria's hand, and she waved it under Willard's nose just as he took a huge swig of tea. He sneezed heartily and spewed tea all over the table and the food he and Fitz had been sharing.

"You stupid oaf!" Fitz said. "Have you no manners at all?"

" 'Tweren't my fault. I tell you, there's something weird going on here." He rubbed a finger across his nostrils and sneezed again.

"The weirdest thing is being paired with *you*," Fitz said in disgust. "I hope that woman knows what she's doing."

"She'll be here soon enough and you can ask her," Willard said petulantly.

Allyson was doubled over, trying not to dissolve into loud, unladylike guffaws of laughter, when Maryvictoria returned.

"It . . . was better . . . than a . . . Punch and Judy show at a country fair," she said, ending on a smothered laugh.

Maryvictoria smiled smugly, and said, "I am glad you enjoyed the show."

"What on earth did you do to poor Rex, though?"

"I thanked him for his help, but when he became too frisky, I told him he would likely end up joining the hounds of hell."

"Oh. Well, it was effective."

Maryvictoria's tone became more serious. "I must leave you for a while, Lady Allyson."

Allyson felt a moment of panic. "Leave me? *Why?*"

"I must run an errand, but I promise I shall return."

Chapter 19

When Nathan returned to Rutherford House, Melton directed him immediately to the library. There he found the earl and his countess seated side by side on a sofa. They were holding hands, and the countess had obviously been crying.

"I have told him everything." Her voice was shaky. "Everything," she repeated, exchanging a long look with her husband.

"I know, my love," he said, putting his other hand over their clasped hands. "We should have discussed this years and years ago, but I did not want to bring up a subject that might cause you pain."

"I never wanted you to find out what an utter fool I had been," she said.

The earl focused his attention on the footman. "Have a seat, Nathan. Since you know so much of our story, you may as well have the rest of it."

Nathan sat in a winged back chair facing them. "Very well, my lord, but it is not nece—"

"It is," the older man countered. "Before I start, though, I should tell you that I suspected immediately Cranston might possibly be involved in abducting Allyson."

"Why?" Nathan asked.

"I am not quite so obtuse as I sometimes appear, Captain. I have noticed the worry and stress Lady Rutherford has suffered whenever he appears at a social gathering."

"And I thought I hid it so well," she said with a weak smile.

"Should we not be out looking for him?" Nathan asked, fretting inwardly at this delay in any rescue of Allyson.

"I have several Bow Street Runners out doing precisely that," Rutherford said. "They are to bring him here, using force if necessary."

Nathan nodded. "Good. I suppose we wait, then."

"Yes, hard as that is." The earl paused. "So allow me to tell you the story of one foolish man—"

"And his equally foolish wife," the countess interposed.

The earl patted her hand again. "Katherine was very young when we married; she had not yet had her eighteenth birthday. I was—what?—three and thirty, I think. It was an arranged marriage. We may have had a total of four or five hours together before the wedding. It was not a love match—then." He shared a smile with his wife, then went on.

"Family pressure prompted me to marry—it was time—so I did. Pretty and pleasant, she suited me well enough. My life would not change substantially. I would still have my usual interests of estates, government, and my clubs. A wife would not make much difference, or so I thought. The truth is, I was both indifferent and neglectful."

Lady Rutherford interrupted. "Duncan, darling, you blame yourself too much." She looked at Nathan. "I was young, and very foolish, and I suddenly had all the freedom in the world. No chaperon accompanying me everywhere; no one to tell me what to do, when. It . . . It went to my head. I became involved with a rather fast group—gambling, all-night parties—but I never went too far with it; I kept my vows." This last was directed to her husband.

"I know you did," he said firmly, then turned back to Nathan. "So, there you have it: a pretty young wife neglected by her husband was ripe for the picking when a handsome scoundrel came along to shower her with attention and dreams of romance."

"It started out as a mere flirtation," Lady Rutherford said thoughtfully. "I think now that I must have been trying to get you to notice me. Then it took on a bizarre life of its own. There was a certain intensity and excitement that had been missing—"

"Anyway, to shorten this considerably," the earl said, "I came to my senses, realized what I had almost lost, and began to woo my wife."

"It looks as though you won the fair lady," Nathan said lightly.

"Luckily, I did."

Nathan was determined to focus on Allyson. "So you think Cranston is behind Al—your daughter's abduction?"

"Frankly, I am more inclined to believe it is the French," the earl said. " 'Tis rather early in Cranston's game to resort to such a desperate measure. And the French, with autumn coming on, are, indeed, desperate."

"That was my thought, too, my lord. The French make more sense."

There was a knock on the door. At the earl's bidding, Melton entered to announce the arrival of two Bow Street Runners accompanying Mr. Cranston. Both the earl and Nathan rose.

"All right! I am here," Cranston snarled at the Runners. "Take your hands off me and untie me."

The two Runners, both fit-looking men in their thirties, looked to Lord Rutherford, who nodded. They released Cranston's bonds and stood aside.

"Just what is the meaning of this . . . this abduction?" Cranston blustered, and then mocked, "Katherine, my own love, never tell me you have betrayed me?"

"If you value that pretty face of yours," Rutherford said calmly, "you will not say another word to or about my wife."

Cranston stared at the earl for a moment, then looked away. "So what is it you want of me?"

"The subject *is* abduction," the earl said. "My daughter has been kidnapped, and it has come to my attention that you recently threatened such an action against her person."

"Abducted? Lady Allyson?" Cranston's surprise seemed genuine to Nathan, who was watching him closely. Cranston gave a nervous laugh. "And you think I did it?"

"Did you not threaten my wife with precisely such a consequence if she failed to succumb to your extortion?"

"Well . . . Yes, I suppose I did, but, as you well know, a threat and a deed are very different things." Again, Cranston sounded a bit blustery.

"Are you saying you know nothing of my daughter's kidnapping?"

Cranston sneered. "Are you so sure she is your daughter?"

Rutherford raised a clenched fist, then slowly lowered it. "Yes, I am quite sure," he said calmly. "If you were a gentleman, I would call you out for such a suggestion."

Cranston flushed at the insult Rutherford had just delivered and seemed to take the earl's measure. He apparently came to the conclusion that Nathan had foreseen: that it was contempt, not cowardice, that motivated Lord Rutherford.

"I know nothing about the girl, except that she invaded my home one night and spent some time there alone with a man." He swiveled toward Nathan. "This man, if I am not mistaken."

"Is that so?" the earl asked softly.

"I am wondering how that sort of news will play with the *ton*?" Cranston's tone was suggestive.

"I suppose—for a price—you will see that that information does not get out?" Again, the earl's tone was deceptively soft.

Cranston nodded smugly. "Ah, I see we understand each other perfectly."

"Perhaps not quite so perfectly," Rutherford said, walking to his desk. He opened a drawer and withdrew a handful of papers of varied sizes. "Ever since I noticed you annoying my wife earlier in the Season, I have been quietly buying up your debts. Tradesmen's bills, gambling debts—all of them. And Bow Street is well aware of your other shady dealings."

"What—?" The bluster was fading.

Rutherford read through several of the papers, naming creditors and the amounts owed. He finished with, "You are not a peer, sir. You can, and possibly will, go to debtor's prison." His voice turned steely. "Now—*where* is my daughter?"

"I . . . I do not know." Cranston's tone was much more subdued. "I know nothing; I had nothing to do with—"

Rutherford and Nathan exchanged glances. Nathan shook his head negatively, and Rutherford nodded agreement.

"Very well," the earl said. "We shall take you at your word, for a time at least. If it turns out you did know, you will hang. I promise you that. When Allyson is found, and if you had nothing to do with her disappearance, you, sir, will quit England. Permanently. Is that clear?"

"Oh, quite clear." Cranston pointed at Rutherford's fistful of papers. "You hold all the cards."

"Meanwhile," Rutherford said, "these fellows"—he gestured to the Runners—"will see that you do not leave London until my daughter is found."

Cranston grimaced in defeat and said not another word as the Runners escorted him out.

"Now, we wait," Rutherford said in a resigned tone as he took his seat again beside his wife.

Nathan remained standing. "Perhaps I should be about my duties. I am sure Melton can find several tasks that need my attention."

"Nonsense, Captain," Lord Rutherford said.

"Captain?" the countess queried, apparently having missed her husband's earlier such reference to Nathan.

"Captain," her husband affirmed. "My dear, allow me to present to you Captain Lord Nathan Christopher Thornton."

"Thornton? Thornton. Why, that is Halstead's family name," she said. "The Duke of Halstead was here to see *you*."

Nathan bowed. "To ring a peal over my head, actually."

"I recall now, there was—is—a younger son. And Eastland never let on!" she exclaimed.

"He, too, was sworn to secrecy," Nathan explained as he took the seat Rutherford gestured toward.

"I see no need to keep it a secret any longer, at least not from my wife and daughter," the earl said. "Unless I miss my guess, this whole business is reaching a boiling point."

"I am so frightened," his wife said. "Who knows what French agents will do to her?"

Almost on cue, Melton knocked and entered, bearing a thick message on a salver.

"This just arrived, my lord."

"Is the messenger still here?" Rutherford asked.

"Yes, my lord. I have him in the entranceway—a lad of perhaps ten years. Jamie is with him."

"Hold on to him for a few minutes, Melton."

"Yes, my lord." The butler left the room.

The earl read the note. " 'Tis what we thought—French. They want a whole range of information about our forces and alliances on the Continent." He handed the note over to Nathan, who scanned it quickly.

"Good God! Oh! My apologies, Lady Rutherford."

She inclined her head as if to say his transgression was of little importance, which, in the scheme of things, was true. Nathan read on, his stomach churning into a hard knot with each word.

"They will release her unharmed only when they have verified the information," he read. He stood and began pacing. "That could take a week, or more likely, a fortnight. I—we—cannot leave her in their hands!"

If the earl and his wife were astonished by the intensity of his outburst, neither one chose to make an issue of it.

"Sit down, Captain," the earl commanded. "You are making me dizzy. Bear in mind that we do not know where they are holding her."

"Perhaps the boy knows something." Instead of sitting,

Nathan went out to the entrance, where a frightened young boy sat on a leather-covered bench and looked from Melton to Jamie.

"Ye can't keep me here," the child said belligerently.

"Who'd want to?" Jamie sneered. "Dirty thing like you?"

Nathan sat beside him, but not so close as to frighten the lad. "What is your name?" he asked in a conversational tone.

"Ch-Charles."

"Charles—after a former king, eh? That's a good strong name, Charles."

The boy relaxed a bit. " 'Tis after me gran'da. *He* were named for a king."

"Tell me, Charles. Who gave you the message to deliver here?"

Charles shrugged. "I never seen 'im afore. He give tuppence to bring it."

And probably followed to ensure it was delivered, Nathan thought. "Can you describe the man?"

"I dunno. Maybe."

"Was he riding or walking?"

"Riding. A big gray with a black blaze on its head." The boy's eyes lit up. "I like horses."

"So do I," Nathan said, his tone casual despite his excitement, for the child had given a fair description of one of the horses in the park. "Was he a big man? Fat? Thin?"

"Not too big. Not fat, but not thin."

"Was he more my size," Nathan asked, "or more Jamie's, here?"

"Hmm. More yours, I think. He had odd-colored eyes."

"Odd-colored?"

"They was kind of like a shiny tin kettle, you know?"

"I have seen eyes like that," Nathan agreed. And he had, when he had been relieved of certain documents in Sussex. "How was the man dressed?"

"Well . . . He weren't bang up to the mark, but he were a nob, all the same."

"Did you notice his boots?"

"They was real shiny, like they just been done."

"Did you notice anything about the way he talked?"

"Oh, yeh. He talked like a nob, kind of like you," the boy said.

Nathan saw Jamie look startled, and then a speculative look crossed the young footman's face. Nathan put a hand on the boy's shoulder. "Thank you, Charles. You have been a great help. Mr. Melton will give you another tuppence and let you go home now."

"Really?" The boy's eyes glowed.

Melton nodded as Nathan returned to the library and explained to the earl and his wife what he had learned and his conjecture that the note came via the leader of those who had accosted him in Sussex.

"So we have a tenuous lead on *who,* but the question is, *where* are they holding her?" Rutherford wiped his hand across his eyes.

"Perhaps if we knew anything of that veiled woman," the countess offered tentatively.

"If, indeed, it *was* a woman," Nathan said. "The coach was quite ordinary, like that one of yours Lady Allyson often uses."

They were all silent for a few moments.

"I cannot give up the information they want." Rutherford's anguished voice echoed in the silence. "Hundreds, perhaps thousands, of men would die needlessly."

"I do not want our daughter to become one of the casualties of this interminable war!" Lady Rutherford cried.

"Nor do I, my dear. Nor do I," her husband replied bleakly.

Nathan put his elbow on the arm of the chair and gripped his head, his hand covering his brows. *Think, damn it!* he told himself. *Where could they be holding her? Where?* He fully understood Rutherford's dilemma. God! How he understood! How could anyone even *think* of possibly sacrificing someone you knew and loved passionately for nameless, faceless "others"?

They were not nameless and faceless, though, were they?

Faces and names from every regiment he had ever known swam before him, especially those of men who had died hideous, miserable deaths. But this was *Allyson,* and he did, indeed, passionately love her. A future without her did not bear thinking about. When exactly had that happened? Good grief! Anne had been right. One did not *choose* whom and when to love. He sighed.

"What do you think, Nathan?" the earl asked.

"I think we have to tear this city apart and *find* her," he replied fiercely.

"A city of nearly a million people?" the countess asked gently.

"If that is what it takes, yes. I do not want them to have her for a single day. We can buy a week, perhaps two, for a concerted search."

"You mean by supplying them with doctored information again," the earl said.

Nathan nodded glumly. "I just do not see another way."

"Unfortunately, neither do I," Allyson's father replied.

Lady Rutherford was waging a less than successful battle against her tears. "If only we had *some* idea of where she could be."

Suddenly, a strong breeze passed through the room, blowing several papers across the earl's desk, one of which fell to the floor.

"That is strange. That window is never opened," Lady Rutherford said. "It lets in too much dust and noise from the street."

The earl rose and looked behind the drapery. "It is closed. Must have been a freak wind from the chimney."

"There is no soot on the hearth," his wife observed.

Nathan picked up the piece of paper that had wafted to a rest at his feet. It was a newspaper clipping describing a series of robberies on the docks. "What is this?" he asked, handing it to Rutherford.

"Part of a series of articles on waterfront crimes. Some of the research for a bill Robert Peel is pushing to establish a police force. We need one, but it will never pass," the earl said, restoring order to the papers on his desk. "Strange. I am sure that item was at the bottom of the file, and it appears only the top papers were blown about."

Nathan felt a lightning bolt of inspiration. "That's where Allyson is! I know it! Somewhere on the docks!"

If either of her parents noticed his use of their daughter's given name, they were too caught up in the emotion of the moment to mention it.

"How can you be so sure?" Lord Rutherford asked.

"I cannot explain it," Nathan replied, "I just know it." How could he possibly tell them of a warming pan that seemed to come from thin air, or an apple-sized stone on a previously clean step, or of their daughter's strange habit of "thinking aloud"?

The earl shrugged. "We have to start somewhere. We may as well start our search there, as soon as we can call in a number of our people and solicit their help."

"I am coming, too," the countess announced.

The earl shook his head. "No, Katherine, love. I'd rather you stayed here. It could prove a dangerous venture."

"I promise I will not get in your way, but I *am* coming," she insisted. "She is my daughter, too."

"Very well."

An hour later, the Earl of Rutherford and Captain Thornton set out with several of Rutherford's male servants to search the docks for the missing Lady Allyson. The countess rode in the "plain" coach driven by John Coachman and accompanied by two armed footmen. The others—all heavily armed, as well—rode and were dressed in plain clothing that would allow them to blend in with local denizens of the targeted area. Not one Rutherford retainer had hesitated to accept this dangerous assignment, though all had been given the choice of opting out.

Chapter 20

Arriving in the London docks area shortly after dark, the Rutherford party left the countess, the coach, and their own horses hidden in a side alley. They were in the care of the coachman, two footmen, and a very young groom who had begged to be included. Nathan thought this lad, like Jamie, was infatuated with Lady Allyson. He smiled to himself as he considered the fact that she was always kind to the servants, thanking them for small services and asking about their families when they returned from half-days off. No wonder they loved her so. The only Rutherford servant with whom she was ever less than gracious was Nathan himself. She must have sensed early on that *he* was able to respond in kind.

The smile faded as he contemplated the danger she might be in now. *Lord, let me be right about the location,* he prayed. If Rutherford had not already declared the charade over, Nathan would have done so himself. She would be furious, he predicted, when she found out the truth. Surely she would come around, though. That kiss at Sussex and the electrified atmosphere that so often enveloped them had to mean something.

He drew himself back to the task at hand. No one had

raised a question or even an eyebrow when the footman Nathan had taken charge of the search. He knew there would be speculation later. That would be then; this was now. As planned back at Rutherford House, the men split into groups of two and three and began to visit dockside taverns to question locals about unusual activities. Nathan and Lord Rutherford would question patrons in The Blue Duck and wait for others to report to them there.

Waiting was hard. Nathan wanted to be out there with each team. Would they ask the right questions? Obtain the right information? What if they missed something? Was Allyson all right?

"You are going to worry yourself into a fit of apoplexy, if you don't calm down, son," the earl said. "There has not been time yet for our people to report."

Nathan had not realized he was drumming his fingers on the table and looking frequently toward the door. He and Rutherford had ordered ale and questioned the patrons. The answers had been disappointing.

Nathan felt sheepish at the earl's comment. "I am not skilled at the waiting game." He did not add that never before had the stakes been so very high for him personally.

"Are you having second thoughts about this? Are we on a wild goose chase?"

"No, I don't think so, sir. I feel instinctively that we are right. It is just—"

The earl sighed. "I know." Rutherford took a swallow of his ale, set the tankard down carefully, and peered at his companion. "I think perhaps your worry has a deeper source than the Foreign Office mission."

"I . . . What do you mean?"

"I think, Captain Thornton, that you are in love with my daughter."

"I . . . I am, my lord. Do you find that idea distasteful?" Nathan held his breath. This was not the way he had envisioned presenting himself to Lord Rutherford as a suitor for Lady Allyson's hand.

"No, I do not find it distasteful in the least. You have *my* approval. Gaining Allyson's consent might prove slightly more difficult."

"Thank you, sir." Nathan offered his hand, and the earl gripped it warmly.

"Don't let your personal feelings cloud your judgment tonight, Thornton."

"I shall certainly try not to."

They sat in companionable silence for several more minutes. Then Robert, the underbutler, entered.

"We think we have something," he said in a low, but excited, tone. "There are three warehouses not far from here that are more or less empty since the war with the United States. They were used to store cotton, you see."

"Go on," the earl urged.

"There's not been much activity around any of them, until today. There was a coach there this morning, and two men have been seen going in and out. And there's two lights in one, in the back."

"That's it," Nathan said. "It must be."

"Sounds promising," the earl said cautiously. "Good work, Robert."

Nathan stood. "Let's go. We shall meet the others outside, look this place over, then decide how to approach it."

The warehouse in question was located on the river. Two landing piers extended from large doorways in the warehouse out into the river to allow boats to unload cargo rowed in from ships anchored in deeper water. The front of the building, which ran parallel with the street, was dark. Two large doorways faced the street to allow for distributing goods to wagons. The windows on the ground floor in both the front and the back were barred. A narrow strip of hard earth ran along the back of the building, passing under one end of each pier.

Nathan posted men on the street side to stand watch at either end of the building, then led the rest around to the back.

"Be careful!" he cautioned. "The ground is not very solid

out there where the tide washes at it. Misleading when the tide is low, as it is now."

He and Robert crept along the back, stooping to pass under the piers, to look into the lighted windows. Rain and fog and the city's unremitting appetite for coal had encrusted the neglected windows so that one could barely see through them. However, one of the windows was raised about two inches. Two men were idly playing cards at a table in that room.

"Oh, no," Nathan murmured to himself on spotting a large black dog at the feet of the two men.

The dog sensed him about the same time and, jumping to its feet, trotted toward the window, growling, then barking.

"Here, Rex, what's going on?"

One of the men, the better dressed of the two, rose and walked toward the window. Nathan flattened himself against the wall and motioned for Robert to do the same. The window edged up another few inches.

"There's nothing here, I tell you. Now you settle down and behave. We shall have no repeat of that earlier fracas," the man said.

Robert edged along to the other window. "Here, Nathan," he whispered.

There she was! Allyson sat calmly on a pallet on the floor, her arms around her drawn-up knees. Her eyes seemed focused at her feet, on the end of the pallet. And she was . . . Yes, she was talking to herself, though he could not hear her. This window was closed. He tried to edge it up. It would not budge.

"How do we get in?" Robert whispered.

"Entrance to this room seems to be through the other one," Nathan whispered back, "and entrance to that one seems to be from inside the warehouse."

"So we have to get inside somehow."

"Should not be too difficult," Nathan said. "We will try that far door." He gestured to the other end of the building.

"It's locked. And it might be barred from the inside."

"We shall see."

Once again, Nathan had come equipped to pick a lock and made short work of the old-fashioned device. Soon, he and Robert, along with Lord Rutherford and the grooms, Alfred and Harry, slipped inside. It was midnight dark in the interior.

"Wait 'til our eyes adjust," Nathan warned quietly.

"It smells like a stable in here," someone whispered.

Finally, as their eyes adjusted, they could see at the far end of the gigantic open room a sliver of light, which Nathan determined came from the room with the two men. They could also make out huge shapes here and there in the main storage area—rejected or neglected cargo, perhaps?

As they made their way cautiously toward the sliver of light, they heard a sharp whistle from outside, one of their own signals. Then there was a great rattle at one of the doors on the street side of the warehouse. Nathan and his men dived for cover behind the large shapes.

A small coach driven by a pair and carrying lanterns on the sides came right into the building. Obviously, they intended eventually to drive straight through to the next street door on leaving. *That explains the stable smell,* Nathan thought. There were two men on the driver's seat. One of them jumped down and opened the door of the coach opposite the Rutherford party. The watchers could not see the two people who exited the coach, but they did hear a voice—a woman's voice.

"We shall not be long, John," she said.

"Yes, my lady. I'll just have a look at this harness if I can get Ned here to hold their heads."

"My God!" Rutherford exclaimed in a whisper. "Beatrice!"

"Beatrice?" Nathan asked.

"Lady Eggoner."

Nathan instantly recalled that Lady Eggoner was a close friend of Lady Rutherford. "I am sorry, my lord."

Nathan called up Robert and Alfred, Rutherford's head groom. "We need to take care of these two," he said quietly, though the occasional stamp of horses' hooves on the stone floor and the rattle of the carriage or a harness was making their exchanges easier. "Alfred, I assume you can handle the horses?"

"Yes, of course."

In less time than it had taken to explain to the other two, the Eggoner servants had each been quietly dispatched into a long sleep. Each was then tied and gagged in case the sleep proved to be shorter than expected.

With Alfred left to see that the Eggoner team did not bolt and create a huge disturbance, Nathan now had himself and three others remaining on his team—Lord Rutherford, Robert, and Harry.

"There is the woman and three men," Nathan explained softly. "We will have to presume that they are all armed just as we are. However, we shall, I think, have the element of surprise on our side."

He took a deep breath. "Let's go!"

"Oh, I am so glad you came back!" Allyson exclaimed when Maryvictoria reappeared.

"I *told* you I would."

"I know, but I was afraid something might happen—"

"To me?" Maryvictoria scoffed. "You forget, my friend, that anything that could harm me in your world already did—many, *many* years ago."

"Oh, so now we are friends, are we?" Allyson asked lightly. "Good. I rather like that idea."

"What happened while I was gone?"

"Those two have been bickering. They seem to be waiting for some female and another person. I . . . I think they plan to . . . to take me somewhere else." Allyson's voice rose in a note of fear. "How will anyone ever find me?"

"Now, now. Not to worry. I daresay help is on the way."

"Do you know that for a certainty?"

"Well . . . No," Maryvictoria admitted. "But any looby should be able to read signs right under his nose!"

"I have no idea what you are talking about."

"Just be patient. If they move you, I shall go along. Have I not told you everything will be all right?"

"Yes, but you are not the one shivering with cold, hungry, angry, feeling begrimed and violated, and . . . and altogether miserable!" Allyson ended on a restrained wail.

"Please, Lady Allyson, you must, as they say, 'screw your courage to the sticking place.' "

Allyson caught hold of herself. "Of course, you are right. I will *not* turn into a watering pot."

There was the clatter of a door opening in the next room. The dog began barking at this intrusion, and continued until Willard quieted him. There were now two more voices, one male and one female, joining those of the bickering Willard and Fitz.

"You should do something about that beast," the woman said disdainfully.

"He's had a rough day," Willard explained.

"I know that woman's voice." Allyson scooted over to the keyhole, but saw only Fitz clearly, though she could barely make out part of a woman's skirt. "Who *is* she?"

The woman spoke again. "I hear her talking. Who is in there with her? Have you somehow compromised our plan?" She sounded indignant.

"Hold on, my lady," Fitz said lazily. "She talks to herself. If you ask me, Lady Allyson is a bit wrong in the upper story."

Allyson sputtered. "Did you hear that?"

Maryvictoria giggled.

"I do not believe it," the woman said. "I have known her since she was born; she is quite, quite intelligent."

"Only she talks to herself from time to time," Willard chimed in with a crude laugh.

"Oh, my heavens!" Allyson could hardly believe her ears. "Lady Eggoner! One of Mama's closest friends."

The man who had come in with Lady Eggoner now spoke. Allyson detected a slight accent. French? Belgian?

"Bring her out here. We will have her write a note to her papa to reinforce the one we sent earlier; then, while you deliver the note, we shall take the lady into the country."

Before Allyson could become indignant or fearful at this news, the door, which had apparently not been latched behind Lady Eggoner and her companion, crashed open. There was the sound of others entering the room.

"Perhaps you would like to tell him yourself," a familiar, dear voice said.

"Nathan!" Allyson breathed.

Another familiar and dear voice added, "Yes, I should be very interested in such."

"Papa!" Allyson called out.

Her cry may have distracted her rescuers, for Allyson could see Fitz's hand reaching into his coat, which hung on the chair in which he had been sitting before Lady Eggoner came in.

But then Harry was beside Fitz with a gun barrel at Fitz's temple. "Naughty, naughty," Harry said, relieving Fitz of his weapon.

"Robert and I will keep watch on these miscreants while Harry relieves them of the rest of their weapons," Lord Rutherford said. "Nathan, you see to my daughter."

"Yes, my lord."

"Duncan, I can explain—" Lady Eggoner began.

"Oh, you will have ample opportunity to do so," Rutherford replied.

The lock turned in Allyson's door and Nathan came in, still holding a pistol in one hand. Seeing only Allyson in the room, he put the weapon in his waistband and kicked the door closed. Without thinking, Allyson threw herself into his arms.

"Oh, Nathan, Nathan, I am so glad . . . to see you." She sobbed in relief.

He tightened his arms around her and showered kisses on her forehead, her eyes, her cheeks, her nose. "Sh. Sh, my love. You are safe, my darling."

He kissed her again, this time a long, deep kiss on her mouth. She responded fiercely, seemingly unable to get near enough, drinking in his closeness, his warmth, his smell. She moaned softly and clung to him feverishly. He buried his face in her hair and said softly, "It is all right now, love. Please, do not cry, my sweet."

"Oh, Nathan. I love you. I . . . I never realized—"

"I know. I love you, too. I want to marry you, Allyson." Then he added, "What a flat I've turned out to be! I meant to do this properly."

She felt as though someone had thrown cold water in her face. She drew back. "M-marry? Oh. Oh, no. It cannot be."

"You love me, but you refuse to marry me? Why?"

"I could never bring that sort of disgrace on my family. I simply could not do it."

"Because I am a soldier—and a footman? Is that it? If I were the son of a peer, you'd have me?"

"Well . . . Y-yes," she sobbed. Don't you see, it just would not work. I love you, but—"

"No 'buts,' Lady Allyson. You either do or you do not. Love must be unconditional." He released her. "We must finish this later."

"There can be no 'later,' " she said sadly.

"So says your pride now."

He opened the door and pushed her gently toward her father, who, now that Nathan could take over in helping to watch over the four captives, enfolded his daughter in his arms.

"Are you all right?" the earl asked.

"N-no. Yes. I mean, I think so." She *was* all right—physically—apart from being hungry and uncomfortable. However, those moments with Nathan had been soul-shattering. Would she have the courage to refuse him again?

Her father put a finger under her chin and forced her to meet his gaze. "Are you sure you are all right? They did not mistreat you?"

"I will be fine. They did not mistreat me."

"Good," he said. "I shall send you home then in our own coach. Your mother is waiting outside by now. The two of you will be well guarded. I would accompany you, my child, but Nathan and I must clear up this situation in order to report to the secretary and the prime minister tomorrow."

"I understand, Papa."

A few minutes later, she was on her way home, clasped in her mother's arms. Exhausted from tension and emotions, she hardly heard her mother's comforting words. At home, after a rejuvenating bath and a too-lavish meal sent up from the kitchen, she was finally alone in her own bedchamber. No. Not alone. As Allyson pulled the bedcovers up to her chin, Maryvictoria appeared on the winged back chair near the bed.

"Oh, no," Allyson groaned. "I know what you are going to say."

"And what would that be?"

"That I am being a fool. That I should just throw caution to the wind, and let what will be, be."

"Well, you put it rather nicely," Maryvictoria said. "How could I possibly add to that? I mean, does not every female find great comfort and warmth in social pride when she tosses away perhaps her only real chance for happiness?"

"Oh, do go away! And take all that romantic nonsense with you."

"Think about it, my lady. Pride makes a very poor companion—and a worse bed partner."

"Maryvictoria Elizabeth!"

"Oops, sorry. I come from a much franker age than this one. I shall go for now."

And she did, leaving Allyson to lie awake half the night mulling over all that had gone on this day. Surely she was making the right decision. Surely. . . .

Nathan had joined the earl in interrogating the prisoners, who were all bound and seated at the table.

"I feel I know you, Fitz," Nathan said. "Did we not meet on a country road in Sussex?"

"I should have killed you then," Fitz snapped.

"I am rather grateful that you did not do so."

Lord Rutherford addressed the man who had accompanied Lady Eggoner. "Phillipe Gautier, I presume?"

The man started. "How—?"

"Ah, Monsieur Gautier, we have been watching for you to turn up here ever since our people on the Continent lost track of you some weeks ago. And here you are—in the company of a respected English lady—captured in a deserted warehouse. How is it that one of Bonaparte's master spies ends so ignominiously?"

"Bad company?" Gautier said flippantly, his gaze flicking over Lady Eggoner, Willard, and Fitz.

"Please, Rutherford, allow me to explain," Lady Eggoner begged.

"Yes, my lady. Your explanation should prove very interesting. I doubt not that Willard and Fitz here are motivated by money. Gautier is motivated by loyalty to the emperor. An admirable motive, if woefully misguided."

Gautier gave a derisive snort.

The earl went on. "But what is *your* reason for turning traitor, my lady? It cannot be money. I happen to know Eggoner left you very well fixed. Was it boredom? A middle-aged widow seeking excitement? What?"

"They have my son," she said dully. "Now they will kill him."

"Your son?"

"My son Stephen from my first marriage to Mr. Tyndale. Stephen was serving in the Peninsula. He was captured and paroled to Paris. They refused to ransom him. Instead, they threatened to kill him if I did not cooperate."

"He was an officer in Wellington's force?" Rutherford asked. Only officers were routinely considered for parole.

"A lieutenant," she said with a sob.

"Sir," Nathan said. "I knew of a Lieutenant Tyndale. I did not know he had been captured."

"F-five months ago," she said.

"You were not resting that night in the Worthington library, were you?" Nathan challenged. He had suddenly recalled the swishing sound of a woman's skirt just as he and Eastland had entered the room to find Lady Eggoner reclining on a sofa.

She hung her head. "No, I was examining the contents of Lord Worthington's desk."

In the end, the male prisoners were escorted to jail to await further action, and Lady Eggoner was sent home with strict orders not to step outside her house until her case was settled. As they returned to Rutherford House, Nathan and the earl discussed the fate of the prisoners.

"Willard and Fitz will either hang or be transported, I suppose," Nathan said.

"In the scheme of things, that poor nobody Willard will probably hang," Rutherford replied. "Fitz's father was a marquis; perhaps the family—if they care—can wield enough influence to get him transported. Less embarrassment to them that way."

"Gautier might be exchanged for Lieutenant Tyndale," Nathan suggested.

"Gautier is worth far more than one lowly lieutenant."

"Yes, I suppose he is."

"They should be willing to give up the lieutenant, *and* one or two others for Gautier. They have paroled several higher-ranking officers to Paris—colonels, lieutenant colonels, a major. We will consult with Horse Guards to see what—or whom—the army wants."

"And Lady Eggoner?"

"Well, she *did* give up Gautier, did she not?" Rutherford winked. "Seriously, I doubt the secretary will see much profit in prosecuting a mother who feared for her son's life. I would surmise that she will be banished to her country home for at least the duration of the war."

Nathan contemplated the nature of British justice in silence. Somehow it seemed more expedient than just, but perhaps human justice was always, or at least usually, that way.

The more pressing dilemma for him, and one that later kept him awake when his exhausted body cried out for rest, was Allyson. He had no doubt she loved him. Her responses to his kisses had not come merely from the emotion and stress of being abducted.

Why had he not just told her who he was? He could have dispelled her doubts. Instead, he had accused her of letting her pride come between them. Was it not *his* pride that wanted her to accept him first for himself, not for some label, be it as a member of the aristocracy, an officer in the king's army, or even a lowly footman or common soldier?

Well, it would be sorted out on the morrow. Besides, her mother had undoubtedly informed her of his status.

Chapter 21

The next morning Allyson sent word to the stable that she would not be riding that day. Moreover, she took her breakfast on a tray in her room in midmorning rather than her usual early hour in the family dining room.

"Why are you being such a coward?" Maryvictoria asked. She had appeared as soon as the breakfast tray was removed.

"You know why, Miss Know-All."

"Yes, but—"

"No, it is no good. I have spent the night thinking of nothing else. Nathan will surely be leaving today; his job here is finished."

"You really plan to let him walk out of your life, just like that?" She snapped ghostly fingers, but of course there was no sound.

"What choice do I have?"

"I would say you have a great deal of choice. The rich always do—if they are willing to defy society—and somehow society always forgives *them*. Well, usually, anyway."

"What *are* you saying?"

"I am trying to remind you that you will have a very substantial amount of money settled on you when you marry. Is that not true?"

"Ye-es . . ." Allyson conceded.

"So, it will surely be enough that it can secure even the lowliest husband a place in society."

"Perhaps." Allyson was beginning to have an inkling of hope. "But my family, my friends . . ."

"We have already established that Lord and Lady Rutherford would stand by you, no matter what. You forget that the countess wields a good deal of influence in the *ton*."

"Clara and Edmund—"

"Are such toadeaters that they will take their cues from the earl and the countess. Besides, they would see accepting you as a duty—a family obligation—that would allow them to play the role of martyr. As for your young brother, he will probably find a variety of ways to obtain his black eyes, with or without your help."

"What about Nathan himself? He is not the kind of man who could live on his wife's largesse, who could go through life an idle fribble, as 'Mr. Crossleigh.' "

"No, he is not," Maryvictoria agreed. "But do not underestimate him. He has hidden depths. The man is capable of far more than you seem to credit him."

"Oh, Maryvictoria, you make it sound so simple."

"It is. Have the man. Hang the labels!"

"I think . . . I think I will." She laughed joyously. "*I will.*"

A knock sounded at her door. A maid bore the message that she was wanted in the library. She did a quick check in the mirror and tucked in a stray strand of hair. With a sigh, she realized that she was wearing the same light green muslin day dress she had worn when she first met Nathan.

It was not her father pacing the library floor.

It was Nathan—Nathan dressed as a gentleman in simple, understated elegance. He stopped pacing and seemed to drink in the sight of her.

"N-Nathan? I thought Papa wanted me," she said, nervous at having this meeting come before she was prepared for it. She was also mystified by his appearance, but too distracted to dwell on it.

"*I* want you. In every way." He stood still, waiting, it seemed, for a signal from her.

Allyson was too honest to hold back. "And I want *you*," she said shyly.

He closed the space between them in an instant, and she was in his arms. He kissed her thoroughly and was just as thoroughly kissed in return.

"I take it this means you will have me?"

"Oh, yes, Nathan. Yes. You were right. Love should be un-conditional. We will do very well. I will have a comfortable marriage portion; perhaps you will want to buy a commis-sion; my friends who matter will stand by me and—"

"Allyson—"

She babbled on. "We shall have to live in more modest circumstances than these, but I am certain—"

"Allyson, listen, love—"

But her enthusiasm was now unstoppable. "Of course, my parents may object at first, but as you have pointed out on more than one occasion, Papa usually lets me have my way—"

"Allyson!" He stopped her babbling with another kiss, one that went on until she was weak-kneed. A knock at the library door parted them slightly. Her parents entered.

"Well, Captain," the earl said affably, "did we give you enough time?"

"Yes, my lord. Your daughter has agreed to marry me."

"Oh, Allyson!" Her mother had happy tears in her eyes.

"Captain!" Allyson exclaimed, twisting away from him.

"You have not told her?" the earl asked Nathan.

"I thought Lady Rutherford must have told her last night or this morning while you and I were out," Nathan said.

"Told me *what?*" Allyson demanded, already feeling a twinge of embarrassment.

"Allow me, daughter, to present to you your fiancé, Captain Lord Nathan Christopher Thornton." Lord Rutherford smiled benignly at the two of them.

"Captain. Lord. Thornton." She pronounced each word

precisely. "Thornton . . . Thornton! Good heavens! Your father is the Duke of Halstead." She felt her anger erupting. "Well, Captain—Lord—Thornton, how nice to meet you." Her cold tone belied her words, and she gave a very formal, haughty little bow of her head. She continued in the same cold tone. "I do hope you have enjoyed your little joke at my expense. I think we have just witnessed the shortest betrothal in the history of England!"

She spotted Maryvictoria hovering behind her father.

"Why did you not tell me?" she wailed.

"It was not my place to do so," the ghost child said.

Her father coughed and said, "It was important to keep the mission confidential."

"Even after last night?" she challenged both her father and Nathan, but especially Nathan.

Her mother was wringing her hands. "Oh, Allyson, I am so sorry. I should have told you, but I thought you knew."

"We seem to have a comedy of errors going on here," the earl said. "Come, Katherine. I think it best we leave these two to sort it out."

"Never mind. I am going, too," Allyson said emphatically.

"No, you are *not,*" both Nathan and Lord Rutherford said, one in the tones of the training field, the other of parliamentary debate.

"Talk!" the earl ordered as he swept his wife and himself out of the room.

Allyson sat in a round chair and folded her arms stubbornly across her chest.

Nathan began pacing again, running a hand through his hair. "I realize this came as a surprise to you, but, really, how can it make a difference in how we *feel* about each other? Not ten minutes ago, you were willing to marry a nobody, a footman. I love you. You love me. Is that not enough?"

"People who love each other do not keep important secrets from each other," Allyson said.

Maryvictoria again made her presence known, but she did not say anything.

"Oh, go away," Allyson said impatiently to the sprite.

"I am not going anywhere, my lady," Nathan said. "I am staying right here until you come to your senses and realize that you *must* marry me."

"*Come to my senses? Must?*" she asked dangerously.

"Allyson, please. Face facts. The whole *ton* will know the story soon enough. They will know that we have spent hours alone together, and if word of that night at Cranston's gets out—and it still may—your reputation will be ruined."

"Now, you listen to me, Captain Lord Nathan Thornton. If I *ever* marry, it will be out of desire, not coercion. Let them talk, if they must."

"Was it not *ton* gossip that made you hesitate when you thought I was a mere footman?"

"You made a fool of me, letting me ramble on about my marriage portion and . . . buying you a c-commission—Captain!"

He squatted on one knee in front of her. "Is that it? You are refusing me because you are *embarrassed?* Good grief, woman, you would not allow me a word in edgewise!"

"Enough, I am not listening to another word."

She stood up so quickly he had to catch himself to keep from falling. He stood as well and reached for her arm, but she shook him off, afraid he might see the tears that threatened.

She turned toward the door, but suddenly found herself tripping over a wrinkle in a carpet that had been smooth seconds earlier. She gave a little yelp as she felt herself falling. Then strong arms broke her fall and enfolded her in a world of comfort and safety.

He hugged her close. "Please," he whispered, "don't leave. I need you. I need *you* to make my life complete."

Her arms went around his neck, and she sighed in defeat—or contentment. "And I need you the same way." She gave a soft, rueful laugh. "I knew I would be undone if I let you touch me."

He chuckled and kissed her soundly once again. Then he

sat in the chair she had vacated and pulled her onto his lap. They traded kisses and the secrets of lovers. "When did you know . . . ?" And they made plans for a future together. They also sat in silence, savoring each other's presence.

Allyson nuzzled his neck. "Nathan?"

"Hmm?"

"How would you feel about naming our first daughter Maryvictoria Elizabeth?"

"Whatever you wish, my love."

Allyson heard a ghostly giggle fading away.